A Book Of

INDUSTRIAL CHEMISTRY

T.Y.B.Sc. CH-345 : Semester IV
As Per New Revised Syllabus w.e.f. June 2015

Dr. G. S. Gugale
Associate Professor & Head of Chemistry Deptt.
Haribhai V. Desai College
PUNE

Dr. A. V. Nagawade
Associate Professor, Dept. of Chemistry
Ahmednagar College
AHMEDNAGAR

Dr. R. A. Pawar
Associate Professor & Head of Chemistry Deptt.
Baburaoji Gholap Mahavidyalaya
Sangvi, PUNE

Dr. K. M. Gadave
Associate Professor
Department of Chemistry
Prof. Ramkrishna More College
Akurdi, PUNE

NIRALI PRAKASHAN
ADVANCEMENT OF KNOWLEDGE

N1861

T.Y.B.Sc. Industrial Chemistry (CH-345) (Semester - IV)   ISBN 978-93-5164-920-5

First Edition : December 2015

© : Authors

Published By :
NIRALI PRAKASHAN
Abhyudaya Pragati, 1312, Shivaji Nagar,
Off J.M. Road, PUNE – 411005
Tel - (020) 25512336/37/39, Fax - (020) 25511379
Email : niralipune@pragationline.com

✦ DISTRIBUTION CENTRES

PUNE

Nirali Prakashan : 119, Budhwar Peth, Jogeshwari Mandir Lane, Pune 411002, Maharashtra
Tel : (020) 2445 2044, 66022708, Fax : (020) 2445 1538
Email : bookorder@pragationline.com, niralilocal@pragationline.com

Nirali Prakashan : S. No. 28/27, Dhyari, Near Pari Company, Pune 411041
Tel : (020) 24690204 Fax : (020) 24690316
Email : dhyari@pragationline.com, bookorder@pragationline.com

MUMBAI

Nirali Prakashan : 385, S.V.P. Road, Rasdhara Co-op. Hsg. Society Ltd.,
Girgaum, Mumbai 400004, Maharashtra
Tel : (022) 2385 6339 / 2386 9976, Fax : (022) 2386 9976
Email : niralimumbai@pragationline.com

✦ DISTRIBUTION BRANCHES

JALGAON

Nirali Prakashan : 34, V. V. Golani Market, Navi Peth, Jalgaon 425001,
Maharashtra, Tel : (0257) 222 0395, Mob : 94234 91860

KOLHAPUR

Nirali Prakashan : New Mahadvar Road, Kedar Plaza, 1st Floor Opp. IDBI Bank
Kolhapur 416 012, Maharashtra. Mob : 9850046155

NAGPUR

Pratibha Book Distributors : Above Maratha Mandir, Shop No. 3, First Floor,
Rani Jhanshi Square, Sitabuldi, Nagpur 440012, Maharashtra
Tel : (0712) 254 7129

DELHI

Nirali Prakashan : 4593/21, Basement, Aggarwal Lane 15, Ansari Road, Daryaganj
Near Times of India Building, New Delhi 110002
Mob : 08505972553

BENGALURU

Pragati Book House : House No. 1, Sanjeevappa Lane, Avenue Road Cross,
Opp. Rice Church, Bengaluru – 560002.
Tel : (080) 64513344, 64513355,Mob : 9880582331, 9845021552
Email:bharatsavla@yahoo.com

CHENNAI

Pragati Books : 9/1, Montieth Road, Behind Taas Mahal, Egmore,
Chennai 600008 Tamil Nadu, Tel : (044) 6518 3535,
Mob : 94440 01782 / 98450 21552 / 98805 82331,
Email : bharatsavla@yahoo.com

niralipune@pragationline.com | www.pragationline.com

Also find us on 🇫 www.facebook.com/niralibooks

Preface ...

The new approach to the subject matter in chemistry in well defined manner introduced by the University of Pune from June 2015 is a welcome step. We are happy to place this text book of **"Industrial Chemistry"** **(CH-345)** in the hands of students of T.Y.B.Sc. Semester - IV.

This book has been written according to the new revised syllabus introduced from June 2015 for Semester - IV. We have tried our best using our versatile experience to make this book quite informative as well as simple and lucid. Wherever possible an attempt is made to provide additional information to raise the standard of education.

Topics like Polymer Chemistry; Sugar and Fermentation Industry; Soaps, Detergents and Cosmetics; Dyes, Paints and Pigments; Chemistry of Pharmaceutical Industries; and Pollution Prevention and Waste Management; are revised as per new revised syllabus.

The concepts are illustrated with examples wherever necessary. A large number of exercises have been given at the end of each topic. We are sure that this book will be equally useful to the teachers and students. We are confident that this book will cater to the exact requirements of students.

We are grateful to our dynamic publisher Shri. Dineshbhai Furia, Shri. Jignesh Furia of Nirali Prakashan for publishing this book with utmost care in a very short time. We are also thankful to Nirali Prakashan Staff especially Mr. Akbar Shaikh, Mr. Kiran Velankar and Ms. Chaitali Takle for completing the publication of this book well in time.

Any comments, criticism and suggestions from the readers for improving the book will be highly appreciated.

December 2015
Pune

Authors

Syllabus ...

1. Polymer Chemistry (10)

Classification of Polymers: Organic and Inorganic Polymers.

(a) Basic concepts, Nomenclature, Degree of polymerization, Classification of polymerization reactions, Thermodynamic and Transport properties of polymer.

(b) **Commercial Polymers and their Importance:** (a) Nylon, Polyesters (Terylene and Dacron), Rubber, Vulcanization of Rubber, Synthetic Rubber, Buna 2-N Rubber, Copolymers of Butadiene, PVC, Acrylic, Teflon, Polyethylene and Acrylonitrile; (b) Silicone Polymers: Silicone oils, Rubber, Grease and Resin; (c) Resins: Phenol-formaldehyde resins, Urea-formaldehyde resins, Epoxy resins, Melamine-formaldehyde resins.

2. Sugar and Fermentation Industry (08)

Sugar: Occurrence, Manufacturing of refined cane sugar from sugar cane, General idea of carbonation and sulphitation processes and their comparison, By-products and their use.

Fermentation Industry: Introduction, Importance, Basic requirements of fermentation process, Manufacture of industrial alcohol from Molasses, Fruits, Food grains and Ethylene, Manufacturing of Wine, Beer, Whisky, Rum; Importance of Power alcohol.

3. Soap, Detergents and Cosmetics (08)

(A) Chemistry of soap, Raw material, Chemical reaction, Types of soap.

(B) Meaning of the terms: Detergent and Surfactants, Emulsion and Emulsifying agents, Wetting and Non-wetting, Hydrophobic and Hydrophilic nature, Amphipathic structures, Types of surfactants, Raw materials for detergents, Washing action of Soaps and Detergents, Detergent builders, Additives.

(C) **(a) Raw materials:** Emulsifiers (natural, synthetic and finely dispersed solids), Lipid components (oils, waxes, fats), Humectants, Colours (dyes and pigments), Preservatives and Antioxidants.

    (b) Cosmetics for skin: Types and problems of skin, Key ingredients of Skin cleaning, Toners, Moisturizers, Nourishing, Protective sunscreen, Talcum powder and Bleaching products.

    (c) Hair care: Classification, Ingredients, Special additives for conditioning and scalp health, Hair colourants (temporary, semi-permanent and gradual colourants), the plant materials (herbs) used in hair cosmetics.

4. Dyes, Paints and Pigments

(a) **Dyes:** Introduction, Classification of dyes: Structures and applications, Nitro, Nitroso, Azo, Heterocyclic, Phthalenes, Xanthenes, Rhodamines, Thiazine, Cyanine, Anthraquinone, Indigoids, Thioindigoids, Phthalocyanines, Vat dyes.

(b) **Paints:** Introduction of paints, Ingredients and Classification, New technologies; Properties of coatings; Solvents, Plasticizers, Dyes and Bioactive additives.

(c) **Pigments:** Introduction, Classification and General Physical Properties.

5. Chemistry of Pharmaceutical Industries (08)

(a) General aspects of drug action: Introduction, Classification, Nomenclature, Structure-activity relationship, Action of drugs, Factors affecting drug action, Metabolism of drugs, Chemical structures, Methods of Production and Pharmacological activity.

(b) Meaning of the terms: Prescriptions, Doses, Analgesic, Antipyretic, Diuretic, Anesthetics, Antibiotics, Anti-inflammatory, Anti-viral, Tranquilizer, Antiulcer, Antialargic and Bronchodilators, Cardiovascular, Cold preparations, Anti-hypertensive, Cough preparation, Anti-neoplastic, Sedatives and Hypnotics, Steroidal, Contraceptive, Histamine and Antihistamine.

(c) Synthesis and uses: Paracetamol, Aspirin, Sulphanilamide.

6. Pollution Prevention and Waste Management (06)

Introduction, Importance of Waste Management, Concept of Atom Economy, Terms involved in Waste Minimization: Source reduction, Recycling, Product changes, Source control, Use and Reuse, Reclamation, Assessment procedures, Types of wastes, Treatment and Disposal of Industrial Waste. Treatment of Wastes or Effluents with Organic Impurities. Treatment of Wastes or Effluents with Inorganic Impurities.

The Nature, Effect and Treatment of some important Chemical Wastes - (Pulp and Paper industries, Soap and Detergent Industries and Food Processing Industries).

■■■

Contents ...

1. Polymer Chemistry   **1.1 - 1.30**

   1.1   Classification of Polymers   1.1
   1.2   Basic Concepts of Polymer   1.2
   1.3   IUPAC Nomenclature of Polymer   1.3
   1.4   Classification of Polymerization Reactions   1.8
   1.5   Thermodynamics and Transport Properties of Polymers   1.10
   1.6   Commercial Polymers and their Importance   1.11
   1.7   Silicone Polymers   1.21
   1.8   Resins   1.24
     1.8.1   Phenol-Formaldehyde (PF) Resins   1.24
     1.8.2   Urea-Formaldehyde (UF) Resins   1.26
     1.8.3   Melamine-Formaldehyde Resins   1.27
     1.8.4   Epoxy Resins   1.28
   •   Exercises   1.28

2. Sugar and Fermentation Industry   **2.1 - 2.26**

(A) SUGAR INDUSTRY

   2.1   Introduction   2.1
   2.2   Importance of Sugar Industry   2.2
   2.3   Cultivation and Harvesting of Sugar Cane   2.2
   2.4   Manufacture of Direct Consumption (Plantation White) Cane Sugar   2.3
     2.4.1   Raw Materials   2.3
     2.4.2   Processes/Steps involved in Cane Sugar Manufacture   2.3
   2.5   Utilization of By-products of Sugar Industries   2.10
     2.5.1   Bagasse   2.10
     2.5.2   Molasses   2.11
     2.5.3   Furnace Ash   2.11

(B) FERMENTATION INDUSTRY

   2.6   Introduction   2.11
   2.7   Importance of Fermentation Industry   2.12
   2.8   Basic Requirements of Fermentation Process   2.12
   2.9   Factors Favouring Fermentation   2.13
   2.10 Fermentation Operations   2.13
   2.11 Manufacture of Industrial Alcohol (Ethyl Alcohol) from Molasses   2.15
     2.11.1 Commercial Production using Molasses as a Raw Material   2.15
     2.11.2 Commercial Production using Starch as a Raw Material (Food Grains) 2.17
     2.11.3 Manufacture of Ethanol from Hydrocarbons   2.20
     2.11.4 Manufacture of Wine   2.22
     2.11.5 Manufacture of Whisky and Rum   2.22
     2.11.6 Importance of Power Alcohol   2.23
   •   Exercises   2.24

3. Soaps, Detergents and Cosmetics   **3.1 - 3.28**

   3.1   Introduction   3.1

(A) SOAP

   3.2   Chemistry of Soap   3.1
   3.3   Raw Materials of Soaps   3.2
   3.4   Chemical Reaction for Manufacture of Soap   3.3
   3.5   Types of Soap   3.4

(B) DETERGENTS

   3.6   Introduction   3.6
   3.7   Meaning of the Terms   3.7
   3.8   Types (Classification) of Surfactants   3.9
   3.9   Raw Materials for Detergents   3.11
   3.10 Washing Action of Soaps and Detergents   3.14
         3.10.1 Washing Action of Soap   3.14
         3.10.2 Washing Action of the Detergent   3.15
   3.11 Comparison of Soaps and Detergents   3.16

(C) COSMETICS

   3.12 Introduction   3.17
   3.13 Raw Materials for Cosmetics   3.18
   3.14 Cosmetics for Skin   3.20
   3.15 Hair Care   3.23
   •   Exercises   3.26

4. Dyes, Paints and Pigments   **4.1 - 4.24**

(A) DYES

   4.1   Introduction   4.2
   4.2   Qualities of a Good Dye   4.2
   4.3   Dye Intermediates   4.2
   4.4   Classification of Dyes   4.4
         4.4.1   Classification of Dyes According to Chemical Constitution   4.4
         4.4.2   Classification of Dyes According to Mode of Application   4.5
   4.5   Theory of Colour   4.6
         4.5.1   Chromophore   4.6
         4.5.2   Auxochrome   4.6
   4.6   Structures and Applications of Some Dyes   4.6
         4.6.1   Nitro Dyes   4.6
         4.6.2   Nitroso Dye   4.7
         4.6.3   Azo Dyes   4.7
               4.6.3.1   Acid Azo Dye   4.7
               4.6.3.2   Basic Azo Dyes   4.8
               4.6.3.3   Direct or Substantive Azo Dyes   4.9

	4.6.4	Phthaleins	4.9
	4.6.5	Xanthene Dyes	4.10
	4.6.6	Rhodamines	4.11
	4.6.7	Thiazine Dyes	4.11
	4.6.8	Anthraquinone Dyes	4.11
	4.6.9	Indigoids	4.13
	4.6.10	Thioindigoid Dyes	4.14
	4.6.11	Cyanine Dyes	4.15
		4.6.11.1 Phthalocyanines	4.15
4.7	Vat Dyes		4.16
4.8	Heterocyclic Dyes		4.17

(B) PAINTS

4.9	Introduction	4.17
4.10	Classification of Paints	4.17
4.11	Methods of Applying Paints	4.19

(C) PIGMENTS

4.12	Introduction	4.20
4.13	Classification of Pigments	4.21
4.14	Physical Properties and Uses of Pigments	4.22
•	Exercises	4.23
5.	**Chemistry of Pharmaceutical Industries**	**5.1 - 5.18**
5.1	General Aspects of Drug Action	5.2
	5.1.1 Introduction	5.2
	5.1.2 Classification of Drugs	5.2
	5.1.3 Nomenclature	5.3
	5.1.4 Structure-Activity Relationship (SAR)	5.4
	5.1.5 Action of Drugs	5.4
	5.1.6 Factors Affecting Drug Action	5.5
	5.1.7 Metabolism of Drugs	5.6
	5.1.8 Methods of Production	5.6
	5.1.9 Pharmacological Activity	5.6
5.2	Meaning of Terms	5.7
	5.2.1 Prescriptions	5.7
	5.2.2 Doses	5.7
	5.2.3 Analgesics	5.7
	5.2.4 Antipyretics	5.8
	5.2.5 Diuretics	5.8
	5.2.6 Anesthetics	5.8
	5.2.7 Antibiotics	5.8
	5.2.8 Anti-inflammatory	5.8
	5.2.9 Anti-viral	5.9
	5.2.10 Tranquilizer	5.9
	5.2.11 Anti-ulcer	5.9
	5.2.12 Anti-allergic and Bronchodilators	5.9
	5.2.13 Cardiovascular	5.9

	5.2.14 Cold Preparations	5.10
	5.2.15 Anti-Hypertensive	5.10
	5.2.16 Cough Preparation	5.11
	5.2.17 Anti-Neoplastic	5.12
	5.2.18 Sedatives and Hypnotics	5.12
	5.2.19 Steroidal	5.13
	5.2.20 Contraceptive	5.13
	5.2.21 Histamine and Antihistamine	5.13
5.3	Synthesis and Uses	5.14
	5.3.1 Paracetamol (p-Acetyl Aminophenol)	5.14
	5.3.2 Aspirin (Acetyl Salicylic Acid)	5.15
	5.2.3 Sulphanilamide (p-Amino Benzene Sulphonamide)	5.16
•	Exercises	5.17

6. Pollution Prevention and Waste Management   **6.1 - 6.20**

6.1	Introduction	6.2
6.2	Importance of Waste Management	6.2
6.3	Atom Economy	6.3
6.4	Terms Involved in Waste Minimization	6.4
	6.4.1 Source Reduction and Waste Reduction	6.5
	6.4.2 Recycling and Reuse	6.5
	6.4.3 Biological Reprocessing (Product Changes)	6.5
	6.4.4 Energy Recovery	6.6
	6.4.5 Avoidance and Reduction Methods (Source Control)	6.7
6.5	Assessment Procedure	6.7
6.6	Types of Wastes	6.11
6.7	Treatment and Disposal of Industrial Waste	6.11
6.8	Treatment of Waste or Effluents with Organic Impurities	6.13
	6.8.1 What is Organic Waste?	6.13
	6.8.2 Waste Volumes and Contribution	6.13
	6.8.3 Organic Wastes Degradation by Aerobic and Anaerobic Biology	6.13
	6.8.4 Recycling and Reuse	6.14
6.9	Treatment of Waste with Inorganic Impurities	6.14
	6.9.1 Disposal of Waste	6.14
	6.9.2 Recyclables	6.15
6.10	The Nature, Effect and Treatment of Some Important Chemical Wastes	6.15
	6.10.1 Pulp and Paper Industries	6.15
	6.10.1.1 Chemical Processes	6.15
	6.10.1.2 Advanced Treatment by Chemical Oxidation of Pulp and Paper Effluent from a Plant Manufacturing Hardboard from Waste Paper	6.15
	6.10.2 Soap and Detergent Industry	6.16
	6.10.2.1 The Removal of Phosphate from Waste Water	6.17
	6.10.3 Food Industry	6.18
•	Exercises	6.19

■■■

Chapter 1 ...

Polymer Chemistry

Contents ...

1.1 Classification of Polymers

1.2 Basic Concepts of Polymer

1.3 IUPAC Nomenclature of Polymer

1.4 Classification of Polymerization Reactions

1.5 Thermodynamics and Transport Properties of Polymers

1.6 Commercial Polymers and their Importance

1.7 Silicone Polymers

1.8 Resins

    1.8.1 Phenol-formaldehyde (PF) Resins

    1.8.2 Urea-formaldehyde (UF) Resins

    1.8.3 Melamine-Formaldehyde Resins

    1.8.4 Epoxy Resins

• Exercises

1.1 Classification of Polymers

• Polymers are classified by number of ways.

(a) Natural and synthetic polymers:

It is classified on the basis of their origin.

Natural polymers: It is isolated from natural materials. For example, wool, cotton, silk, rubber, cellophane, leather etc.

Synthetic polymers: It is artificially prepared from low molecular weight compounds. For example, PVC, polyethylene, terylene, teflon, nylon etc.

(b) Organic and Inorganic polymers:

It is classified on the basis of backbone chain of polymer.

Organic polymers: The backbone chain of polymers containing carbon atom is termed as organic polymer. Most of the synthetic polymers are organic polymers.

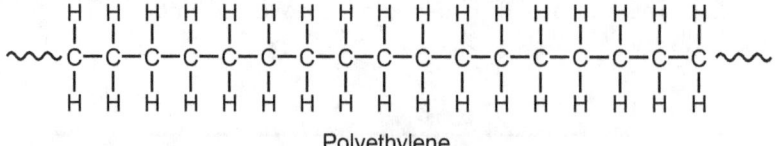

Polyethylene

1.1

Inorganic polymers: The backbone chain of polymer containing no carbon atom is termed as inorganic polymer. For example, glass, polygermene, silicone etc.

$$\sim\!\!\sim O-\underset{\underset{R}{|}}{\overset{\overset{R}{|}}{Si}}-O-\underset{\underset{R}{|}}{\overset{\overset{R}{|}}{Si}}-O-\underset{\underset{R}{|}}{\overset{\overset{R}{|}}{Si}}-O-\underset{\underset{R}{|}}{\overset{\overset{R}{|}}{Si}}-O-\underset{\underset{R}{|}}{\overset{\overset{R}{|}}{Si}}-O-\underset{\underset{R}{|}}{\overset{\overset{R}{|}}{Si}}-O-\underset{\underset{R}{|}}{\overset{\overset{R}{|}}{Si}}-O-\underset{\underset{R}{|}}{\overset{\overset{R}{|}}{Si}}\sim\!\!\sim$$

Silicone

(c) **Thermoplastic and thermosetting polymers**:

It is classified on the basis of behavior to the heat treatment.

Thermoplastic: When polymer softens on heating and converted into any shape that they can retain on cooling is termed as thermoplastic polymer. For example, PVC, nylon, polyethylene etc

Thermosetting: When polymer is heated it undergoes some chemical change and converted into an infusible mass which is termed as thermosetting polymer. For example, polyurethanes, vulcanized rubber, bakelite, etc.

(d) **Plastics, elastomers, fibers and liquid resins:**

It is classified on the basis of ultimate form and use.

Plastics: On application of heat and pressure polymer is shaped into hard and tough utility articles which are termed as plastics. For example, polyethylene, PVC, polystyrene etc

Elastomers: After vulcanization, polymer gets converted into rubbery products exhibiting good strength and elongation, which is termed as elastomers. For example, natural rubber, silicone rubber, synthetic rubber etc.

Fibers: Polymer drawn into long filament like materials whose length is 100 times greater than its diameter is termed as fibers. For example, Nylon, Terylene etc.

Liquid resins: It is used as adhesives, potting compounds, sealant etc. in liquid form which is used as liquid resin. For example, polysulphide sealant, epoxy adhesives etc.

1.2 Basic Concepts of Polymer

1. **Polymer:** It is a macro molecule formed by repetition of small, simple chemical units to form long chain. For example, polyethylene.

$$nH_2C = CH_2 \longrightarrow \sim\!\!\sim CH_2 - CH_2 - CH_2 - CH_2 - CH_2 - CH_2 \sim\!\!\sim$$

Ethylene ($H_2C=CH_2$) is a monomer and $-CH_2-CH_2-$ is a repeating unit. It is represented as polyethylene structure as follows.

$$-\!\!\left[\!\!-CH_2 - CH_2\!-\!\right]_n\!\!-$$

where n is a degree of polymerization.

2. **Monomer:** Simple chemical units or repeating units used in the formation of polymer is called as monomer.

3. **Degree of polymerization:** The number of repeating units or monomeric units present in polymer chain is called as degree of polymerization.

   Repeating unit: The repetition of which constitutes a regular manner in chain is called as repeating unit.

4. **Homopolymer:** The polymer formed from only one type of monomer is called as homopolymerization and the polymer formed is called as homopolymer. If A and B are monomers to form following structure.

$$\sim\sim A—A—A—A—A—A—A—A—A\sim\sim$$
$$\sim\sim B—B—B—B—B—B—B—B—B\sim\sim$$

5. **Copolymer:** The polymer formed from two types of monomer is called as copolymerization and the polymer formed is called as copolymer. If A and B are two monomers to form following structures of copolymers.

(i) Random copolymer

$$\sim\sim A—B—B—A—A—A—B—A—A—B\sim\sim$$

(ii) Alternating copolymer

$$\sim\sim A—B—A—B—A—B—A—B—A—B\sim\sim$$

(iii) Block copolymer

$$\sim\sim A—A—A—B—B—B—A—A—A—B—B—B—A—A—A\sim\sim$$

(iv) Graft copolymer

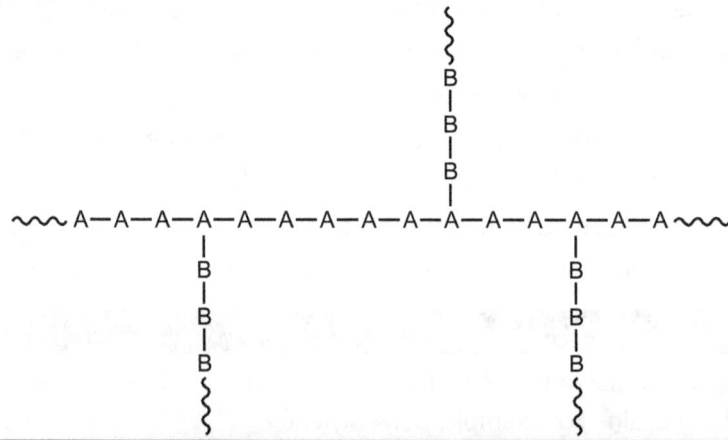

1.3 IUPAC Nomenclature of Polymer

- The polymer is named according to different ways:
  (a) Source based,
  (b) Structure based nomenclature,
  (c) Nomenclature of inorganic and inorganic-organic polymer and
  (d) Traditional names.

(a) Source based nomenclature:

(i) Homopolymers: This type of polymer gives names using real monomer from which it is derived.

For example, poly(methyl methacrylate) monomer can be named using IUPAC recommendation or established traditional name. When ambiguity arises, class names can be added.

For example, source based name poly(vinyloxirane) structure is shown below:

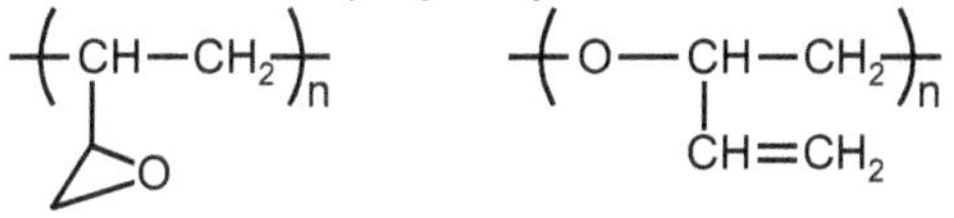

(a)   (b)

To clarify, the polymer name is named using the polymer class name followed by a colon and the name of monomer, i.e. class name: monomer name.

Thus structure (a) is named as polyalkylene:vinyloxirane and structure (b) as polyether:vinyloxirane.

(ii) Copolymers: Copolymer structure can be described using most appropriate connectives as shown below in Table 1.1.

Table 1.1: Qualifiers used in copolymer

Type of Copolymer	Qualifier or connective	Example
Unspecified	*co (C)*	Poly(A-co-B) e.g. Poly(styrene-co-isoprene)
Statistical	*stat (C)*	Poly(A-stat-B) e.g. Poly[isoprene-stat-(methyl methacrylate)]
Random	*ran(C)*	Poly(A-ran-B) e.g. Poly[(methyl methacrylate-ran-butylacrylate)]
Alternating	*alt(C)*	Poly(A-alt-B) e.g. Poly[styrene-alt-(maleic anhydride)]
Periodic	*per(C)*	Poly(A-per-B-per-C) e.g. Poly[styrene-per-isoprene-per-(4-vinylpyridine)]
Block	*block(C)*	Poly(A-block-B) e.g. Poly(buta-1,3-diene)-block-poly(ethane-co-propene)
Graft	*graft (C)*	Poly(A-graft-poly B) e.g. Polystyrene-graft-poly(ethylene oxide)

(iii) Non-linear polymers: Non-linear polymers and copolymers are named using qualifiers in italic symbols as shown below in Table 1.2. The qualifiers such as branch is used as prefix(P) when naming a copolymer or connectives (C) between two polymer names.

Table 1.2: Qualifiers for non-linear copolymer and polymer

Type of copolymer	Qualifier or connective	Example
Blend	**blend (C)**	Poly(3-hexylthiophene)-*blend*-polystyrene
Comb	**comb (C)**	Polystyrene-*comb*-polyisoprene
Complex	**compl (C)**	Poly(2,3-dihydrothieno[3,4-*b*][1,4]dioxine)-*compl*- Poly(vinylbenzenesulfonic acid)
Cyclic	**cyclo (P)**	*Cyclo*-polystyrene-*graft*-polyethylene
Branch	**branch (P)**	*Branch*-poly[(1,4-divinylbenzene)-*stat*-styrene]
Network	**net (C or P)**	(*net*-polystyrene)-*ipn*-[*net*-poly(methyl acrylate)]
Interpenetrating network	**ipn (C)**	(*net*-polystyrene)-*ipn*-[*net*-poly(methyl acrylate)]
Semi-interpenetrating polymer network	**sipn (C)**	(*net*-polystyrene)-*sipn*-polyisoprene
Star	**star (P)**	*star*-polyisoprene

(b) Structure based nomenclature:

(i) Regular single-strand organic polymer: In this nomenclature uses constitutional repeating unit (CRU).

It can be determined as follows:

1. Largest portion of the polymer chain is drawn to show the structural repetition.

   e.g.

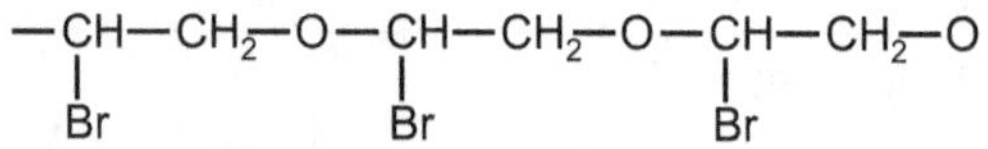

$$-CH-CH_2-O-CH-CH_2-O-CH-CH_2-O$$
$$|||$$
$$BrBrBr$$

2. Smallest portion of the polymer is constitutional repeating unit.

$$-CH_2-O-CH- \qquad -O-CH-CH_2- \qquad -CH-CH_2-O-$$
$$|||$$
$$BrBrBr$$

$$-CH_2-CH-O- \qquad -CH-O-CH_2- \qquad -O-CH_2-CH-$$
$$|||$$
$$BrBrBr$$

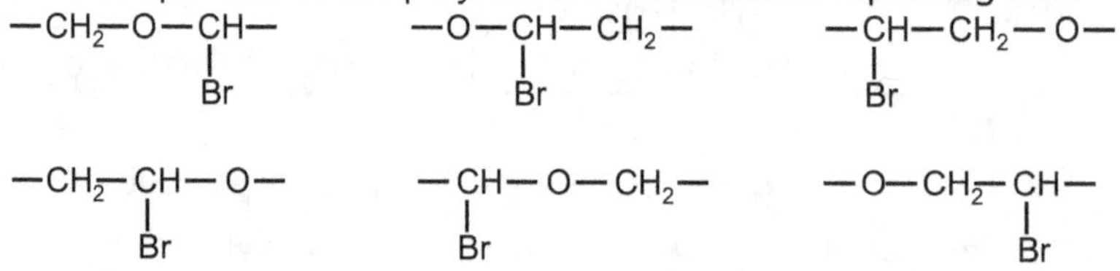

3. To identify the subunits of structure i.e. largest divalent groups that can be named according to IUPAC nomenclature of organic compounds. Names of divalent groups in polymers are shown in Table 1.3.

Table 1.3: Representations of divalent groups in polymers

Name	Group	Name	Group
oxy	$-O-$	Hydrazine-1,2-diyl	$\overset{1}{-}NH-\overset{2}{N}H-$
sulfonyl	$-SO_2-$	phthaloyl	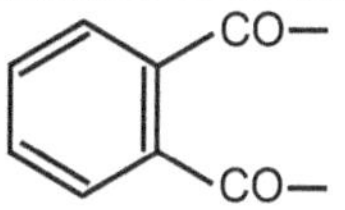
diazenediyl	$-N=N-$	1,4-phenylene	
imino	$-NH-$	Cyclohexane-1,2-diyl	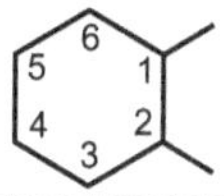
carbonyl	$\overset{O}{\underset{-C-}{\parallel}}$	1-bromoethane-1,2-diyl	$\overset{1}{-}CH\overset{2}{-}CH_2-$ with Br
oxalyl	$-\overset{O}{\underset{\parallel}{C}}-\overset{O}{\underset{\parallel}{C}}-$	methylmethylene	$-CH-$ with CH_3
methylene	$-CH_2-$	propylimino	$-N-$ with $CH_2CH_2CH_3$

4. The correct order of the subunit seniority is determined. Following Fig. 1.1 shows determination of order of seniority.

   In the oxy subunits in the CRUs are heteroatom chains. From Fig. 1.1, oxy subunits are senior to the acyclic carbon chain subunits, the largest of which are bromo-substituted $-CH_2-CH_2-$ subunits. 1-bromoethane-1,2-diyl is chosen in preference to 2-bromoethane-1,2-diyl as the former has a lower locant for the bromo-substituent. The preferred CRU is therefore oxy (1-bromoethane-1,2-diyl) and the polymer is thus named as poly[oxy(1-bromoethane-1,2-diyl)]. Please note the enclosing marks around the subunit carrying the substituent.

   Polymers that are not made up of regular repetitions of a single CRU are called irregular polymers. For these, each constitutional unit (CU) is separated by a slash, e.g. poly(but-1-ene-1,4-diyl/1-vinylethane-1,2-diyl).

5. CRU is chosen as that with lowest possible locant for substituents.

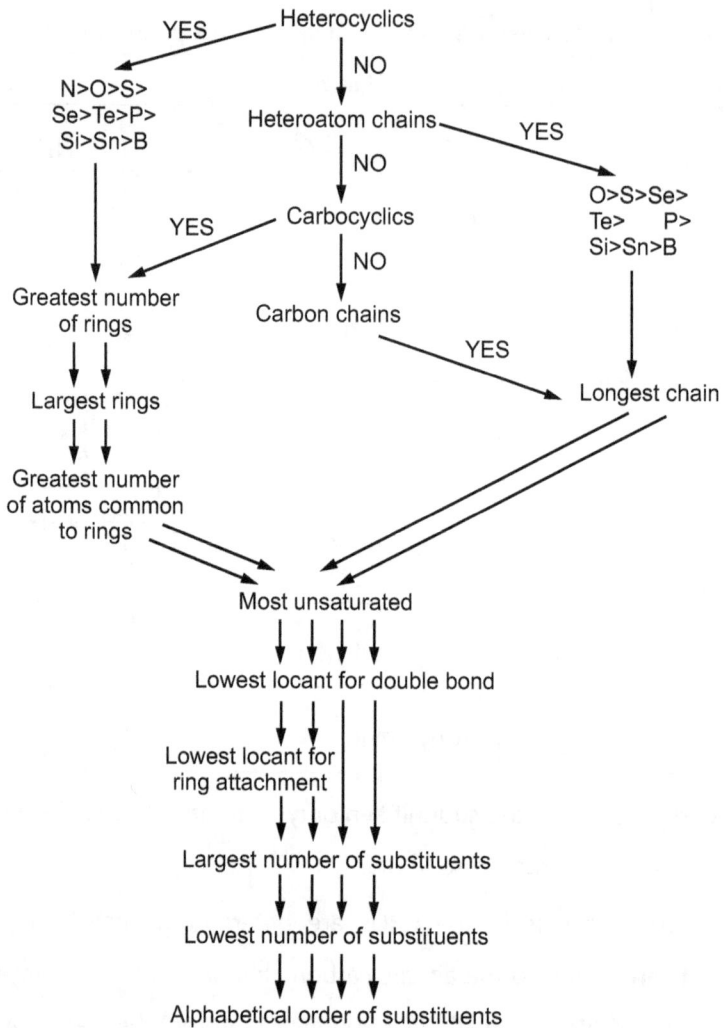

Fig. 1.1: The order of subunit seniority. The most senior is at the top centre. Subunits of lower seniority are found by following the arrows. The type of subunit, be it a heterocycle, a heteroatom chain, a carbocycle, or a carbon chain.

(ii) **Regular double-strand organic polymers:** Uninterrupted chains of rings are present in double-strand polymers. In a Spiro polymer, each ring has one atom in common with adjacent rings. In a ladder polymer, adjacent rings have two or more atoms in common. To identify the preferred CRU, the chain is broken so that the senior ring is retained with the maximum number of heteroatoms and the minimum number of free valencies. An example is

The preferred CRU is an acyclic subunit of 4 carbon atoms with 4 free valencies, one at each atom, as shown.

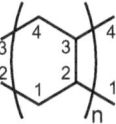

It is oriented so that the lower left atom has the lowest number. The free-valence locants are written before the suffix, and they are cited clockwise from the lower left position as: lower-left, upper-left: upper-right, lower-right. This example is thus named poly(butane-1,4:3,2-tetrayl). For more complex structures, the order of seniority again follows Fig. 1.1.

(c) Nomenclature of inorganic and inorganic-organic polymers:

Some inorganic polymers such as regular single-strand can be named like organic polymers using the rules given above.

e.g. 1. $[O-Si(CH_3)_2]_n$- are named as poly[oxy(dimethylsilanediyl)]

2. $[Sn(CH_3)_2]_n$- are named as poly(dimethylstannanediyl).

Inorganic polymers can also be named in accordance with inorganic nomenclature, but it should be noted that the seniority of the elements is different from that in organic nomenclature.

For example, those containing metallocene derivatives, are at present best named using organic nomenclature. e.g. poly[(dimethylsilanediyl)ferrocene-1,1'-diyl].

(d) Traditional names:

Some trivial and traditional names for polymers are commonly usage. e.g. polystyrene, polyethylene, polypropylene etc.

1.4 Classification of Polymerization Reactions

Polymerization is brought by two types of reactions (a) Chain polymerization and (b) Step polymerization

(a) Chain polymerization: In this polymerization, monomer undergoes self addition. It is very rapid reaction and no byproduct is formed. The monomer containing double bond undergoes chain polymerization reaction. For example, vinyl compounds ($CH_2=CHX$), olefins ($CH_2=CHR$), allyl compounds ($CH_2=CH.CH_2X$), dienes ($CH_2=CR-CH=CH_2$) etc. It consists of three steps: (i) Initiation, (ii) Propagation and (iii) Termination.

Chain polymerization is further classified into three different types.

1. **Free radical polymerization:** Polymer chain growth is initiated by free radicals produced by decomposition of compound which is called as initiator and the reaction is called as free radical polymerization.

   Formation of free radicals: Hydrogen peroxide is an initiator to form hydroxyl free radical.

$$HO-OH \longrightarrow \dot{O}H + \dot{O}H$$
$$\text{Initiator} \qquad \text{Free radicals}$$

   Initiation: To start polymerization reaction is called initiation.

$$\dot{O}H + CH_2\!\!=\!\!CH \longrightarrow HO-CH_2-\dot{C}H$$
$$\qquad\qquad\quad | \qquad\qquad\qquad\qquad |$$
$$\qquad\qquad\quad X \qquad\qquad\qquad\qquad X$$

   Propagation: After initiation add more and more monomers to form long polymer chain which is called as propagation of polymer chain.

$$HO-CH_2-\dot{C}H + CH_2\!\!=\!\!CH \longrightarrow HO-CH_2-CH-CH_2-\dot{C}H + CH_2\!\!=\!\!CH \longrightarrow$$
$$\qquad\quad | \qquad\qquad\quad | \qquad\qquad\qquad\qquad | \qquad\qquad | \qquad\qquad\quad |$$
$$\qquad\quad X \qquad\qquad\quad X \qquad\qquad\qquad\qquad X \qquad\qquad X \qquad\qquad\quad X$$

$$HO-CH_2-CH-CH_2-CH-CH_2-\dot{C}H \text{ and so on}$$
$$\qquad\qquad | \qquad\qquad | \qquad\qquad |$$
$$\qquad\qquad X \qquad\qquad X \qquad\qquad X$$

   Termination: The propagation of chain growth is stopped by free radical site being killed by adding some impurities or by terminating agent. Termination takes place by different ways.

   Termination by coupling, chain transfer reaction, by addition of inhibitors etc.

2. **Ionic polymerization:** There are two types of ionic polymerization: (i) Cationic polymerization and (ii) Anionic polymerization. Polymer chain reaction initiated by positive ion is called as cationic polymerization and when polymer chain reaction initiated by negative ion is called as anionic polymerization.

3. **Coordination polymerization:** Polymerization reaction catalyzed by organometallic compound is called as coordination polymerization. Ziegler-Natta catalyst is used in this polymerization.

(b) **Step polymerization:** In this polymerization takes place by stepwise manner. It is a slow reaction and small molecules like H_2O, NH_3 etc. are eliminated or not in polymerization. It is further classified into three types.

1. **Poly condensation polymerization**: Monomers containing two or more reactive functional groups (such as –OH, –COOH, –NH$_2$ etc.) undergo condensation with each other by eliminating small molecules such as H$_2$O, NH$_3$, alcohol etc. For example, polyester, polyamide etc. formed by polycondensation polymerization.

n HO—R$_x$—OH + n HO—C—R$_y$—C—OH ⟶ HO$\left[\text{R}_x\text{—O—C—R}_y\text{—C—O}\right]_n$H + nH$_2$O

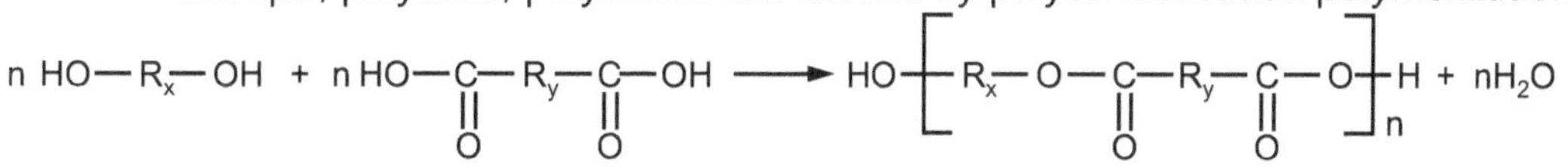

| Diol   Dicarboxylic acid   Polyester   Water |

2. **Poly addition polymerization:** In this reaction, there is migration of atoms from one monomer molecule to another or to intermediate product. Vinyl monomers or monomer pairs with reactive functional groups can undergo polyaddition polymerization. For example, polystyrene formed from styrene in presence of perchloric acid by this method. Polyurethane polymer formed from diisocyanate and diol by polyaddition method.

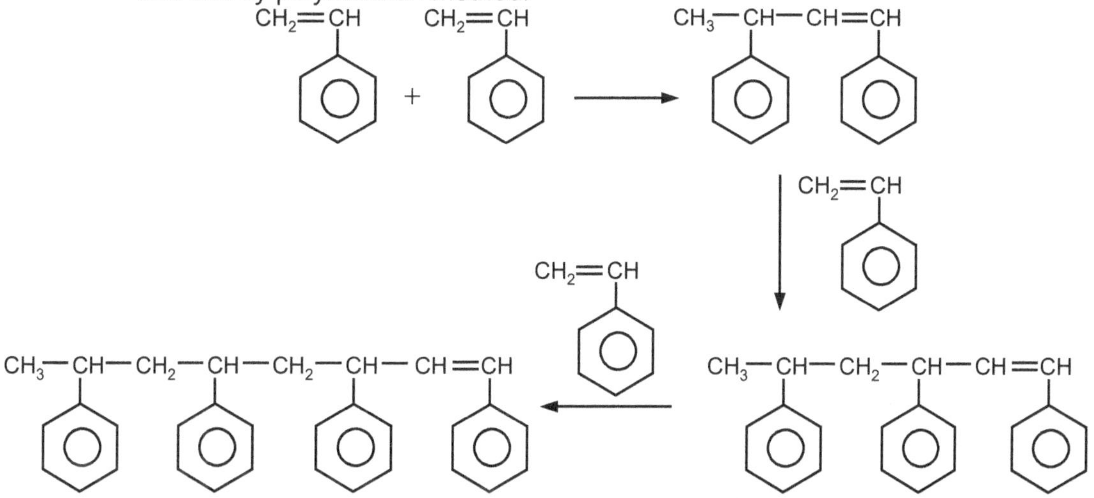

and so on.

3. **Ring opening polymerization:** Monomers having a ring structure can open and polymerize. **For example, Nylon-6 formed from caprolactam by ring opening polymerization.**

1.5 Thermodynamics and Transport Properties of Polymers

- Polymer behavior different from that of commonly known chemical compounds is a characteristic and different from that of small or low molecular weight compound.
- For example, small compound like solid benzene heated melt sharply at 5.5°C and on further heating it boils and converts into gaseous benzene. High molecular weight polymer compound such as polyethylene polymer if heated it does not melt sharply at one particular temperature. Initially it softens and then converts into viscous, molten polymer and on further heating it does not convert into polyethylene gas but it converts into decomposed products of various gases. Second difference is of behavior of polymers

toward solvents i.e. solubility. For example, low molecular weight compound sodium chloride added slowly to a fixed volume of water. It dissolves till its saturated point and further added sodium chloride does not dissolve further but settle solid at bottom. When viscosity of salt solution and water is measured there is no large difference in viscosity. If when high molecular weight polymer like polyvinyl alcohol is added to a fixed volume of water, it does not go into solution immediately. It first absorbs water, swell and gets distorted in shape and after longer time go into solution. Furthermore if more polymer is added to a fixed volume of water without saturation point is reached, viscosity of polymer solution also increases.

- Information obtains about size and shape of polymer molecules from studies of their solution properties.
- Solubility occurs when the free energy of mixing is negative.

$$\Delta G = \Delta H - T\Delta S$$

- Entropy of mixing ΔS is always positive and therefore sign of ΔG is determined by the sign and magnitude of the heat of mixing ΔH. For non-polar molecules and absence of hydrogen bonding, ΔH is positive and is assumed to be the same as that derived for the mixing of small molecules. For this case, the heat of mixing per unit volume can be approximated as

$$\Delta H = V_1 V_2 (\delta_1 - \delta_2)^2$$

where, 'V' is the volume fraction and subscripts 1 and 2 refer to solvent and polymer respectively. The quantity δ_2 is the cohesive energy density or for small molecules, the energy of vaporization per unit volume. The quantity δ is known as the solubility parameter.

- Transport properties such as diffusivity relate to how rapidly molecules move through the polymer matrix. These are very important in many applications of polymers for films and membranes.

1.6 Commercial Polymers and their Importance

1. **Nylon:** It is also called as polyamides. It is formed between diamines and dicarboxylic acids. Its general formula is as follows.

$$\left[\begin{array}{c} N-R_x-N-C-R_y-C \\ | \quad\quad | \quad \| \quad\quad \| \\ H \quad\quad H \ O \quad\quad O \end{array} \right]_n$$

Aliphatic polyamides are called as nylon. It is a different type of nylon and it is denoted by numbering systems such as nylon-6, 6; nylon-6, 10, nylon-6 etc. It is prepared by self polycondensation or ring opening polymerization.

$$HO-C-(CH_2)_4-C-OH + H_2N-(CH_2)_6-NH_2 \xrightarrow[\text{High pressure}]{553 \text{ K}} \left[C-(CH_2)_4-C-NH-(CH_2)_6-NH \right]_n$$

Adipic acid   Hexamethylene diamine   Nylon-6,6

Nylon 6, 6 is used as a plastic as well as fibre. It has good tensile strength, abrasion resistance and toughness upto 150°C. It is used to produce tyre cord, to make monofilament and rope. It is tough plastic and hence it is a good substitute for metals in gears and bearings. It is also used to make textile fibres for use in dresses and undergarments. Nylon-6, 10 is not used as important textile fibre but is used to make articles like brushes and bristles. Nylon-11 is used in textile fibre.

Nylon 6 is widely used for gears, fittings and bearings. It is used as sitars, violins, violas and cellos. It is also used in the manufacture of large variety of treads, ropes, nets, filaments and tire cords. It is used in hosiery and knitted garments.

2. **Polyesters (Terylene and Dacron)**: It contains ester linkages. Its general structure is as follows.

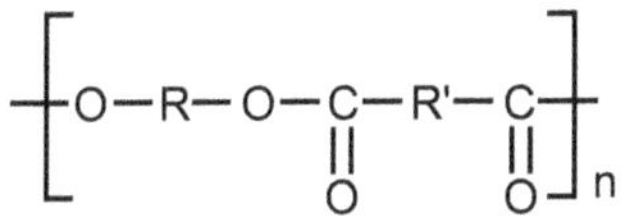

Dacron is a synonym of Terylene. It is also called polyethylene terephthalate and it is used for making thread and cloth. Polyester is manufactured by polycondensation between diol and dicarboxylic acid. Aliphatic polyester is not industrially important because of its low melting point. The low melting point of aliphatic polyester overcomes by introducing the aromatic ring into the polymer chain. For example,

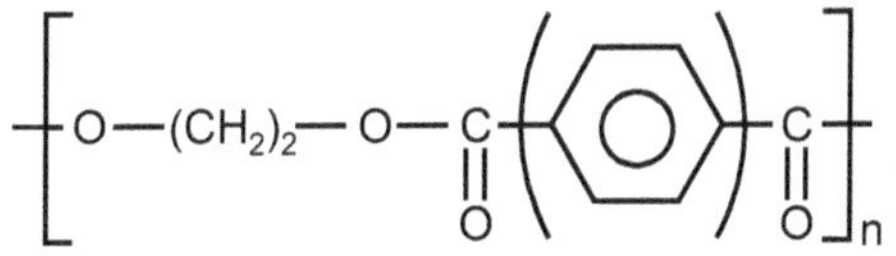

(M.P. 265°C)

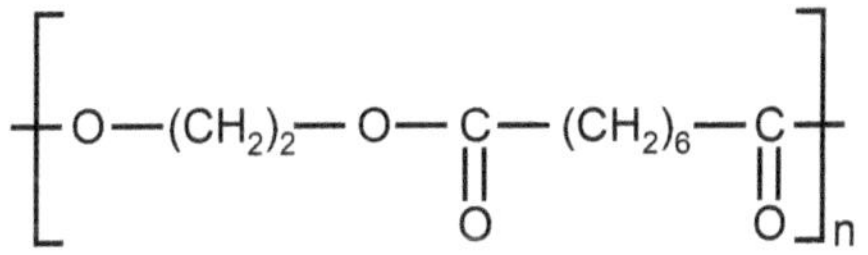

(M.P. 65°C)

Polyethylene terephthalate (PETP) have high M.P. (265°(C) because of its presence of aromatic ring in the polymer chain. It has very good mechanical strength upto 175°C. This polymer is commercially most important and its trade name is Terylene or Dacron. It is prepared from ethylene glycol and terephthalic acid. PETP is obtained by melt condensation method using DMT (dimethyl terephthalate) and ethylene glycol. In the first step the reaction is carried out at reflux temperature of ethylene glycol under low vacuum. In the second step, the reaction is carried out at high temperature at 200-250°C under high vacuum.

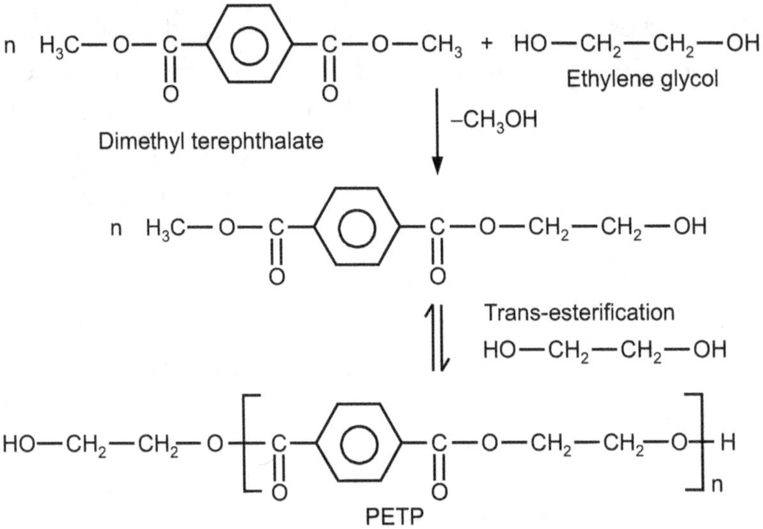

n H_3C—O—C—⟨○⟩—C—O—CH$_3$ + HO—CH$_2$—CH$_2$—OH
                                              Ethylene glycol

Dimethyl terephthalate

—CH$_3$OH ↓

n H_3C—O—C—⟨○⟩—C—O—CH$_2$—CH$_2$—OH

Trans-esterification
HO—CH$_2$—CH$_2$—OH ↕

HO—CH$_2$—CH$_2$—O⎡C—⟨○⟩—C—O—CH$_2$—CH$_2$—O⎤H
                                                                    n
PETP

It is excellent water and moisture barrier material. Plastic bottles made from this polymer are widely used for soft drinks.

Polyester is used to prepare textile fibres. The garments formed from these fibres are wrinkles resist. PETP is used to make films. Films are used for manufacturing of magnetic recording tapes. For industrial use, aliphatic unsaturated polyesters are formed by taking unsaturated dicarboxylic acid such as maleic acid. It is polymerized with ethylene glycol to give aliphatic unsaturated polyester.

n HOOC—CH=CH—COOH + HO—CH$_2$—CH$_2$—OH $\xrightarrow{-(2n-1)\ H_2O}$ H⎡O—C—CH=CH—C—O—CH$_2$—CH$_2$—O⎤H
  Maleic acid   Ethylene glycol n

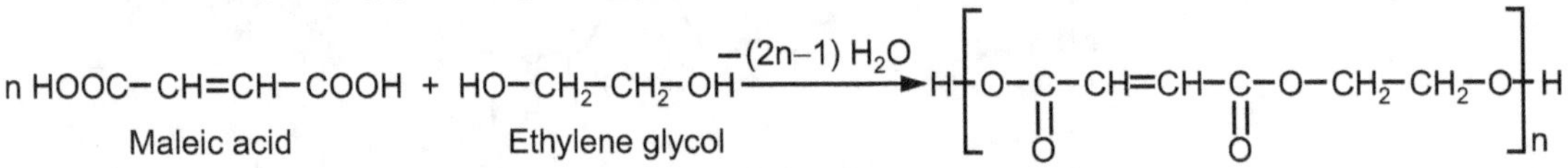

The presence of double bond in aliphatic unsaturated polyester is used for cross linking with styrene. The resin matrix is obtained after cross linking is used in fibre-reinforced plastics. It is also used for decorative coatings.

3. **Rubber:** Rubber is an example of an elastomeric type polymer. Rubber is of two types: (i) Natural rubber and (ii) Synthetic rubber.

   (i) Natural Rubber: It is containing cis-isoprene repeating unit and its general structure is as follows.

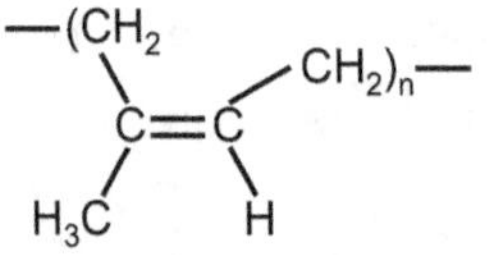

—(CH$_2$ CH$_2$)$_n$—
            C=C
        H$_3$C   H
(Cis-1,4 polyisoprene)

Natural rubber is obtained from milky white fluid known as latex from rubber trees (Hevea brasiliensis). Coiled structure is of natural rubber (cis-isomer).

(ii) Synthetic rubber: It is produced from petroleum based hydrocarbons such as butadiene, isoprene, chloroprene, styrene and isobutylene.

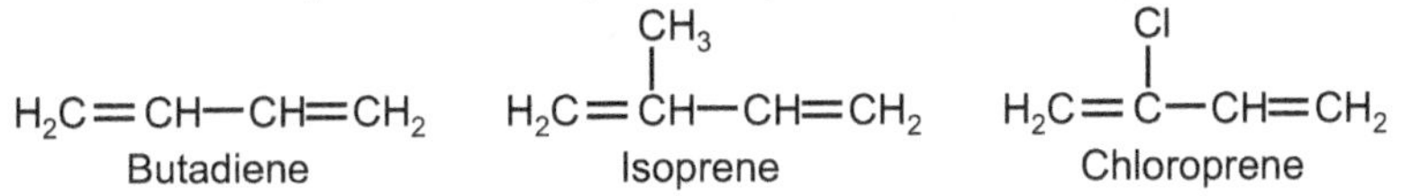

$$H_2C{=}CH{-}CH{=}CH_2 \qquad \underset{\text{Isoprene}}{H_2C{=}\overset{\overset{\displaystyle CH_3}{|}}{C}{-}CH{=}CH_2} \qquad \underset{\text{Chloroprene}}{H_2C{=}\overset{\overset{\displaystyle Cl}{|}}{C}{-}CH{=}CH_2}$$

Butadiene

Types of synthetic rubber:

(a) Synthetic polyisoprene rubber [trans- isomer is Gutta-Perch(a)] is obtained by free radical polymerization of isoprene.

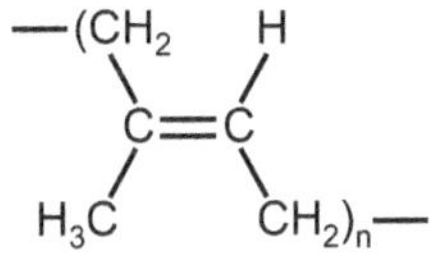

(Trans-1,4 polyisoprene)

Polymerization of isoprene give varying degree of cis-1, 4 and trans 1, 4 as well as 1, 2 or 3, 4 addition.

It depends upon the type of initiator and solvent used in polymerization. Polymerization is carried out under controlled condition. Polyisoprene containing upto 96% cis configuration can be obtained by using lithium alkyl initiator.

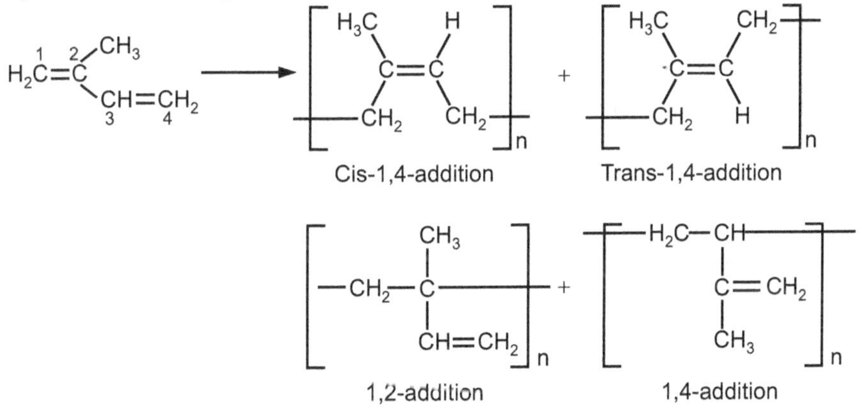

Cis-1,4-addition   Trans-1,4-addition

1,2-addition   1,4-addition

Trans isomer is more crystalline structure. It is highly zig-zag chain which cannot be stretched. Therefore it is non-elastic. Raw polymer and vulcanized properties of polyisoprene are similar as like natural rubber. Both synthetic and natural polyisoprene exhibit good inherent tack, high compounded gum tensile, good hysteresis and has good tensile properties. Synthetic polyisoprene is widely used in industrial applications requiring low water swell, high gum tensile strength, good resilience. Gum compound based polymer is used in rubber bands, cut thread, baby bottle nipples. Black loaded compounds based are used in pipe gaskets, shock absorber bushing etc.

(b) Polysulphide rubber: The first commercial synthetic rubber produced is polysulphide rubber. It is also called as thiokol rubber synthesized in 1929. It is excellent resistant to natural oxidants such as oxygen and ozone and to organic solvent. They also have excellent oil resistance. The reaction between sodium polysulphide with ethylene dichloride is to form thiokol rubber.

$$nCl-CH_2-CH_2-Cl + n\ Na_2S_x \longrightarrow \left[CH_2-CH_2-S_x \right]_n + 2n\ NaCl$$

Polysulphides are generally formed from alkyl dihalides reacting with alkali polysulphides. The obtained polysulphides are generally cured with the help of lead dioxide. It is used to make sealants, gaskets, gasoline hoses, fabric coatings, balloons etc. It is used to make excellent fuel material. It is mixing with inorganic oxidizers such as ammonium perchlorate then it is used as solid propellants for rockets.

(c) Polychloropene rubber: Polymerized chloroprene is developed by DuPont and its given trade name is Neoprene. It is synthesized by emulsion polymerization technique. Trans -1,4 configuration is produced during polymerization. It can be readily vulcanized by use of ZnO or MgO. The rubber produced by vulcanized rubber have excellent tensile strength. It is inferior to natural rubber but in some properties is superior in its resistance to oil and organic solvent. The elastomer is used for providing oil-resistant insulation coatings to wires and cables. It is also used for producing shoe soles, solid tyres, gloves. It is used in the manufacture of industrial hoses, gaskets, conveyor belts, stoppers and printing rollers.

Butyl rubber is copolymerized from isobutylene and small percentage of isoprene.

(d) Polybutadiene rubber: It is the second largest synthetic rubber produced after SBR rubber. Anionic polymerization of butadiene with lithium metal or Ziegler-Natta catalyst is to form syndiotactic 1, 2-polybutadiene (90% vinyl unit). Ziegler polymerization using $VOCl_2$ and $(C_2H_5)2AlCl$ of butadiene is to form high cis-polybutadiene. Due to high abrasion resistance, cis-polybutadiene is used in automobile tyre.

Use of alkyl lithium or anionic catalyst produces a polymer with 40% cis, 50% trans and 10% vinyl.

| 1,3-butadiene | Cis-1,4 | Vinyl | Trans-1,4 |

High trans-polybutadiene can be made by use of transition metal catalyst. It is highly crystalline plastic material.

4. **Copolymer of butadiene:** Certain synthetic rubber is formed by copolymerization of butadiene.

    Styrene-butadiene rubber (GRS or SBR or Buna-S): SBR rubber formed from styrene and butadiene is mixed in 1:3 ratio respectively. It is also called as BUNA-S. SBR is made by free radical polymerization and emulsion techniques using redox initiator such as H_2O_2. To control molecular weight, use dodecyl mercaptan as a chain modifier. In this copolymer contains 80% of 1, 3 (both cis- and trans-) and 20% 1, 2 or 3, 4 repeating units. When polymerization is carried out at 5°C the rubber obtained is called as cold rubber. If polymerization is carried out at 30°C then that rubber is called as warm rubber. The product obtained is latex and coagulated to form solid rubber. The rubbers are vulcanized using sulphur.

$$n\ H_2C{=}CH\ +\ n\ H_2C{=}CH{-}CH{=}CH_2 \longrightarrow \left[CH_2{-}CH{-}CH_2{-}CH{=}CH{-}CH_2 \right]_n$$

Styrene	1,3-Butadiene		SBR

SBR rubber is very tough and substitute for natural rubber. It possesses high abrasion resistance. It also possesses high load bearing capacity. It is used in the manufacturing of automobile tyres, making floor tiles, footwear articles, cable insulation.

Nitrile rubber is copolymerized from butadiene and acrylonitrile.

$$n\ H_2C{=}CH{-}CH{=}CH_2 + n\ H_2C{=}CH \xrightarrow{H_2O_2,\ \Delta} \left[CH_2{-}CH{=}CH{-}CH_2{-}CH_2{-}CH \right]_n$$

Butadiene	Acrylonitrile	Polybutadiene acrylonitrile

It is also called Buna-N rubber or polybutadiene acrylonitrile copolymer or nitrile rubber. Nitrile rubbers are highly resistant to oil and hydrocarbon and hence it is used as oil seals and oil resistant applications, tank lining etc.

Terpolymer is formed using three monomers such as butadiene, acrylic acid and acrylonitrile by emulsion polymerization technique. This polymer is used for curing reaction to form cross linked elastomeric structure.

5. **Vulcanization of rubber:** Vulcanization of rubber was first time discovered by Good Year in 1839. Cross linking is carried out in rubber using sulphur to improve in being tougher, resistant to heat and cold and increase in elasticity. This process is called as vulcanization of rubber.

$$
\begin{array}{ccc}
CH_2 & CH_2 & CH_2 \qquad CH_2 \\
| & | & |\qquad\quad | \\
CH & +\ S_8\ +\quad CH & \longrightarrow\quad CH{-}S_x{-}CH \\
|| & || & |\qquad\quad | \\
CH & CH & CH{-}S_x{-}CH \\
| & | & |\qquad\quad | \\
CH_2 & CH_2 & CH_2 \qquad CH_2
\end{array}
$$

Vulcanization also takes place without affecting double bond by using sulphur and eliminate H_2S.

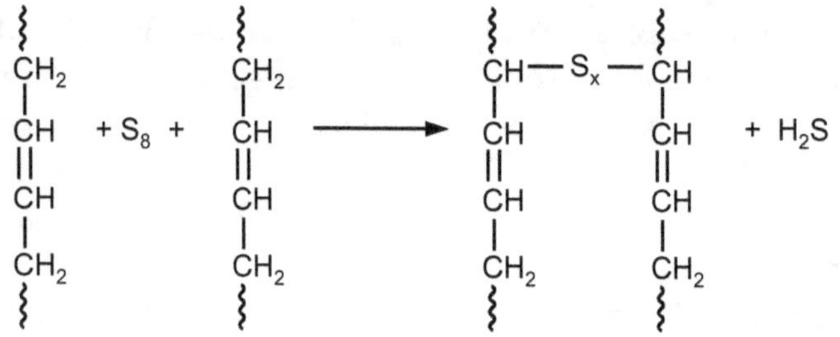

$$
\begin{array}{cccc}
CH_2 & CH_2 & CH\!-\!S_x\!-\!CH & \\
| & | & | \quad\quad | & \\
CH \;+\; S_8 \;+\; & CH & \longrightarrow \;\; CH \quad\quad CH & +\; H_2S \\
\| & \| & \| \quad\quad \| & \\
CH & CH & CH \quad\quad CH & \\
| & | & | \quad\quad | & \\
CH_2 & CH_2 & CH_2 \quad\quad CH_2 &
\end{array}
$$

The cross-linking also takes place by use of S_2Cl_2.

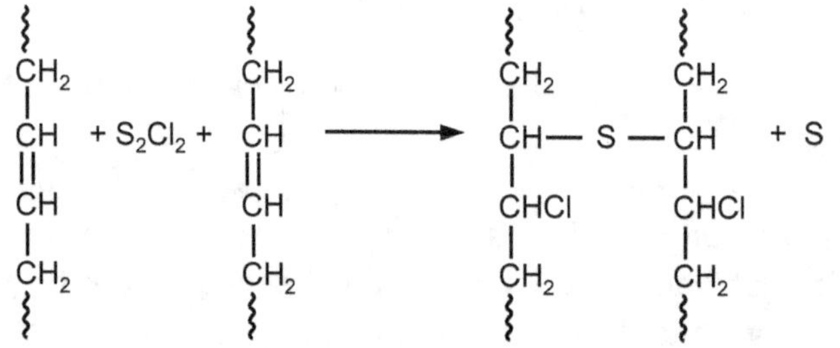

$$
\begin{array}{cccc}
CH_2 & CH_2 & CH_2 \quad\quad CH_2 & \\
| & | & | \quad\quad | & \\
CH \;+\; S_2Cl_2 \;+\; & CH & \longrightarrow \;\; CH\!-\!S\!-\!CH & +\; S \\
\| & \| & | \quad\quad | & \\
CH & CH & CHCl \quad CHCl & \\
| & | & | \quad\quad | & \\
CH_2 & CH_2 & CH_2 \quad\quad CH_2 &
\end{array}
$$

Vulcanization is also carried out by use of different types of sulphur compounds such as thioacids, mercaptans or mercaptoacids etc.

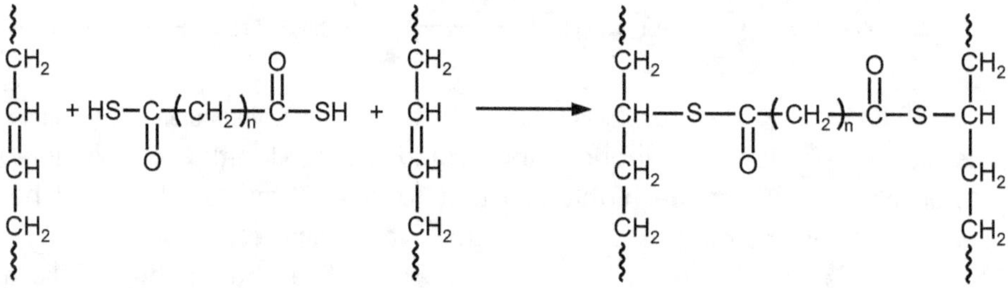

$$
\begin{array}{ccccc}
CH_2 & & CH_2 & CH_2 \quad\quad\quad CH_2 & \\
| & \quad\quad O & | & | \quad\quad\quad\quad | & \\
CH \;+\; HS\!-\!C\!-\!(CH_2)_n\!-\!\overset{\displaystyle O}{\overset{\|}{C}}\!-\!SH \;+\; & CH & \longrightarrow \;\; CH\!-\!S\!-\!C\!-\!(CH_2)_n\!-\!\overset{\|}{\underset{O}{C}}\!-\!S\!-\!CH & \\
\| & \underset{O}{\|} & \| & CH_2 \quad\quad\quad\quad CH_2 & \\
CH & & CH & | \quad\quad\quad\quad | & \\
| & & | & CH_2 \quad\quad\quad\quad CH_2 & \\
CH_2 & & CH_2 & &
\end{array}
$$

Without use of sulphur, cross linking is also brought by use of ZnO. For example, in polychloroprene, cross linking takes place by use of ZnO.

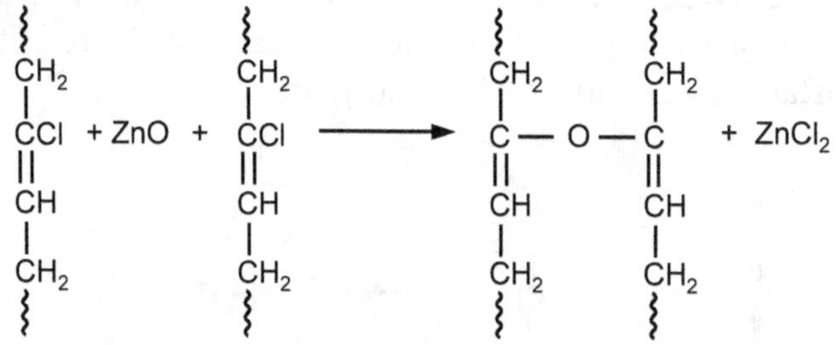

$$
\begin{array}{cccc}
CH_2 & CH_2 & CH_2 \quad\quad CH_2 & \\
| & | & | \quad\quad | & \\
CCl \;+\; ZnO \;+\; & CCl & \longrightarrow \;\; C\!-\!O\!-\!C & +\; ZnCl_2 \\
\| & \| & \| \quad\quad \| & \\
CH & CH & CH \quad\quad CH & \\
| & | & | \quad\quad | & \\
CH_2 & CH_2 & CH_2 \quad\quad CH_2 &
\end{array}
$$

Vulcanized rubber has excellent elasticity, lower water absorption tendency, it is resistant to action of organic solvent, it is resistant to attack of oxidizing agents.

6. **Polyvinyl Chloride (PVC):** Its structure is as follows.

$$\left[CH_2 - \underset{\underset{Cl}{|}}{CH} \right]_n$$

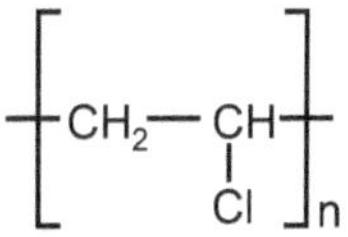

The polymerization is carried out of vinyl chloride monomer ($CH_2=CHCl$) by suspension or emulsion techniques to form PVC. It is also made by bulk polymerization techniques. Bulk and suspension polymerization use azo compounds as a initiator and redox initiator for emulsion techniques.

It is the cheapest plastic. It is widely used as plastic. It is used for making pipes, laminated materials, equipment parts, cable insulations and fibre. It is not thermally stable beyond 200°C. It undergoes degradation with evolution of HCl. Due to formation of conjugated double bond in polymer chain, it results in discoloration of PVC. To avoid this, suitable stabilizer is added in PVC. Stabilizers such as organometallic salts, epoxy compounds, alkali earth oxides etc. are used.

PVC is partially syndiotactic and does not have regular structure. PVC is horn like material and it is very difficult to process. Due to this property it is compounded with plasticizer. Fully rigid to flexible material can be formed by adding varying amount of plasticizer. PVC is used in certain formulations such as in plastisols and organosols. The percentage of chlorine in PVC increases by dissolving suitable solvent such as chlorobenzene and chlorinating at 100°C. This polymer is called as chlorinated PVC. The advantage of chlorination is that polymer becomes more resistant to acids and bases. But thermal stability of chlorinated PVC decreases. Chlorinated PVC is widely used in the manufacture of adhesives, coatings and fibres.

7. **Acrylic:** The compound containing acryloyl group is called as acrylic.

    (a) Polyacrylic acid: It has the following structure.

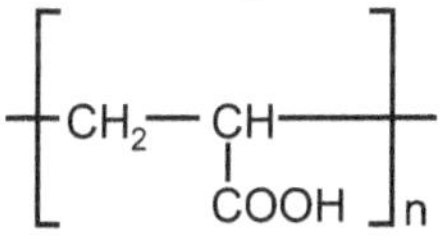

$$\left[CH_2 - \underset{\underset{COOH}{|}}{CH} \right]_n$$

It is dissolved in water and undergoes ionization and exhibits typical behavior of polyelectrolyte. It shows very high viscosities in solutions. It is not used as important plastic because it is water soluble property. It is used as a thickening agent in adhesives.

    (b) Acrylic fibres are synthetic fibres of acrylonitrile. It is called as polyacrylonitrile (PAN) or polyvinyl cyanide. Its structure is as follows:

$$\left[CH_2 - \underset{\underset{CN}{|}}{CH} \right]_n$$

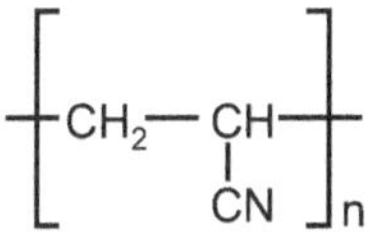

It is soluble in dimethyl formamide and dimethyl sulphoxide. It is used to make PAN fibres.

(c) Acrylic glass or Polymethylmethacrylate (PMMA) is transparent thermoplastic. Its structure is as follows:

$$\left[CH_2 - \underset{\underset{COOCH_3}{|}}{\overset{\overset{CH_3}{|}}{C}} \right]_n$$

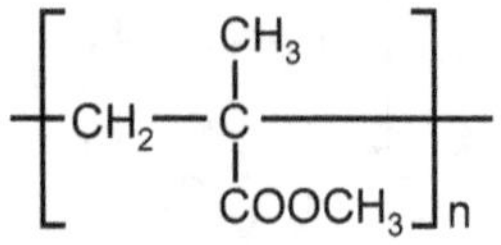

It is resistant to most of chemicals but soluble in organic solvents such as ketones, esters and chlorinated hydrocarbons. It is excellent substitute for glass. It has good mechanical properties. The main characteristic of these plastics is optical clarity. It is similar to glass in having poor scratch resistance. It is used to make signboards and lenses for automobile lighting. It is also used for decorative purposes in buildings, acrylic paint, and fast drying paint containing pigment suspension in acrylic polymer emulsion.

(d) Acrylic resin: Acrylic resins are group of thermoplastic or thermosetting plastic or copolymers of acrylic acid, methacrylic acid, and esters of these acids or acrylonitrile used to produce paints, synthetic rubbers and light weight plastics, textiles, coatings and adhesives etc. It can be cast and molded.

8. **Teflon (Polytetrafluoroethylene):** Its general structure is as follows.

$$\left[CF_2 - CF_2 \right]_n$$

Emulsion polymerization technique is used for the preparation of Teflon using peroxide as a initiator. It is a highly linear and crystalline polymer. Its M.P. is around 330°C. Mechanical strength of polymer is unchanged in the temperature range between −100 to 350°C. It is not dissolved in fuming nitric acid. It is highly chemical resistant. Alkali metal in molten form is only reacting with this polymer.

$$n\, F_2C = CF_2 \xrightarrow[\text{High pressure}]{\text{Persulphate catalyst}} \left[CF_2 - CF_2 \right]_n$$

This polymer is useful for making articles such as pump valves and pipes where chemical resistance is required. It is also useful for making non-lubricated bearings and its fibers are used to form belts, filter cloth and similar materials where chemical resistance is required. The major application of PTFE (polytetrafluoroethylene) is for wiring in aerospace and computer application. It has excellent dielectric properties.

9. **Polyethylene:**

$$\left[CH_2 - CH_2 \right]_n$$

It is of two types of varieties: Low density polyethylene (LDPE) and high density polyethylene (HDPE).

Low density polyethylene is formed by high pressure polymerization of ethylene using oxygen as a initiator at 180-285°C. It is polymerized using bulk or solution polymerization.

$$n \; H_2C{=}CH_2 \xrightarrow[\text{O}_2 \text{ or } \text{H}_2\text{O}_2]{\text{1000 to 2000 atm}} \text{Low Density Polymer (LDPE)}$$

Low density polyethylene has density around 0.91 to 0.92 gm/cc. During polymerization process either by intramolecular or intermolecular chain transfer reaction undergoes to form branched polymer. LDPE is used for packing and wrapping of frozen food, textile materials etc. LDPE is used for making pipes for agricultural, domestic, and irrigation water line connections. It is also useful for insulations of electric cables.

It is inert to chemicals and its resistance to breakage is useful to make bottles and containers.

HDPE is formed by coordination polymerization reaction and its density is 0.965 gm/cc. Its M.P. is 144-150°C.

$$nCH_2 = CH_2 \xrightarrow[\substack{\text{6 to 7 atm., in presence} \\ \text{of Zieglar Natta catalyst}}]{\text{333 to 343 K}} \text{High density polymer (HDPE)}$$

HDPE is useful for making toys and household articles. Whenever high tensile strength and stiffness are required, HDPE is more useful.

10. **Polyacrylonitrile (PAN):** It is also called as polyvinyl cyanide and its general structure is as follows.

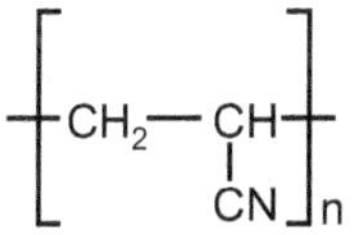

$$\left[\begin{array}{c} CH_2{-}CH \\ | \\ CN \end{array}\right]_n$$

It is prepared by free radical polymerization using peroxide as initiators.

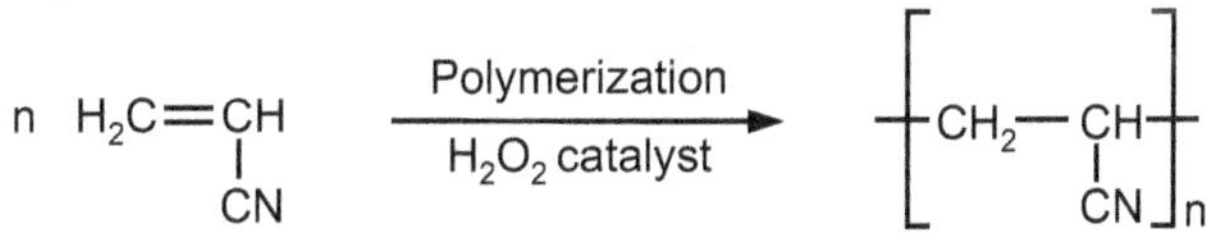

$$n \; H_2C{=}CH \underset{CN}{|} \xrightarrow[\text{H}_2\text{O}_2 \text{ catalyst}]{\text{Polymerization}} \left[\begin{array}{c} CH_2{-}CH \\ | \\ CN \end{array}\right]_n$$

It is soluble in dimethyl formamide and dimethyl sulphoxide. It is hard, horny and has high melting point. It has good mechanical properties and heat resistance upto 220°C. It is used to produce PAN fibres. These fibres are used for making cloth, carpets and blankets. It is when copolymer with butadiene produce nitrile rubber which is very great industrial important material.

1.7 Silicone Polymers

- It is a quartz like polymers in which the three dimensional network of SiO_2 has been modified by introducing of organic groups. The mainly used methyl groups are directly bonded to silicon by silicon –carbon bond. The general structure of silicone polymer is as follows.

$$HO-\left[\begin{array}{c} R \\ | \\ Si-O \\ | \\ R \end{array}\right]_n H \qquad OR \qquad \sim\sim \begin{array}{ccc} R & & R \\ | & & | \\ Si-O- & Si-O \sim\sim \\ | & & | \\ R & & R \end{array}$$

- The synthetic route to silicones proceeds via methylchlorosilanes. In industry almost all methylchlorosilanes are made from silicon and methyl chloride by the Muller-Rochow direct synthesis. The reaction is carried out at temperatures of 250-300°C and 2-5 bar in the presence of copper catalyst to form $(CH_3)_2SiCl_2$.

- Important silane $(CH_3)_2SiCl_2$ are required for production of silicone fluid and silicone rubber obtained is of about 80% yield. The starting materials for producing silicone polymer are alkyl chlorosilane, aryl chlorosilane or substituted esters of orthosilicic acid. These groups are easily hydrolyzed by water to form hydroxyl groups.

- The hydroxyl group is called silanol. Silicones are polymers made up of repeating unit of siloxane.

$$n \begin{array}{c} H_3C \\ \\ H_3C \end{array}\!\!\!\!Si\!\!\!\!\begin{array}{c} Cl \\ \\ Cl \end{array} + nH_2O \xrightarrow{-2nHCl} n \begin{array}{c} H_3C \\ \\ H_3C \end{array}\!\!\!\!Si\!\!\!\!\begin{array}{c} OH \\ \\ OH \end{array} \xrightarrow{-nH_2O} \left[\begin{array}{c} CH_3 \\ | \\ O-Si \\ | \\ CH_3 \end{array}\right]_n$$

- The silane diols are used to form chain like polymers. If silane triols are used the formation of two or three dimensional network is possible.

$$\begin{array}{ccccc}
& O & & O & \\
& / & & \backslash & \\
\sim O\!\!\diagdown & Si-R & & R-Si & -O- \\
& Si-R & & R-Si & \\
& | & & | & \\
& O & & O & \\
& | & & | & \\
& R-Si & -O- & Si-R & \\
& | & & | & \\
& O & & O & \\
& | & & | & \\
-O- & Si-R & & R-Si & -O- \\
& | & & | & \\
& O & & O & \\
& \backslash & & / & \\
& R-Si & -O- & Si-R & \\
& / & & \backslash & \\
& O & & O & \\
& / & & \backslash &
\end{array}$$

- Silicones are typically heat resistant and rubber like and have applications in sealants, adhesives, lubricants, medicine, cooking utensils, thermal and electrical insulation. Silicones are present in common form such as silicone oil, silicone grease, silicone rubber, silicone resin etc.

1. **Silicone oils:** It is clear, colourless and odorless liquid. It is soluble in benzene, gasoline, carbon tetrachloride and other organic solvents. They are stable in temperature at −70 to 270°C in pure form. It is chemically inert, neutral and water repellent. The methyl and methylphenyl silicone oils have important value.

$$H_3C-\underset{\underset{CH_3}{|}}{\overset{\overset{CH_3}{|}}{Si}}-O\left[\underset{\underset{R}{|}}{\overset{\overset{CH_3}{|}}{Si}}-O\right]_n\underset{\underset{CH_3}{\diagdown}}{\overset{\overset{CH_3}{|}}{Si}}-CH_3$$

where R = CH_3 Methyl silicone oil and R = C_6H_5 Methyl phenyl silicone oil.

The effect of temperature on viscosity of methyl silicone oils is very little and it has very good compressibility. Due to this reason they are good brake and hydraulic liquids. In the industry of plastic and rubber, they are used in solutions and aqueous emulsions as separation and unmolding media. They are also added to polishes, paints and varnishes and are used in medicine, pharmacy and cosmetics. They are used as impregnating agents for textiles, leather and paper. The impregnation of textiles is usually accompanied by an anti-wrinkle treatment.

Methylphenyl silicone oils provide high and low temperature lubricants and after filling with lithium stearate, a basis of silicone for silicone grease. Silicone oils are used in transformers and switches, as the working fluid in diffusion pumps, as antifoam and floatation agents, dirt-repelling additive to polishes and window cleaning fluids and heat transfer liquids.

2. **Silicone greases:** It is prepared by thickening the oils with components such as finely powdered silicate, talcum, graphite or metal soaps; these are used mainly as special sealants and lubricants resistant to high temperatures. The addition of molybdenum (IV) sulfide is to improve lubricating properties.

3. **Silicone rubber:** Vulcanization of linear dimethyl polysiloxanes with chain lengths of 6000 to 7000 siloxane units (Mol. Wt. 500000) produces silicone rubber.

   Silicone rubber is vulcanized by free radical mechanism by use of benzoyl peroxide or by radiation techniques.

   The cross linking takes place by following way.

4. **Silicone resin:** It is branched cage like structure. Its general formula is $R_nSi\ X_mO_y$, where R is methyl (Me) or phenyl (Ph) and X is functional group: hydrogen (H),

hydroxyl (OH), chlorine (Cl) or alkoxy group (OR). These groups are further condensed to give highly cross linked insoluble polysiloxane network.

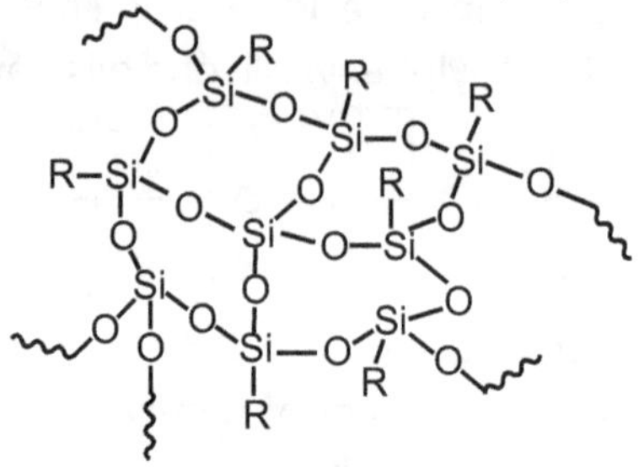

Application of resins are used for binding agents, as starting materials for porous ceramics, matrix sources with impregnation, fibre spinning and ceramic adhesions.

1.8 Resins

1.8.1 Phenol-Formaldehyde (PF) Resins

- Phenol-Formaldehyde resins are formed by polycondensation reaction between phenol and formaldehyde and this reaction is catalyzed by either acids or bases. Acid catalyzed reaction is as follows:

1. $HCHO - H^{\oplus} \longrightarrow {}^{\oplus}CH_2OH$

2.

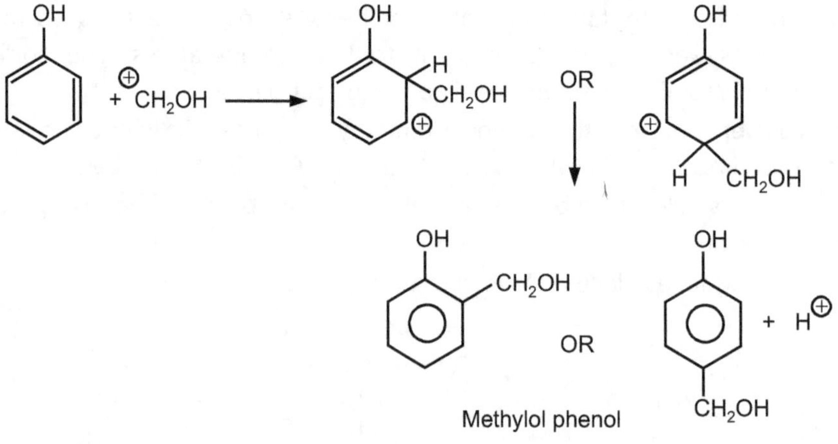

Methylol phenol

3.

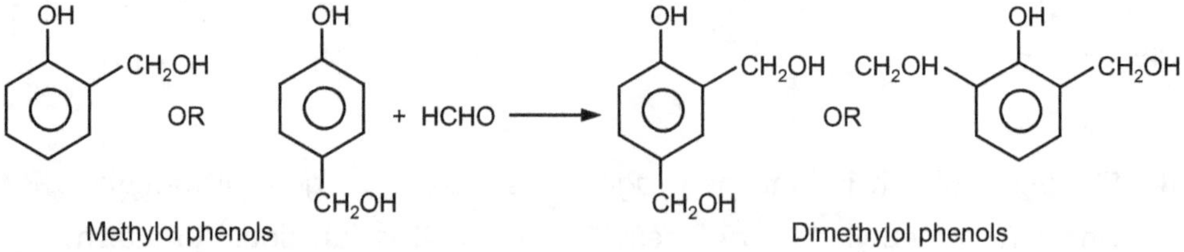

Methylol phenols   + HCHO ⟶   Dimethylol phenols

Alkali catalyzed reactions are as follows:

1.

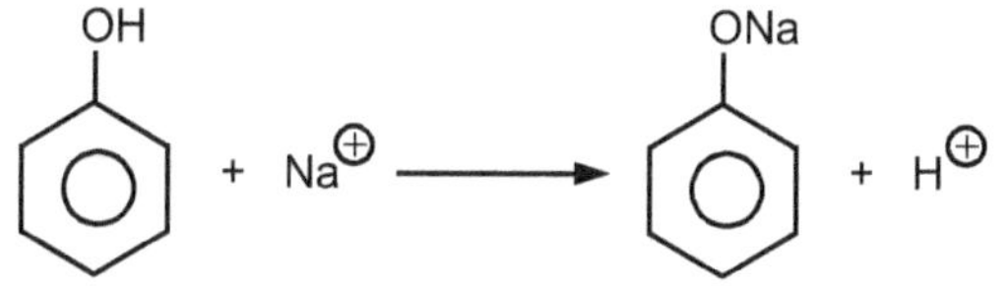

2.

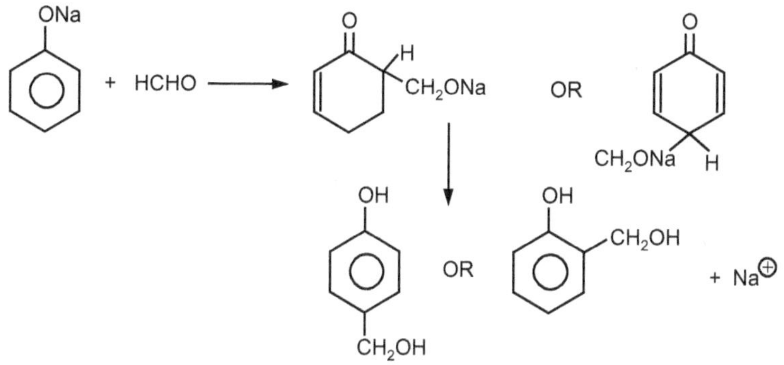

- Dimethylloyl phenol and phenol undergo condensation reaction to give following compound.

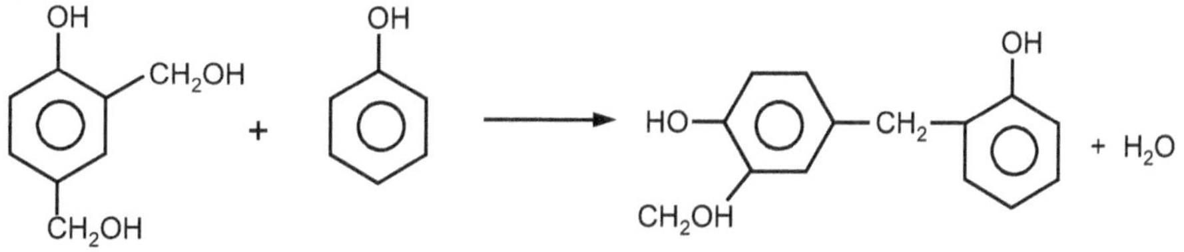

- Methylloyl phenol and phenol react to give the methylene compound.
- When excess of formaldehyde is added and the reaction is continued to react all the ortho- and para-positions of phenol molecules and form following three dimensional cross linked polymer.

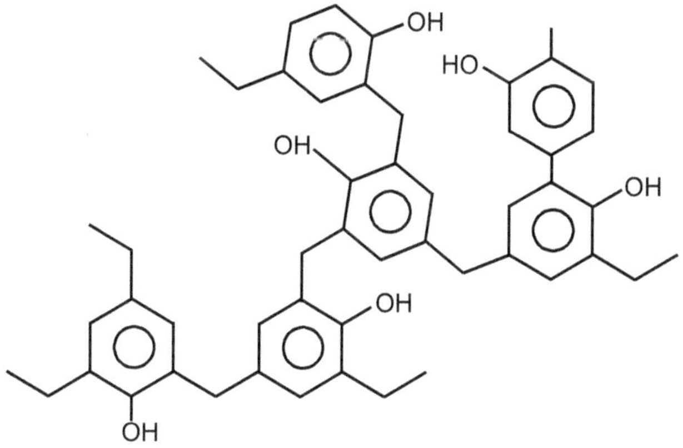

Linear polymer is also formed by two ways.

In the first way phenol is reacted with 75% formaldehyde using an acid catalyzed reaction.

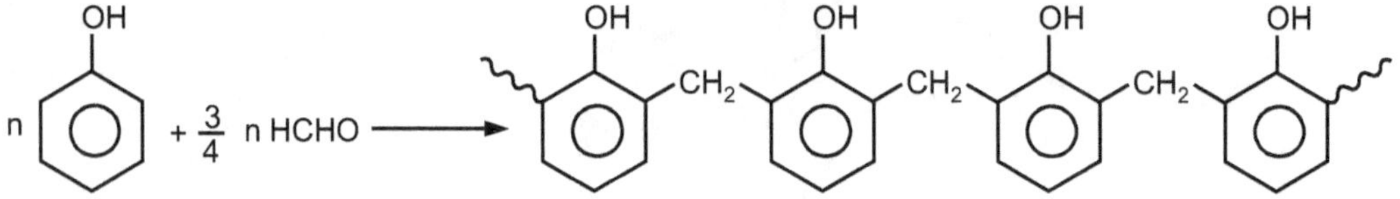

$$n \text{ (phenol)} + \tfrac{3}{4}\, n\ HCHO \longrightarrow$$

- The resin formed can be stored for longer time without hardening and cross-linking. The cross linking can be done whenever necessary by adding excess of formaldehyde and then heating. This PF resin is also called as **Novolak** or **Bakelite resin**.

- In second way equimolar quantities of phenol and formaldehyde are reacted using alkaline catalyst under carefully controlled rate of reaction. The resins formed contain methyllol group at ortho and para position as following type of linear structure.

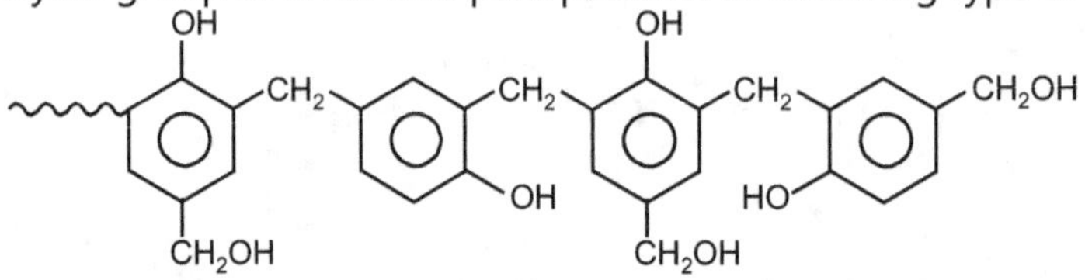

When it is stored it undergoes slow reaction to form hard resin. Such type of resin is called **resol.**

- The novolak and resol can undergo reaction to form cross linked network as shown below.

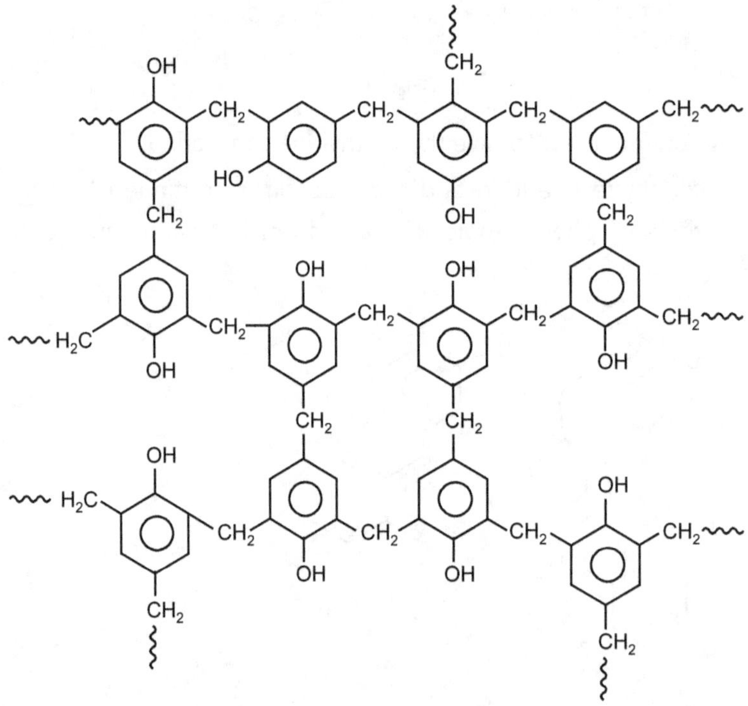

- Bakelite resins are compounded with asbestos powder or saw dust as filler and it is used for moulding electrical items, telephone instruments. Resol is useful for making laminates paper, fabric or asbestos cloth are impregnated with resols.

- Novolak and resol resins are used as coating composition. Mixed with sand, they find use as core binders in foundries.

1.8.2 Urea-Formaldehyde (UF) Resins

- It is formed by polycondensation reaction between urea and formaldehyde to form urea-formaldehyde (UF) resins as follows. It is also known as urea-methanal resin.

$$n \ HCHO \ + \ n \ NH_2CONH_2 \longrightarrow H{\left[NHCO-NH-CH_2\right]}_n OH \ + \ (n-1)H_2O$$

- When excess of formaldehyde is used then hydrogen of imide group of linear polymer is replaced by methylol group.

$$\text{\textasciitilde} NHCO-NH-CH_2 \text{\textasciitilde} \ + \ HCHO \longrightarrow \text{\textasciitilde} NHCON-CH_2 \text{\textasciitilde}$$
$$|$$
$$CH_2OH$$

- If linear polymer of UF resin is heated subsequently with excess of formaldehyde, a three dimensional network of polymer will be formed.

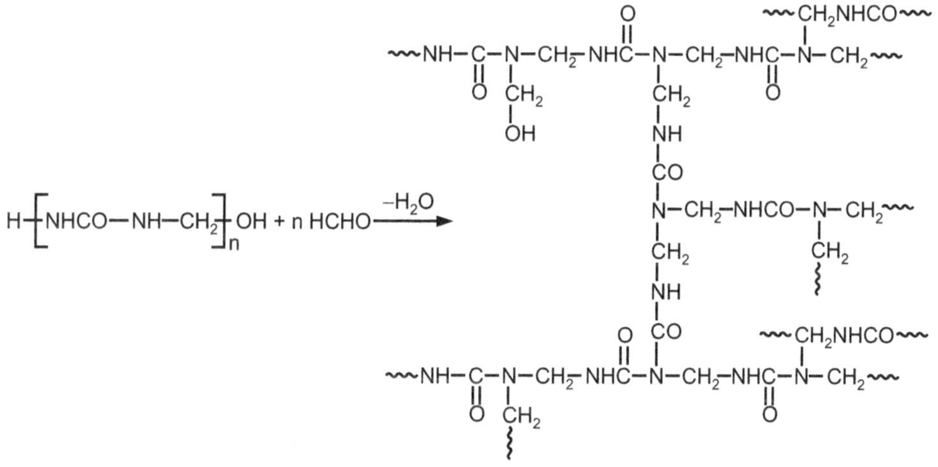

- UF resin has high tensile strength, high heat of distortion temperature, low water absorption and high surface hardness. UF resin is non-transparent thermosetting resin or plastic. Urea-formaldehyde resins are used as adhesives, finishes, particle board.

1.8.3 Melamine-Formaldehyde Resins

- It is formed in two stages. In the first stage melamine and formaldehyde react to give methylol derivatives at 80°C-90°C shown below.

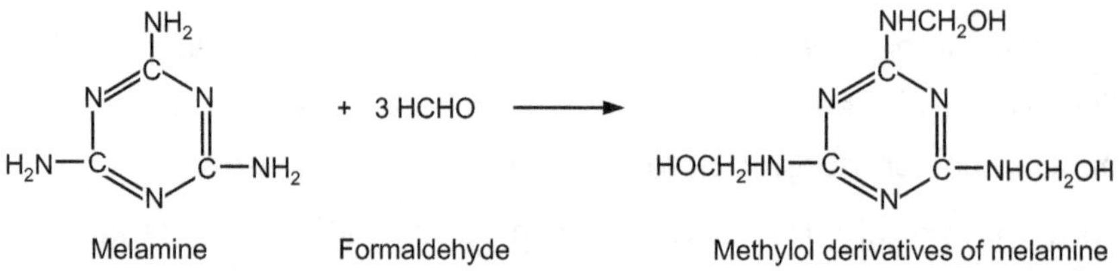

Melamine   Formaldehyde   Methylol derivatives of melamine

- In the second stage subsequent polycondensation of methylol derivative of melamine takes place with addition of excess quantities of melamine in acidic medium at 50°C-60°C to form linear polymer. After addition of formaldehyde, it is further reacted to linear polymer to give three dimensional network of the polymer as shown below.

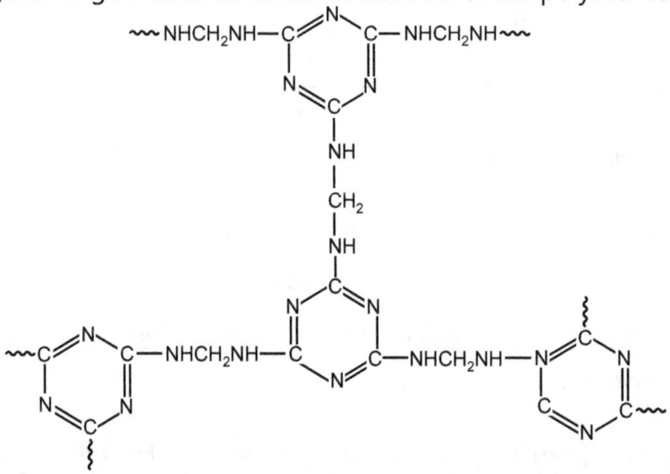

- It is amorphous, white product and readily soluble in water but insoluble in organic solvents. It is used in the manufacture of plastics, carbamide glue, and varnishes. Melamine is used in the manufacture of decorative laminates. It is used in lacquer's preparation.

1.8.4 Epoxy Resins

- Its general structure is as follows:

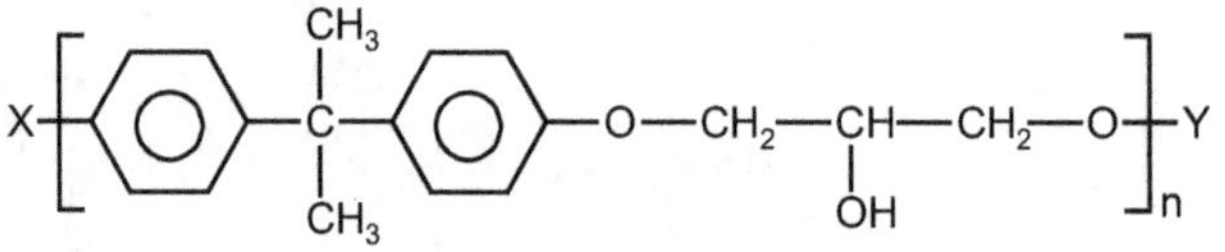

- It is polyether. It is prepared from epichlorohydrin and bisphenol.

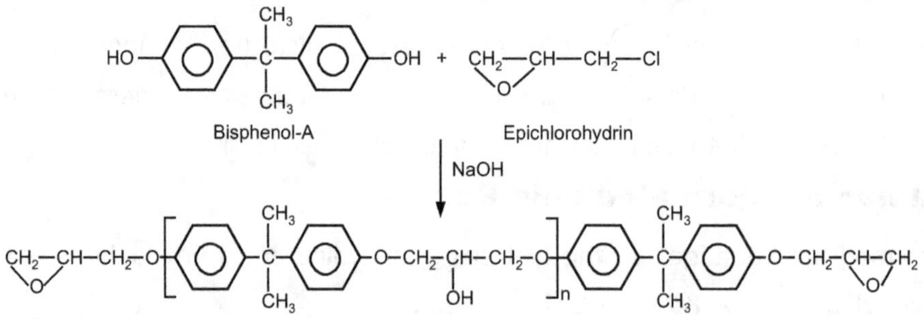

Bisphenol-A   Epichlorohydrin

- Instead of bisphenol, other compounds like glycols, glycerol and resorcinol are also used for preparation. It is highly chemical resistance and have good adhesion. It is used as adhesive. It is also used as protective coatings and materials like electronic circuit boards and for patching holes in concrete pavement when it is cured to form very tough materials. They are used for industrial floorings, potting materials for electrical insulation, foams etc.

Exercises

(A) Answer the following:

1. Define and explain the following terms:
   - (a) Polymer
   - (b) Monomer
   - (c) Repeating unit
   - (d) Degree of polymer
   - (e) Homopolymer
   - (f) Copolymer
   - (g) Chain polymerisation
   - (h) Ionic polymerisation
   - (i) Free radical polymerisation
   - (j) Polymerisation
   - (k) Step polymerisation
   - (l) Co-ordination polymerisation
   - (m) Polycondensation polymerisation
   - (n) Poly addition polymerisation
   - (o) Ring opening polymerisation

2. Give classification of polymers.

3. Give classification of polymerization reaction.

4. What is nylon? Give commercial importance of Nylon.

5. What is polyester? Give commercial importance of polyesters (terylene and dacron).

6. What is the commercial importance of rubber?

7. What is vulcanization of rubber?

8. What is the commercial importance of synthetic rubber, Buna 2-N rubber?

9. What is copolymer? Give importance of copolymers of butadiene.

10. What is the commercial importance of PVC?

11. What is the commercial importance of acrylic polymer?

12. What is teflon? What is the commercial importance of teflon polymer?

13. What is the commercial importance of polyethylene?

14. What is the commercial importance of acrylonitrile polymer?

15. What is silicone polymer? What are uses of silicone oils, rubber, grease and resin?

16. Give the synthesis and uses of phenol-formaldehyde resins.

17. Give the synthesis and uses of urea-formaldehyde resins.

18. Give the synthesis and uses of epoxy resins.

19. Give the synthesis and uses of melamine-formaldehyde resins.

20. Write a note on thermodynamics and transport properties of polymers.

21. What is source based nomenclature of polymer?

(B) Multiple Choice Questions (MCQs):

(i)   Polytetrafluoroethylene is called as _____.

   (a) Teflon   (b) Novolak   (c) Acrilan fibres   (d) Polyester

(ii) Terylene polymer is also called as _____.

   (a) Polyamide   (b) Nylon   **(c) Polyester**   (d) Polyether

(iii) Terylene is a _____type of polymer.

   (a) Plastic   (b) Elastomer   **(c) Fibre**   (d) Resin

(iv) Polymethylmethacrylate (PMMA) is transparent _____ polymer.

   (a) thermosetting   **(b) thermoplastic**   (c) elastomer   (d) resin

(v)   Low density polyethylene has density around _____.

   (a) 0.91 gm/cc   (b) 0.965 gm/cc   (c) 0.521 gm/cc   (d) 0.715 gm/cc

(C) State True or False:

(i)   Epoxy resin is a polyether polymer.

(ii)   Whenever necessary cross-linked phenol-formaldehyde resin is formed by adding excess of formaldehyde and then heating.

(iii) Cis-1, 4 polyisoprene is a synthetic rubber.

(iv) SBR is a homopolymer.

(v)   HDPE is formed by coordination polymerization reaction.

(vi) Aliphatic polyester have low M.P. than aromatic polyester.

(vii) Nitrile rubber is also called BUNA-S.

(viii) Vulcanized rubber has excellent elasticity.

> **Ans.:** (i) - True, (ii) - True, (iii) - False, (iv) - False, (v) - True, (vi) - True, (vii) - False
>
> (viii) - True.

■■■

Chapter 2...

Sugar and Fermentation Industry

Contents ...

(A) SUGAR INDUSTRY

2.1   Introduction
2.2   Importance of Sugar Industry
2.3   Cultivation and Harvesting of Sugar Cane
2.4   Manufacture of Direct Consumption (Plantation White) Cane Sugar
    2.4.1   Raw Materials
    2.4.2   Processes/Steps involved in Cane Sugar Manufacture
2.5   Utilization of By-products of Sugar Industries
    2.5.1   Bagasse
    2.5.2   Molasses
    2.5.3   Furnace Ash

(B) FERMENTATION INDUSTRY

2.6   Introduction
2.7   Importance of Fermentation Industry
2.8   Basic Requirements of Fermentation Process
2.9   Factors Favouring Fermentation
2.10 Fermentation Operations
2.11 Manufacture of Industrial Alcohol (Ethyl Alcohol) from Molasses
    2.11.1 Commercial Production using Molasses as a Raw Material
    2.11.2 Commercial Production using Starch as a Raw Material (Food Grains)
    2.11.3 Manufacture of Ethanol from Hydrocarbons
    2.11.4 Manufacture of Wine
    2.11.5 Manufacture of Whisky and Rum
    2.11.6 Importance of Power Alcohol
•   Exercises

(A) SUGAR INDUSTRY

2.1 Introduction

• Food may be classified according to its principal chemical constituents into carbohydrates, fats, proteins, vitamins and minerals. Carbohydrates are abundant in wide variety of foods, including potatoes, rice, wheat, corn etc. They serve as a principal source of energy for physiological functions and other biological process. Carbohydrates are made up of carbon, hydrogen and oxygen atoms.

- Carbohydrates of simple structures are called sugars. Sugar and starch are among those chemicals found so abundantly in nature. Both are available at such percentages in some plants like sugar cane, sugar beet, potato etc. Cane sugar belongs to this class called as sucrose having the formula $C_{12}H_{22}O_{11}$. Chemists designate a large group of related compounds as sugars. They are usually referred to by specific names viz. corn sugar, fruit sugar, milk sugar etc.

2.2 Importance of Sugar Industry

- Sucrose is obtained commercially in substantial amounts from sugar cane and sugar beet plants only. Sugar cane which supplies about 56% of the world total and sugar beet which provide 44%. Sugar in the cane and beet has same chemical composition as sucrose. Sugar is formed in the stalk of the sugar cane by a process of photosynthesis. The primary use of sugar is in the manufacture of food materials or as a food itself. Cane sugar is used all over the world as a sweetening agent. For this purpose, highly refined or purified i.e. white sugar is used.

- Sucrose has a food value. Sugar supplies man with about 13% of the energy required for existence. It supply energy required for the growth of living cells their reproduction and movement. It is best fuel for living cells. Due to its important functions, it is necessary to study the extraction, purification and the properties of sucrose. The cane sugar industrially is based on extraction of sucrose from sugar cane. In India, sucrose is obtained from sugar cane only. Sugar cane contains 70-75% water, 10-15% crystalline sugar, 0.5-1% reducing sugar, 10-18% fiber, 1% ash and 1% organic acids. India has been the chief sugar producing country in the world. Today, the quality of sugar has been improved to great extent as a result of better techniques employed throughout the world.

2.3 Cultivation and Harvesting of Sugar Cane

- Sugar cane is a large perennial tropical grass. It has a bamboo like stalk which grows to a height of 10 to 14 feets and contains 11 to 15% sucrose by weight. The cane is usually planted with cuttings from the mature stalk, in rows separated by 3-6 feet distance. Each cutting should contain two or more buds, which sprout and produce a number of new stalks. Approximately 12 to 15 months are required for first crop, while the subsequent crops require about 12 months. The cane stalk consists of a series of joints or internodes separated by nodes. The nodes are woody nature, while the internodes is soft pith containing sucrose. Generally, after 2 to 5 harvests obtained from the original planting, the fields are replanted (i.e. 2-5 cuttings have been made from the original plantings).

- Sugar cane harvesting is done by hand with machete type knives or by machine depending on the availability of labor. The workers cut off the sugar cane close to the ground level as well as they remove leaves and tops of the stalk. Transportation of sugar cane from field to mill is mainly done by the use of trucks, trailers, cart tandems, etc. After cutting, there can be no delay in transporting the freshly cut cane to the factory, because failure to process it within less than 24 hours after cutting causes loss by inversion to glucose and fructose. Therefore, to avoid the inversion of sucrose and finally yields of sugar, sugar cane should be processed for sugar as early as possible.

2.4 Manufacture of Direct Consumption (Plantation White) Cane Sugar

- Sugar cane is an important source of white crystalline sugar. The quality of sugar has been improved to a great extent as a result of better techniques employed.

2.4.1 Raw Materials

- Manufacture of cane sugar requires raw materials mainly sugar canes and processing materials such as lime, calcium triphosphate or phosphoric acid, carbon dioxide, sulphur dioxide and process water.

2.4.2 Processes/Steps involved in Cane Sugar Manufacture

- The cane sugar manufacture involves number of physical and chemical process. The steps involved in the manufacture of cane sugar from sugar cane are as follows:
  (i)   Preliminary treatment to sugar cane.
  (ii)   Extraction of juice.
  (iii) Purification of juice.
  (iv)   Evaporation or concentration of cane juice.
  (v)   Crystallisation of sucrose.
  (vi)   Centrifugation.
  (vii) Drying.
  (viii) Screening and bagging.

  (i) Preliminary treatment to sugar cane: Before milling sugar canes are given cleaning treatments, such as washing in order to remove mud or dirt (e.g. soil, rock, clay etc.). Washing systems can range from a simple wash with warm water on the carrier or table. In modern plants, washing system consists of conveyors with water jets, baths for removal of adhered dirt.

  (ii) Extraction of juice: For the extraction of sugar cane juice, the following operations are carried out:
    (a) By chopping or cutting the canes into smaller pieces with one or two sets of rotating knives. The speed of rotating knives is about 400-600 revolutions per minute.
    (b) By disintegrating the canes into finer pieces by a crusher or shredder. The crusher consists of two roller mills.

The crushed sugar cane passes through a series of three horizontal rollers (mills). The rollers are fixed at the corners of a triangle. The top roller from each mill rotates in anticlockwise direction while the bottom two rollers rotate clockwise. The heavy pressure on the top roller is exerted by hydraulic rams (about 500 tons). Below each mill a juice pan is placed for collection of extracted juice. In sugar factory, 3 to 5 such roller mills may be arranged. The crusher and first mill extract 60-70% cane juice, while the remaining mills extract 22-24% cane juice.

This extracted sugar cane juice is only about 50% of the total juice present in the sugar cane, i.e. fiber (bagasse) contains remaining 50% juice. The juice that remains with fiber contains the same proportion of sucrose as in the original juice of the cane. If this sucrose is not extracted from the fiber, then it would cause a loss to the factory. It also affects total recovery of sugar. To reduce sucrose in the fiber (bagasse), compound imbibition process is used.

Compound Imbibition process: It is a dilution process which helps to reduce the sucrose content in the fiber by repeated dilution. In this process, the juice from second mill is sprayed on the fiber (bagasse) as it passes from first mill. The juice from the third mill is sprayed on first as well as second mills, while the juice from the fourth mill is sprayed with hot water and the expressed juice from that mill is brought back to the second mill. In this way, the juice in the bagasse is always diluted before crushing. Thus, compound imbibitions process is nothing but dilution. Thus, nearly, 95-98% juice is extracted from bagasse.

The juice from milling station is pumped into a weighing tank. The weighed juice is screened with metallic cloths to remove suspended impurities. This juice is acidic, opaque greenish liquid containing soluble impurities like soils, fats, proteins, waxes, gums and colouring matter.

(III) Purification or Clarification of juice: After weighing, the juice is sent for purification process. To remove soluble impurities, number of processes are used. Good purification depends upon the formation of a stable flocculant precipitate of impurities, which settles rapidly. The clarification processes are as follows:

(a) **Purification by Lime Defecation process:** The screened juice is acidic having pH 4.9 to 5.5. Inversion of sucrose may take place in acidic solution. So to avoid inversion of sucrose, it should be neutralized by adding milk of lime (about 1 pound of CaO per ton of cane) to bring the pH to the range 7.5 to 8.5. Then this solution is heated to a temperature between 90°C to 115°C. The combined action of lime and heat on the juice leads to precipitate tricalcium phosphate. Along with this, remaining colloidal impurities such as proteins, gums, etc. are coagulated and precipitated. The precipitate is removed by sedimentation or settling in clarifier.

The flocculant precipitate or muds which settle on the classifier trays contain about 5% solid matter. Sugar is recovered from the muds by using rotary vacuum filters with perforated metallic screen cloth. The turbid filtrate is returned to the purification system and then press cake is discarded or used as fertilizer.

(b) **Phosphatation:** If the phosphate content of the preclarified juice is less than 300 ppm of phosphate, then a soluble phosphate like phosphoric acid (H_3PO_4) is added to improve the clarification. The mixture is then limed to pH 7.0 to 8.0, aerated with compressed air and sent to clarifier. The precipitated calcium phosphate absorbs much of the impurities present in the juice. If phosphoric acid is used for purification of juice then an excess of lime is required.

(c) **Sulphitation:** In this method, sulphur dioxide is used to clarify sugar juice. The juice can be treated with calcium phosphate and SO_2 is bubbled through the juice until pH becomes 7 to 7.1, which is heated to about 60-70°C. The hot juice is sent to the settling tank where suspended matter and impurities get precipitated out and clear juice is obtained. Then impurities are removed by filtration.

Sulphur dioxide acts on lime for forming a precipitate of calcium sulphite. It can be removed by filtration.

$$Ca(OH)_2 + H_2SO_3 \longrightarrow CaSO_3 \downarrow + 2\,H_2O$$

Sulphurous acid is formed by passing SO_2 gas in the juice, it is a strong bleaching agent.

The sulphur dioxide in purification serves three purposes. They are as follows: (1) It neutralises excess quantity of lime added. (2) It bleaches juice by acting on the colouring matters. (3) It decreases the viscosity of juice.

(d) **Carbonation:** The purification of cane juice is also carried out by passing carbon dioxide. In this process, CO_2 gas acts as a neutralising agent while the lime is used as a clarifying agent. Sugar cane juice is heated at about 60°C and milk of lime is added to it. The CO_2 gas is obtained by burning limestone in the kiln. Then CO_2 gas is passed through limited cane juice till the pH of the resulting solution becomes seven or less. The limited juice then reacts with CO_2 to precipitate excess of lime.

$$Ca(OH)_2 + CO_2 \rightarrow CaCO_3 \downarrow + H_2O$$

The juice along with the precipitate is filtered without settling. If excess of CO_2 gas is passed through juice, then calcium bicarbonate is obtained. By boiling juice, calcium bicarbonate decomposes into $CaCO_3$ and CO_2 gas. The juice is filtered without settling in a rotary press.

Carbonation process removes greatest amount of non-sugars as compared to sulphitation process. Higher recovery of commercial sugar is possible due to carbonation process. Similarly, good quality sugar produced is also superior when carbonation process is used instead of sulphitation process.

(iv) Evaporation or Concentration: The clarified juice is pumped to evaporator, where it is concentrated to a clear heay syrup containing about 65% solids. Evaporation is carried out in 'multiple effect' evaporator in order to achieve maximum steam economy, i.e. evaporation is carried out in a series of evaporators. Generally, four such evaporators are used. Each evaporator is made up of steel plate having cylindrical shape. All evaporators are placed vertically and are heated by means of steam. This arrangement allows the juice to be drawn from one vessel to the next and permits the juice to boil at low temperature. The steam is produced under vacuum and it is circulated through 'multiple evaporators' system. When steam enters in second evaporator, which have less temperature, still the evaporation becomes rapid. This is because higher vacuum is maintained in the second evaporator, i.e. higher vacuum in evaporator decreases the boiling temperature of juice. Occasionally, surfactants are added to the juice to improve the rate of evaporation.

The vacuum and corresponding temperature maintained in each evaporator along with steam temperature is as follows:

Description	Evaporators			
	I	II	III	IV
(i) Temperature of heating steam (°C)	111	98.8	86.1	76.1
(ii) Boiling temperature of juice (°C)	99	86.2	76.4	60
(iii) Vacuum maintained (inch/Hg)	1.1	12	20	24.5

From above data, it is seen that most of the water is removed at comparatively lower temperature, which does not allow sugar loss due to evaporation. From the fourth evaporator, the pale yellow syrup is obtained containing about 60% solid matter.

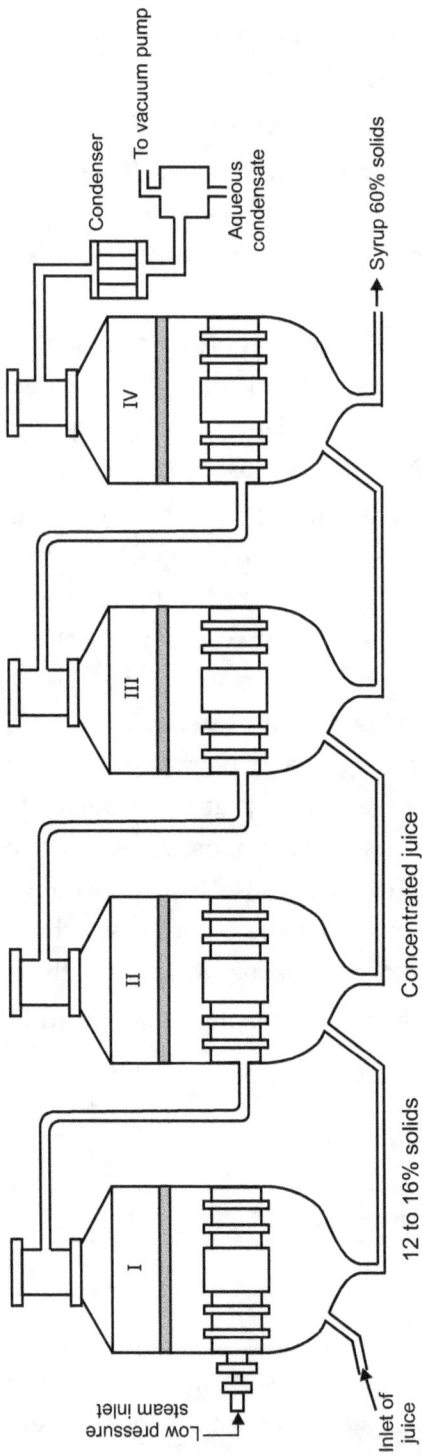

Fig. 2.1: Concentration by Multiple Effect Evaporator

(v) Crystallisation: The concentrated dark brown viscous syrup from the evaporator is pumped to a single effect 'vacuum pan' where it is evaporated to supersaturation. The vacuum pan is designed to handle viscous material, it is a vertical cylinder. A typical vacuum pan is 8 m in height and 5 m in diameter. The working capacity of vacuum pan is about 100 cubic feet of massecuite (mixture of syrup and crystals). Vacuum pan is fitted with a mechanical stirrer for maintaining the uniform temperature (Refer Fig. 2.2).

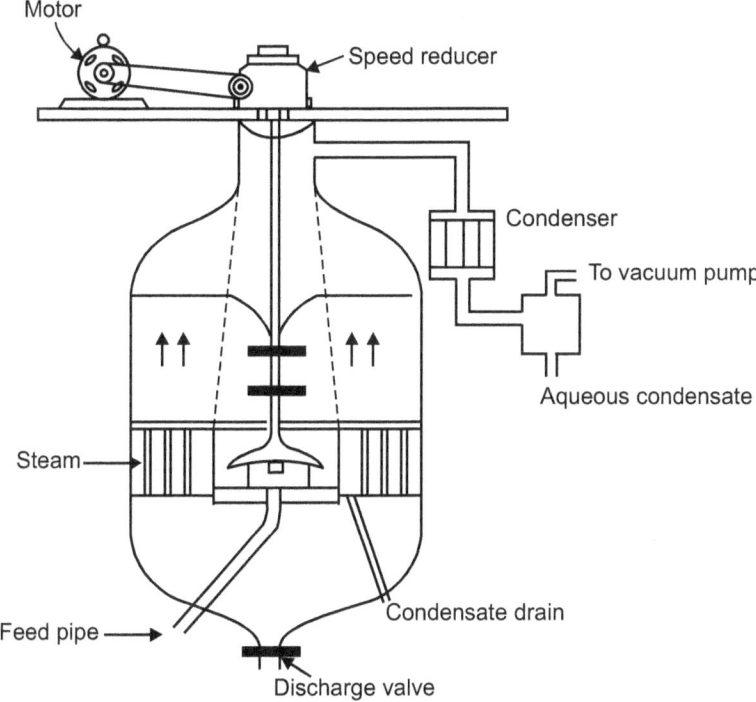

Fig. 2.2: Cross-section of vacuum pan

The crystallization is carried out in four different stages: (a) Seeding or graining, (b) Establishing the seeds, (c) Growth of crystals and (d) Concentration.

The 'seed grain' is added in the first compartment, which serves as a nuclei for the sugar crystals. Additional syrup is added to control the fluidity of the massecuite. Approximately, 20% of the syrup is introduced at the concentrator and 80% of the syrup is fed to the various compartments.

The crystallization of sugar in vacuum pan is called 'sugar boiling' and each boiling is termed as 'strike'. A single crystallization is not sufficient to recover all the sugar from the syrup and hence it is necessary to follow three or four boiling. The products of first boiling (massecuite) would be given the letter 'A' and its products after centrifugation are A-sugar and A-molasses. Similarly, products of second and third boiling would be assigned the letters B and C respectively. The products of first and second boilings are termed as A and B massecuites and are sent to centrifugals for separation of crystals. While the product of third boiling (C-massecuite) is a low purity, highly viscous material containing a large amount of recoverable sucrose remained in the solution. Centrifugation of the 'C'-massecuite yields final molasses and C-sugar is used for seeding the sugars A and B.

Curing of Sugar: The A-massecuite from crystallizer is sent to the centrifugal machine by using magwa pump for separating sugar from molasses A.

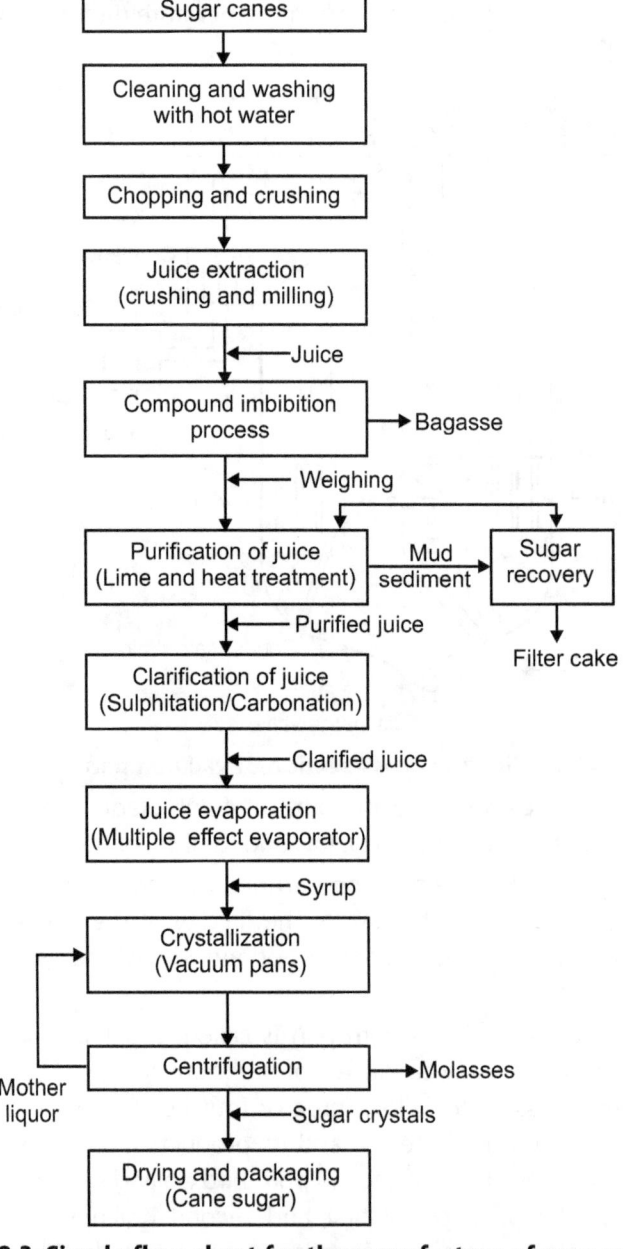

Fig. 2.3: Simple flow-sheet for the manufacture of cane sugar

(vi)   Centrifugation: Massecuites A and B from vacuum pan are sent to the centrifugal machines where, the crystals are separated from the mother liquor. A centrifugal machine consists of a cylindrical perforated basket. It is lined with a perforated metal sheet. The basket is placed on a shaft which can rotate the massecuite from a vertical layer on the screen lining. The basket rotates with the speed 1000-1800 revolutions per minute (r.p.m.). The perforated lining helps to separate the sugar crystals which wash with a spray of water. Due to this the molasses adhering on the crystals are removed. The basket continues rotating until the sugar is dry.

(vii) Drying: The sugar crystals obtained from centrifuge contain small amount of mixture ranging from 1 to 2% depending upon the type and condition of the centrifugal, character of the grain, the purity of the massecuites, etc. The wet sugar is fed to drying equipment called granulators which are nothing but rotating horizontal drums. Heated air is passed through the dryer counter current with the flow of sugar. The temperature of the hot air must be controlled, otherwise high temperature removes the luster of the sugar crystals.

(viii) Screening and bagging: The resulting dried crystals are screened to remove the larger and the finer fractions, i.e. they are graded according to size. The separation of various size grains is usually accomplished by mechanical screens. Finally, the sugar is weighed and packed automatically in various bags, boxes, barrels and sacks.

2.5 Utilization of By-products of Sugar Industries

- Following are important by-products of sugar industry.

2.5.1 Bagasse

- The fibrous portion of cane from which juice is extracted is known as bagasse. It contains about 46-52% moisture, 43-52% fibre and 2-6% soluble solids (mostly sugar). A large quantity of bagasse is produced during the cane sugar manufacture and its application in many areas.

Uses of Bagasse:
(i)   Bagasse is primarily used as a fuel for the generation of steam which is utilized in electricity production. It is also used as a fuel for furnaces in sugar factories and as a substitute for charcoal or wood used for cooking purpose.

(ii) The bagasse is utilized as a raw material for the pulp, paper, paper board and wall board industries.

(iii) Bagasse charcoal is manufactured from bagasse, which on destructive distillation gives charcoal, combustible gases, methyl alcohol, acetic acid and tar.

(iv) Pith is separated by gravity separators from bagasse and used in the manufacture of explosives.

(v)   Bagasse is used in the manufacture of α-cellulose, plastic, furfural and bagasse concrete.

(vi) Bagasse mixture with molasses and the ammoniated bagasse are used as animal feed.

(vii) The compost of bagasse contains potassium 0.3%, P_2O_5 0.005%, nitrogen 0.4% and hence used as a neutral fertilizer.

(viii) A high quality wax has also been extracted from bagasse.

(ix) Producer gas is made by burning to bagasse ash by means of a mixture of air and steam; the resulting gas being a mixture of burnt and combustible gas.

2.5.2 Molasses

Molasses is a dark coloured viscous liquid left after crystallization of cane sugar from cane juice. A residual mother liquor left in the crystallization of sugar, from which no additional sugars can be recovered economically, is a by-product, commonly called black-strap molasses i.e. it is concentrated cane juice, from which no cane sugar has been extracted. It contains a significant quantity of both sucrose and reducing sugars.

Uses of Molasses:

(i) Molasses is extensively used for cattle feed, although it provides carbohydrates.

(ii) Molasses is used in the manufacture of organic chemicals like acetone, citric acid, glycerol, acetic acid and vinegar, lactic acid etc.

(iii) Edible syrup is manufactured from molasses.

(iv) Molasses is utilized to produce compressed yeast, which contains enzymes invertase and zymase responsible for fermentation.

(v) It is used in the distilleries for the production of rum and ethyl alcohol by the process of fermentation.

(vi) It is also used as a neutral fertilizer as for every one metric tonne of molasses spread in the field, the land receives on the average 5.2 kg nitrogen, 2.5 kg P_2O_5 and 51.3 kg K_2O.

2.5.3 Furnace Ash

• The bagasse ash contains silica (SiO_2) and oxides of other metals like Ca, Mg, K, Na, Al, Fe and P. The quantity of ash produced averages 0.3-0.5% of the weight of the cane.

Uses of Furnace Ash:

(i) It is mostly used as a natural fertilizer because it contains K_2O - 10%, and P_2O_5 - 3%.

(ii) It is also used in the glass industry, as it is easy to grind, it resist to water below 100°C.

(B) FERMENTATION INDUSTRY

2.6 Introduction

• Fermentation of sugars by yeast is the oldest synthetic chemical process used from ancient times. It is still of economic importance for the preparation of ethanol and certain other alcohols such as organic acids like (acetic, lactic, citric, fumaric, amino acids etc.), antibiotics (penicillin, streptomycin, chloromphenicol etc.), vitamin-C.

• The word fermentation is derived from the Latin word (Ferver = to boil). The term fermentation is defined by different ways.

- It can be defined as, the process in which chemical changes are brought about in an organic substrate (carbohydrate, hydrocarbons, proteins etc.) by the action of biological catalyst known as enzymes produced by specific type of living microorganisms.
- The microorganisms which cause the breakdown of the complex organic compounds into simpler ones, or help the oxidation of some organic compounds are all fungi.
- The other class of microorganisms namely the yeasts are very important in chemical industries because all types of alcoholic fermentations require these yeasts.
- There are two classes of yeasts (1) Cultured yeast i.e. Saccharomyces Cerevisiae and Saccharamyces ellipsoidous and (2) Wild yeast i.e. S Pastorianus.
- The raw material used in alcohol fermentation industries is the cane sugar or glucose. Therefore any natural product which contains these sugars or can be easily converted into them is a good source of ethyl alcohol.
- The raw materials for alcohol industry are:
  1. Substances containing fermentable sugars. e.g. cane juice, beat, dates, molasses and fruit juices.
  2. Substances containing starch e.g. potatoes, rice, barley and maize.

2.7 Importance of Fermentation Industry

- The products of industrial fermentation are the metabolic products formed during the growth of microorganism. The products include:
  (a) Alcoholic products like wine, beer, alcohol etc.
  (b) Organic acids like acetic, lactic,citric,gluconic etc.
  (c) Amino acids like Lysine,glutamic etc.
  (d) Antibiotics like chloromphenicol, tetracycline, erythromycin etc
  (e) Yeasts like Baker and fodder.
  (f) Vitamin C.
- All these products can be obtained from natural substances like agricultural products and by-products which are cheaply available. The products listed above can also be obtained by chemical synthetic route but at higher cost. Some products can only be economically obtained by the fermentation process only.

2.8 Basic Requirements of Fermentation Process

- Success of the industrial fermentation process depends on various factors as follows:
  (a) The raw material must be cheaply and easily available in uniform composition.
  (b) Selected microorganism for fermentation operation must readily propagate. It should maintain its uniform biological and biochemical characteristics during operation to give high yield of the desired fermentation product.
  (c) The rate of fermentation should be high (less time).
  (d) It should give the unique product and recovery of product must be easy.
  (e) The industrial fermentation should be more economic than the chemical process.
- The fermentation process has been brought about by different microorganisms of natural origin, hence certain condition has to be maintained for good fermentation yield.

2.9 Factors Favouring Fermentation

- Formation of high fermentation yields of product depends on following factors.

  (a) **Medium:** An appropriate amount of all desired nutritive components should be present in the medium for the proper growth of the microorganisms. The precursors (minerals) must be added to maintain the proper concentration of all the nutritive components.

  (b) **pH:** The microorganisms are living organism, hence they sustain very narrow pH range. Optimum pH (6.5 to 7.5) of the medium is the basic requirement for better fermentation result. Acidic and basic substances produced by the microorganism during fermentation can alter the pH. This inhibits the growth of the microorganism, so various buffers are used to control the pH.

  (c) **Temperature:** Low temperature decrease the rate of fermentation while high temperature destroys the microorganism. Optimum temperature must be used for the better fermentation yield. The optimum temperature for good fermentation yield is 30-40°C.

  (d) **Aeration:** For aerobic fermentation, dissolved oxygen is required in the medium. It is necessary to bubble the air for aerobic fermentation; so stirring or mixing of the medium during the fermentation may be done at regular intervals of time.

  (e) **Foaming:** During fermentation CO_2 is formed which forms foam or froth during stirring or mixing of the medium. This may lead to infection and loss of material i.e. reduction in fermentation yield. So de-foaming equipments are used or antifoaming agents are added in the medium.

  (f) **Inoculum:** The optimum inoculums size is from 1% to 20% depending upon a particular fermentation process.

  (g) **Sterilization:** Contaminations due to other microorganisms may reduce the fermentation yield by destroying certain nutrients, so that sterilization of the medium is necessary.

2.10 Fermentation Operations

- Fermentation process involves following operations.

(a) Preparation of inoculum:

As far as the industrial fermentation process is involved, it requires the biological catalyst. i.e. micro-organisms e.g. for fermentation of molasses it requires Saccharomyces Cerevisiae species. These species are grown by microbiological operation which is required for fermentation starting from a laboratory slant culture. Pure culture is first developed in a test tube, then in flasks and in seed tank under sterile conditions. Development is carried out in a number of successive stages with increasing volume in each preceding stage. During the growth of the microorganism, proper nutrients are supplied.

(b) Preparation of medium:

The microorganism used for the fermentation process cannot survive at high concentration of alcohol. For this purpose, either natural medium (cane and beet molasses, cornsteep liquor or sulphite liquor) or the synthetic medium (medium containing nutrients like carbon and nitrogen compounds, inorganic salts, vitamins, precursors, buffers etc. in appropriate amount of water) is diluted under controlled pH.

(c) Sterilization of equipments and air:

In order to avoid contamination of undesirable microorganism, sterilization of fermentation equipments, medium and air is essential.

(d) Fermentation:

The fermentation process is started by seeding the fermentation medium by the inoculums in a fermentation tank. During this process certain parameters such as temperature, aeration, foaming, amount of precursors, pH etc. are to be carefully controlled to get the desired fermentation product.

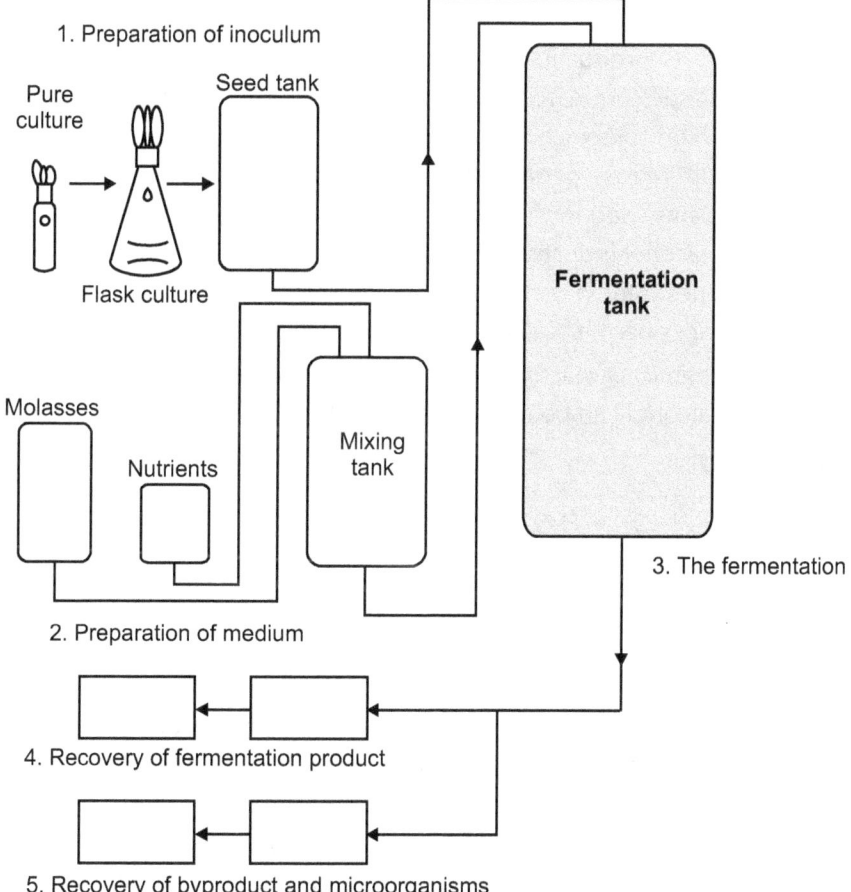

Fig. 2.4

(e) Recovery of fermentation products:

When almost all the raw material is converted into product by fermentation, the products formed are separated or recovered from the medium by different techniques such as precipitation (for organic acids as their Ca or Ba salts); distillation (for volatile liquids like acetone, ethanol etc.); solvent extraction (for penicillin); and adsorption on resins or activated carbon (for streptomycin).

(f) Recovery of byproduct and microorganism:

The microorganism from the fermentation medium is separated by filtration or by gravity settling. The choice of a particular method depends on the nature of microorganism and desired products. The separated yeast may be recycled or used for other purpose.

2.11 Manufacture of Industrial Alcohol (Ethyl Alcohol) from Molasses

- Ethyl alcohol is the most common solvent and raw material. It is next to water and is used in laboratory and chemical industry. Much of this alcohol is obtained synthetically from ethylene. However, its production from microbial fermentation using variety of cheap sugary substrates is still commercially important. It is imperative that the microorganisms used must have a high tolerance for alcohol, must grow vigorously and produce a large quantity of alcohol. Yeasts, particularly Saccharomyces Cerevisiae, represent the best known microorganisms used in the production of ethyl alcohol. Some of the inexpensive substrates used in alcohol industry are molasses from cane sugar or waste sulphite liquor from paper industries. Starch yielding grams (corn), potatoes, grapes may be used as substrate if their prices permit. Some countries use sugar beet for the purpose.

- **Reaction:** The chemical reaction that results in the microbial fermentation of carbohydrate into alcohol can be represented as follows.

- **Inversion of Sugar:**

$$C_{12}H_{22}O_{11} + H_2O \xrightarrow{\text{Invertase}} C_6H_{12}O_6 + C_6H_{12}O_6$$

$$\text{Molasses} \qquad\qquad\qquad \text{D-Glucose D-Fructose}$$

- **Fermentation:** $C_6H_{12}O_6 \xrightarrow{\text{Zymase}} 2C_2H_5OH + CO_2 + 31.2 \text{ kcal}$

2.11.1 Commercial Production using Molasses as a Raw Material

- The industrial production of ethanol involves various steps, control of certain reaction conditions. The high yield of industrial alcohol can be obtained as follows.

    1. **Dilution:** Molasses contain about 50% fermentable carbohydrates (sugars). Big deep tanks of steel or stainless steel are used as containers in the industrial production method. Molasses is diluted to a suitable sugar concentration (15-16%). It is called as Mash or Wort.

2. **Addition of Nutrients and pH adjustment:** A small quantity of nitrogen source (e.g., ammonium phosphate, urea, ammonium sulphate) and sulphuric acid (H_2SO_4) is added in it. pH of this medium is maintained at about 5.0.

3. **Seeding by Inoculum:** An actively growing Saccharomyces Cerevisiae culture is added to the medium. The size (quantity) of inoculums is adjusted as per the size of the medium.

4. **Fermentation:** The fermentation starts and is allowed to proceed for about 24-40 hours at about 25-30°C temperature. The yield of ethyl alcohol ranges about 50% of the fermentable sugar concentration present in the medium. The large amount of CO_2 which is produced during the fermentation process as a result of decarboxylation is recovered and compressed to its solid state. The yeast recovered is usually used as an animal feed. After the successful fermentation, the liquor obtained is called as Beer. It is distilled to separate alcohol from it.

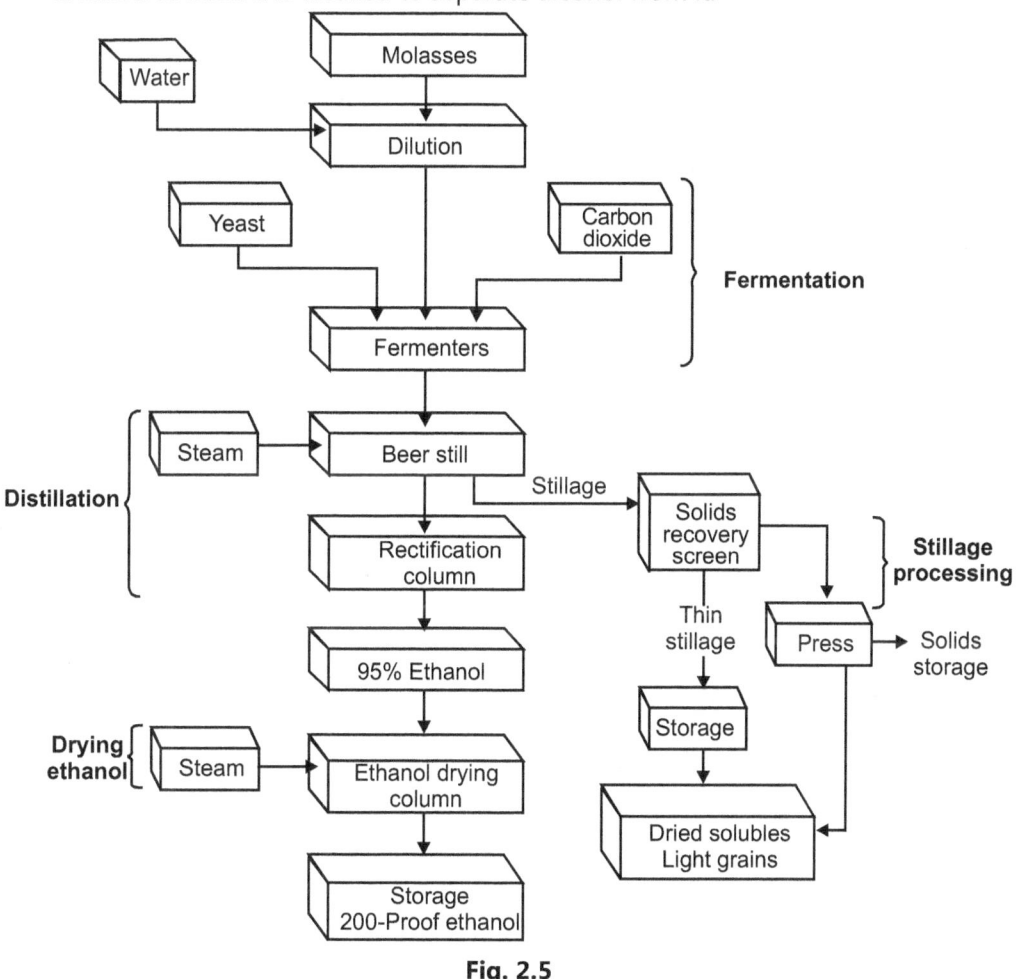

Fig. 2.5

2.11.2 Commercial Production using Starch as a Raw Material (Food Grains)

- When starches such as corn are used as the raw material they have first to be hydrolysed to release simple fermentable sugars. The hydrolysis can be accomplished with enzymes from barley malt or moulds (e.g., Aspergillus oryzae) or by heat treatment of acidified material.

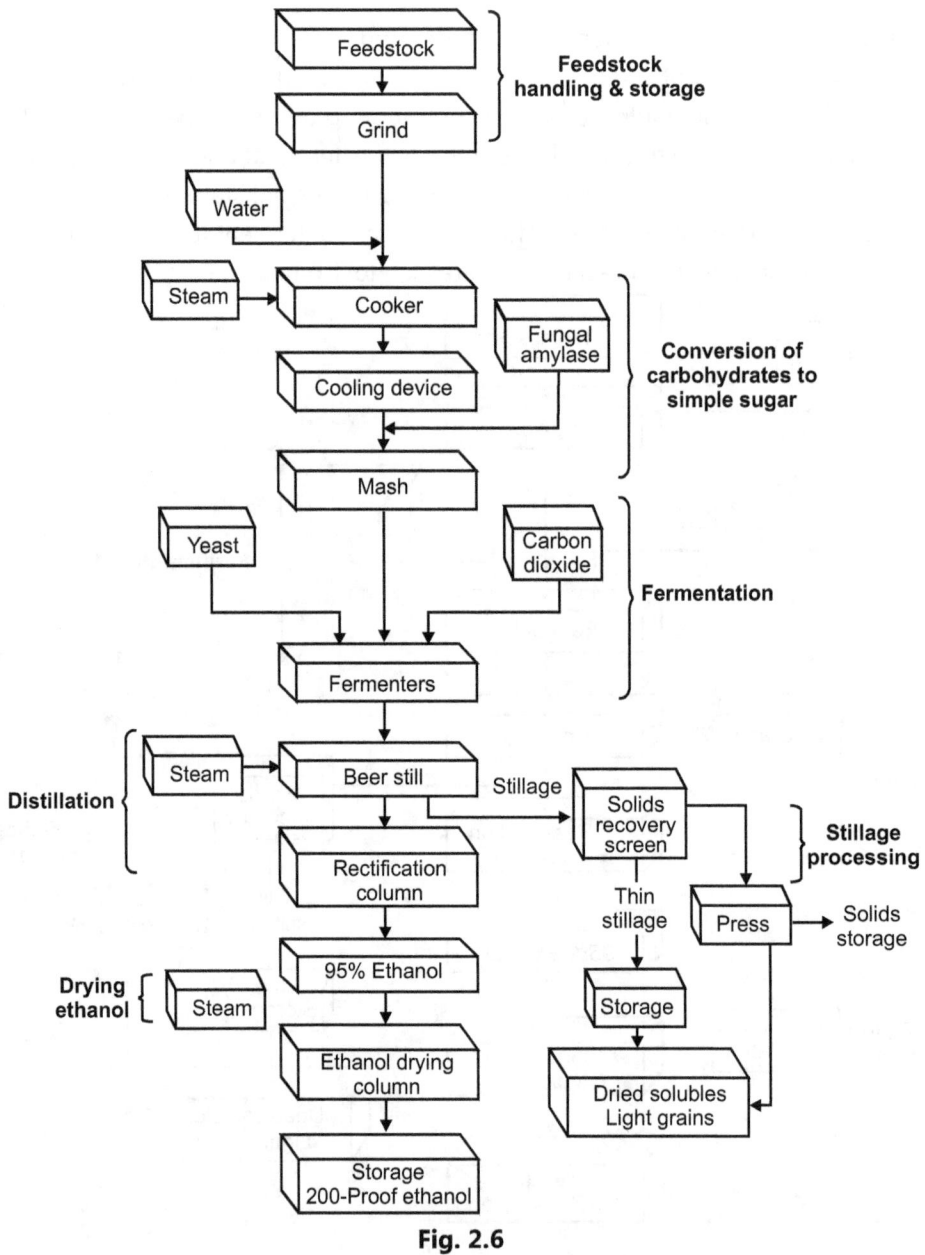

Fig. 2.6

- After the simple fermentable sugars are obtained, the fermentation process proceeds similarly to that of molasses.
- After the fermentation is over the fermented liquid left in the fermentor is called beer. The beer contains 6.5 to 11% alcohol by volume.
- The alcohol is separated by distillation. The beer is first passed over several heat exchangers and then pumped to the upper section of the beer still. As beer passes down the beer column, it gradually loses its lighter boiling constituents. The liquid discharged from the bottom of the still through a heat exchanger is known as slop or spillage. It carries proteins, residual sugar and vitamin products, which are used as a constituent of animal feed.
- The overhead containing alcohol, aldehydes and water is passed through a heat exchanger to the partial condenser or dephlegmator. The condensed liquid frequently known as high wines contains about 50 % alcohol including other volatile liquids.
- The overhead passing through a dephlegmator is partly condensed to keep the stronger alcohol in this column and to provide reflux for the upper parts. The more volatile products (still contain a trace of aldehydes) are then totally condensed. 95 to 95.6% alcohol are carried out to the upper part of the aldehyde still. Further reduction of water is not possible by simple distillation. During distillation a part of the high alcohol passes over into the distillate, the amount is completely separated by repeated distillation. The rectification or refining of alcohol of alcohol-water mixture increases the strength of the alcohol component by virtue of the composition of the vapours being stronger in the more volatile constituent than the liquid from which these vapours arise. However, alcohol cannot be made stronger than 95.6% by rectification, because water form as binary constant boiling mixture of this composition, which boils slightly lower than absolute or anhydrous alcohol. The distillation of dilute alcohol i.e. wort is done by a specially designed still known as Coffey's still.

Coffey's still:
- Aeneas Coffey (1780-1852), the inventor of the Coffey or columnar still, was an Irish (Born in Dublin) excise man and inventor who worked for the British government in Scotland. He has invented a very efficient and fast still that accomplished three consecutive distilling operations in one step. It is less expensive to operate than any alembic still and much faster.

Working of Coffey's still:
- It consists of two tall wooden walled columns lined with perforated copper plates for collection of condensate. Columns are placed side by side on the same level and are well supported in steel frames. The left side column is called analyzer and is connected to from the side at the top with an outlet pipe to the left side of the rectifier column near the bottom. A zigzag stout pipe is fitted inside the rectifier, the inlet of which enters on the right side near the bottom and outlet outs through the left side near the top connected to the top of the analyzer. A thick imperforated plate, pierced in the middle with a pipe for draining away the condensate, is fitted in the rectifier to concentrate solution of the condensate. The outlet pipe fitted to the plate is divided into two branches fitted with two stop cocks. These branches are connected to two worn condensers immersed in cold water. The spirit is condensed in the condenser connected

to inner branch and the outer branch condenser collects weak spirit while a hot feint contains the fusel oil. An outlet tube fitted to the right side plate (near the bottom) of rectifier collects hot feint into the hot feint receiver. The vapours escaping from hot feint are introduced, at the top, through the outer branch into the condenser joined to hot feint receiver.

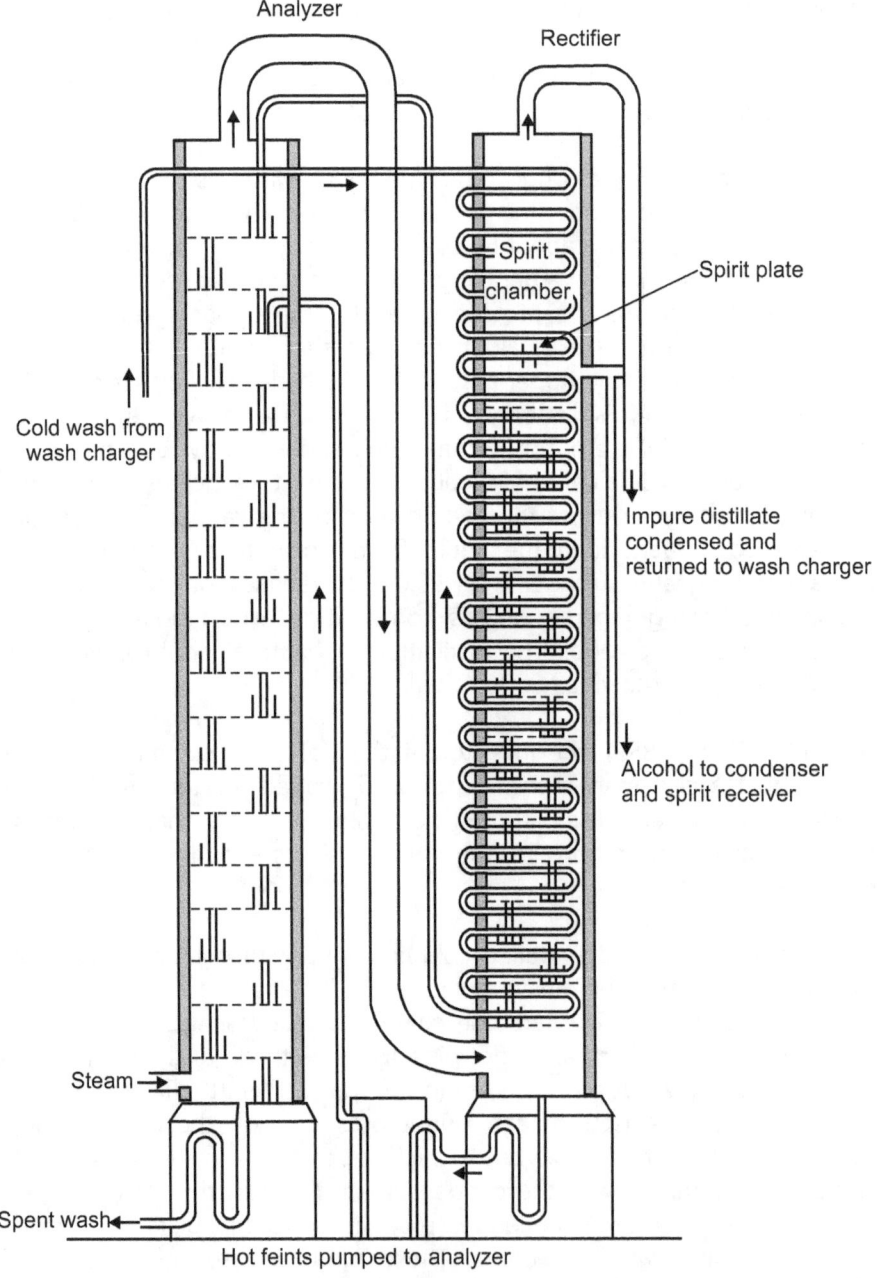

Fig. 2.7

- There is a steam inlet pipe on the left side (near the bottom) of the analyzer. There is an outlet for spent wash at the base of analyzer.

- At the beginning of the distillation, steam is introduced into the analyzer, which then enters into rectifier. Wash is then pumped into the zigzag pipe where it gets heated by rising steam. The ascending vapour is becoming richer in alcohol by the evaporation of the more volatile alcohol and the partial condensation of the less volatile water in its passage through the wort. The alcohol is further concentrated by washing the vapour in a similar way with the dilute alcohol first obtained, the weaker residue being added to the wort.

2.11.3 Manufacture of Ethanol from Hydrocarbons

- Ethanol is manufactured by reacting ethene with steam. The reaction is reversible, and the formation of the ethanol is exothermic.

$$CH_2 = CH_{2(g)} + H_2O_{(g)} \rightleftharpoons CH_3CH_2OH_{(g)} \qquad \Delta H = -45 \text{ kJ mol}^{-1}$$
$$\text{Ethene} \qquad\qquad\qquad \text{Ethyl alcohol}$$

- Only 5% of the ethene is converted into ethanol at each pass through the reactor. By removing the ethanol from the equilibrium mixture and recycling the ethene, it is possible to achieve an overall 95% conversion.

- A flow sheet for the manufacture of ethanol from ethene is given below.

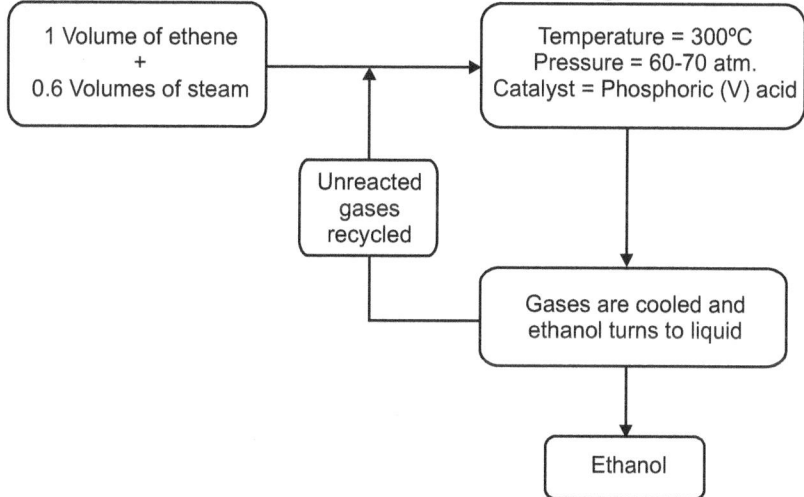

- The forward reaction is exothermic and there is a decrease in volume from reaction. As per the Le-Chatelier's principle the forward reaction is favoured by the low temperature and high pressure. The physicochemical principles involved in the preparation of ethyl alcohol are as follows:

  (i) **The proportion of ethene and steam:** The equation shows that the ethene and steam react in equimolar ratio. In order to get this ratio, you would have to use equal volumes of the two gases.

$$CH_2 = CH_{2\,(g)} + H_2O_{\,(g)} \rightleftharpoons CH_3CH_2OH_{(g)} \qquad \Delta H = -45 \text{ kJ mol}^{-1}$$

Because water is cheap, one can use an excess of steam in order to move the position of equilibrium to the right according to Le-Chatelier's principle.

In practice, an excess of ethene is used.

This is very surprising. Because increase in steam volume should increase the rate of forward reaction.

The reason for this is the nature of the catalyst. The catalyst is phosphoric (V) acid coated onto a solid silicon dioxide support. If you use too much steam, it dilutes the catalyst and can even wash it off the support, making it useless.

(ii) **The temperature:** You need to shift the position of the equilibrium as far as possible to the right in order to produce the maximum possible amount of ethanol in the equilibrium mixture.

The forward reaction (the production of ethanol) is exothermic.

$$CH_2 = CH_{2 (g)} + H_2O_{(g)} \rightleftharpoons CH_3CH_2OH_{(g)} \qquad \Delta H = -45 \text{ kJ mol}^{-1}$$
$$\text{Ethene} \qquad\qquad\qquad\qquad \text{Ethyl alcohol}$$

According to Le-Chatelier's principle, this will be favoured by the lower temperature.

In order to get as much ethanol as possible in the equilibrium mixture, you need as low temperature as possible. However, the optimum temperature is 300°C to increase the rate of reaction.

The lower the temperature you use, the slower the reaction becomes. To increase the yield of ethanol per day, the optimum temperature of 300°C is used to increase the rate of reaction.

(iii) **The pressure:** Equilibrium reaction

$$CH_2 = CH_{2(g)} + H_2O_{(g)} \rightleftharpoons CH_3CH_2OH_{(g)} \qquad \Delta H = -45 \text{ kJ mol}^{-1}$$
$$\text{Ethene} \qquad\qquad\qquad\qquad \text{Ethyl alcohol}$$

There is a decrease in the volume in the forward reaction. There are 2 molecules on the left-hand side of the equation, but only 1 on the right.

According to Le-Chatelier's principle, if you increase the pressure the system will respond by favoring the reaction which produces fewer molecules, that will cause the pressure to fall again.

In order to get as much ethanol as possible in the equilibrium mixture, you need as high a pressure as possible. High pressures also increase the rate of the reaction. However, the pressure used is not all that high.

At high pressures, the ethene polymerizes to make poly(ethene). Apart from wasting ethene, this could also clog up the plant.

(iv) **The catalyst:** The catalyst has no affect whatsoever on the position of the equilibrium. Its only function is to speed up the reaction.

In the absence of a catalyst, the reaction is so slow that virtually no reaction happens in any sensible time. The catalyst ensures that the reaction is fast enough for a dynamic equilibrium to be set up within the very short time that the gases are actually in the reactor.

2.11.4 Manufacture of Wine

- Wine is an undistilled product of fruit juice fermentation brought about by yeast. Wine is produced by the normal alcoholic fermentation of fruit juices, especially the grape juice. The microorganisms used in the wine fermentation are the various strains of Saccharomyces cerevisiae such as S. cerevisiae or S. ellipsoidous.

Commercial Production:

Five major steps are involved in commercial production of wines. They are:

(a) **Crushing:** Grapes are harvested and ripened to a stage they contain highest sugar percentage. These fruits are crushed in a wine press and the crushed fruits with juice are called "must". The must is generally treated with SO_2 to prevent microbial spoilage.

(b) **Fermenting:** The "must" is now inoculated with the starter culture of selected strain of the yeast and is aerated slightly to promote vigorous yeast growth. Once the fermentation starts, the rapid production of CO_2 maintains anaerobic condition. The temperature is kept usually at 25-30°C during fermentation period ranging from 5-11 days in order to inhibit multiplication of wine yeast and undesirable bacteria that live at high temperature.

(c) **Tanking:** When most of the sugar is fermented the juice is separated from solid parts of fruits by allowing it to pass into tanks. These tanks, provided with valves to let the CO_2 escape, are completely filled with juice. The anaerobic condition for alcoholic fermentation is allowed to continue for about 12 days to increase the percentage of alcoholic concentration.

(d) **Maturing:** The wine is then allowed to mature in wooden tanks for 2 to 5 or more years. During maturing period the wine clears and develops the desired flavour of volatile ester.

(e) **Finishing:** The wine may be finally cleared with the addition of gelatin, casein or Spanish clay. The cleared wine is filtered, bottled and pasteurized to prevent microbial spoilage.

2.11.5 Manufacture of Whisky and Rum

- Whisky and rum are the potable bottled alcohols used for the drinking purpose. These alcohols are made from silent spirit (95% ethyl alcohol) by dilution with demineralised water. Appropriate colour and flavor are then added. The resulting liquor is then bottled, sealed, labelled and packed into boxes. Both these brands of potable alcohol are similar with respect to alcohol content. Both are **25UP** (UP is underproof, 100 – UP = Proof, and proof is the double the percentage of alcohol). Hence, 25UP is 100 – 25 = 75 proof that is 37.5% alcohol by weight and 42.7% by volume.

- Whisky, rum, brandy, gin etc. are made in a unit called industry attached to the distillery. Ethyl alcohol is made in distillery by fermentation of molasses. This is normally 95% alcohol called SS that is silent spirit. This SS is pumped through pipes into big tanks where blending is done. Blending is the process of mixing of SS, DM water, colour and flavour in proper proportion.

- The liquor obtained is then filled in bottles, sealed, labeled and packed.

- Rum is the simplest potable alcohol which do not contain any flavor. It only consist of silent spirit, deminerelised water and caramel. Caramel is burnt sugar which gives dark brown colour and peculiar taste to the rum.

- Whisky is the most sold popular drinking alcohol. There are variety of whiskies particularly based on the composition. Ordinary whisky contains SS, DM water, Colour and flavor. Premium whisky contains small concentration of special spirit in addition to all components of ordinary whisky. Special spirit is the silent spirit kept in wooden containers called vats which are buried underground for the number of years. On long storage alcohol reacts with acid to produce esters making alcohol mellow. Scotch whisky is the highest priced drinking alcohol. Scotch is s a malt whisky or grain whisky made in Scotland. It was originally made from malted barley. Now it is made from wheat, rye and other sources of carbohydrates including sugar. Scotch whisky is aged in Oak barrels atleast three years. Aging improves the taste and aroma of alcohol. The price of scotch depends on number of years used for the aging.

2.11.6 Importance of Power Alcohol

- Ethanol is most commonly used to power automobiles, though it may be used to power other vehicles, such as farm tractors, boats and airplanes. Ethanol (E100) consumption in an engine is approximately 51% higher than for gasoline since the energy per unit volume of ethanol is 34% lower than for gasoline. However, the higher compression ratios in an ethanol-only engine allow for increased power output and better fuel economy than could be obtained with lower compression ratios. In general, ethanol-only engines are tuned to give slightly better power and torque output than gasoline-powered engines. In flexible fuel vehicles, the lower compression ratio requires tunings that give the same output when using either gasoline or hydrated ethanol.

- Although fossil fuels have become the dominant energy resource for the modern world, alcohol has been used as a fuel throughout history. The first four aliphatic alcohols (methanol, ethanol, propanol, and butanol) are of interest as fuels because they can be synthesized biologically, and they have characteristics which allow them to be used in current engines. One advantage shared by all four alcohols is octane rating. Biobutanol has the advantage that its energy density is closer to gasoline than the other alcohols (while still retaining over 25% higher octane rating), however, these advantages are outweighed by disadvantages (compared to ethanol and methanol) concerning production, for instance. Generally speaking, the chemical formula for alcohol fuel is $C_nH_{2n+1}OH$.

- Alcohol fuels are usually of biological rather than petroleum sources. When obtained from biological sources, they are known as **bioalcohols** (e.g. **bioethanol**). There is no chemical difference between biologically produced alcohols and those obtained from other sources. However, ethanol that is derived from petroleum should not be considered safe for consumption as this alcohol contains about 5% methanol and may cause blindness or death. This mixture may also not be purified by simple distillation, as it forms an azeotropic mixture.

- Ethanol is already being used extensively as a fuel additive, and the use of ethanol fuel alone or as part of a mix with gasoline is increasing. Compared to methanol its primary advantage is that the fuel is non-toxic, although the fuel will produce some toxic exhaust emissions.

Exercises

(A) Answer the following:

1. Define the following:
   - (i) Sugar boiling
   - (ii) Molasses
   - (iii) Bagasse
   - (iv) Compound Imbibition process
   - (v) Carbonation process
   - (vi) Phosphatation process
   - (vii) Sulphitation process

2. Answer the following:
   - (i) What are multiple effect vacuum evaporators?
   - (ii) Explain curing of sugar.
   - (iii) Give applications of molasses.
   - (iv) Why sugar cane cut from the field should be crushed within 24 hours?
   - (v) Give applications of bagasse.
   - (vi) What is meant by massecuite?
   - (vii) Explain sulphitation process.

3. Write short notes on the following:
   - (i) Clarification of juice
   - (ii) By-product of sugar industry
   - (iii) Multiple effect vacuum evaporator
   - (iv) Curing of cane sugar
   - (v) Crystallization of sugar
   - (vi) Sulphitation process
   - (vii) Carbonation process

4. Attempt the following:
   - (i) What are multiple effect evaporators? How do they bring about great saving of fuel?
   - (ii) What are the by-products of sugar industry? Give its applications.
   - (iii) Explain the use of lime in processing of juice in sugar manufacture.
   - (iv) Explain the process of clarification of juice by sulphitation process.
   - (v) Describe the manufacture of cane sugar with the help of flow sheet.

(vi) Describe manufacture of direct consumption sugar with the help of flow sheet diagram.

(vii) What is meant by fermentation? Discuss the role of various microorganisms in the fermentation process.

(viii) What is yeast? Explain the use of various types of yeast in fermentation process.

(ix) What is fermentation? Discuss conditions favourable for fermentation.

(x) What are the basic requirements for fermentation?

(xi) What is meant by fermentation? What are the basic operations involved in fermentation process?

(xii) Discuss with flow sheet the manufacture of ethyl alcohol from (a) Molasses, (b) Food grains, (c) Hydrocarbons.

(xiii) Discuss with flow sheet the manufacture of ethyl alcohol from molasses with reference to Coffey's still.

(xiv) Discuss the various physicochemical principles involved in the manufacture of alcohol from hydrocarbons.

(xv) How wine is manufactured from grapes?

(xvi) Discuss the construction and working of Coffey's still.

(xvii) What is rum? How it is made?

(xviii) What is meant by silent spirit and rectified spirit?

(xix) What is scotch? How it differs from ordinary whisky?

(xx) What do you mean by potable alcohol?

(xxi) What is denatured alcohol? How it is prepared?

(xxii) Explain the importance of power alcohol.

(xviii) Write short notes on:

   (a) Microorganisms used in fermentation
   (b) Coffey's still
   (c) Raw materials for the fermentation of alcohol.
   (d) Importance of alcohol as a fuel
   (e) Different grades of alcohol.
   (f) Duty and duty-free alcohol.
   (g) Denatured spirit

(B) Multiple Choice Questions (MCQs):

   (i) The function of compound imbibition process is to ....
   (a) concentrate the juice
   (b) clean the crystals of sugar
   (c) reduce the sucrose in the fibre
   (d) remove colouring matter only

(ii)   In multiple effect evaporators, surfactants are added to the juice ....
   (a) to remove floating impurities   (b) to improve the rate of evaporation
   (c) growth of crystals   (d) to remove mud particles

(iii) After clarification of juice by sulphitation process brings the pH to the range ....
   (a) 5.6 to 6.8   (b) 7.0 to 7.1
   (c) 6.3 to 6.9   (d) 9 to 10

(iv)   The screening process is essential to ....
   (a) remove sulphur particles   (b) remove colours
   (c) remove non-sugar   (d) remove floating impurities

(v)   Which enzyme produced by yeast bring about hydrolysis of sucrose into glucose and fructose?
   (a) Zymase   (b) Invertase
   (c) Maltase   (d) Azobacter

(vi)   The wash or wort contains .... % of alcohol.
   (a) 15-20   (b) 25-30
   (c) 6-10%   (d) 40-50%

(vii) The alcohol obtained from Coffey's still is about .... pure.
   (a) 78-80%   (b) 90%
   (c) 96%   (d) 70%

(viii) Fructose is converted into ethanol by .... enzyme.
   (a) Zymase   (b) Maltase
   (c) Invertase   (d) Diastase

(ix)   Fermentation process usually proceeds well only in the presence of ....
   (a) CO_2 (b) SO_2
   (c) H_2S (d) air

(x)   Which fermentation process is carried out at about 15°C temperature?
   (a) Top fermentation   (b) Middle fermentation
   (c) Bottom fermentation   (d) End fermentation

(C) State True or False:
(i)   Sugar cane may be crushed within less than 24 hours after cutting.
(ii)   In India, sucrose is obtained from sugar cane and sugar beet.
(iii) Organic chemicals like acetone, citric acid, butanol etc. are obtained from baggase.
(iv)   High quality wax is obtained from bagasse.
(v)   Sucrose can supply energy required for living cells.
(vi)   Molasses are used as edible syrup and compressed yeast.
(vii) The crusher and first mill extract 80-90% of the cane juice.
(viii) The crystallization of sucrose in vacuum pans is called as sugar boiling.

■■■

Chapter 3...

Soaps, Detergents and Cosmetics

Contents ...

3.1 Introduction

(A) SOAP

3.2 Chemistry of Soap
3.3 Raw Materials of Soaps
3.4 Chemical Reaction for Manufacture of Soap
3.5 Types of Soap

(B) DETERGENTS

3.6 Introduction
3.7 Meaning of the Terms
3.8 Types (Classification) of Surfactants
3.9 Raw Materials for Detergents
3.10 Washing Action of Soaps and Detergents
    3.10.1 Washing Action of Soap
    3.10.2 Washing Action of the Detergent
3.11 Comparison of Soaps and Detergents

(C) COSMETICS

3.12 Introduction
3.13 Raw Materials for Cosmetics
3.14 Cosmetics for Skin
3.15 Hair Care
•   Exercises

3.1 Introduction

• Soap and synthetic detergent products, such as laundry soaps, toilet soaps, detergent powder, cleaning powder, medicated soaps, shaving soaps and creams, shampoos etc. are extensively used in the present day-to-day life. Total consumption of soaps and detergents in a country is a very reliable measure of its civilization.

(A) SOAP

3.2 Chemistry of Soap

• Soap is a necessity in modern civilization. Soaps are the salts of long-chain fatty acids like oleic, stearic, palmitic, lauric and myristic acids (fatty acids containing from

8 to 22 carbon atoms). The sodium and potassium salts of higher fatty acids are water soluble and strongly surface active and hence find extensive applications in cleansing and washing purposes. On the other hand, the water insoluble soaps (e.g. heavy metal salts of fatty acids) are used as lubricants and base for paints. The usual household and industrial soap products in addition to pure alkali metal soaps contain filling materials, germicides, perfumes, dyes etc. for achieving certain important properties in the soap. The hard soaps like sodium salts of fatty acids are moderately soluble in water and do not form lathers easily. Soft soaps like potassium salts of fatty acids are fast dissolving and form lathers readily. Tallow, animal fats and coconut oils are the main sources of hard soap, while linseed oil, caster oil etc. produce soft soaps.

- The cleaning action of soap is appreciably reduced in hard waters. Soap making involves the use of oils and fats which have potential food value. Soap cannot be used in the acidic solution. In hard water as well as in acidic solution, it yields sticky precipitate which gets adhered to textile fibres during processing.

3.3 Raw Materials of Soaps

- The principle raw materials required for soaps are fats and oils (fatty acids), caustic soda or caustic potash and common salt. However, certain additives, filling materials, colouring matters, binding materials, perfumes and medicinal chemicals are also added in soap for achieving certain properties. They are as follows:

  (i) **Fats and oils:** Tallow, fat and coconut oil or their fatty acid derivatives are the important materials in soap making. For getting good quality soap, fatty acids containing only 12-18 carbon atoms are suitable. Further, a high proportion of unsaturated fatty acids (e.g. oleic, linoleic, etc.) give soft soaps. The main sources of animal oils and fats are tallow (beef and mutton), grease, lard, whale oil, fish oil, etc., while vegetable oils and fats obtained from coconut oil, palm oil, olive oil, castor oil, neem seed oil, cotton seed oil etc.

  (ii) **Caustic soda (NaOH) and Caustic potash (KOH):** An aqueous sodium hydroxide is used for saponifying oils and fats or for neutralizing fatty acids making hard soaps. It is available in the form of flakes or in solution. For making soft soaps, an aqueous solution of potassium hydroxide is used. Caustic potash is usually received in drum as solids.

  (iii) **Common salt (NaCl):** It is used for graining in full boiled process of soap making. About 12.5 parts of common salt per 100 parts of oil to be used for saponification.

  (iv) **Soap stocks (Rosin):** It is obtained from the gum of pine trees, which mainly contains abietic acid. The colourless variety of rosin is used in the manufacture of laundry soaps. Rosin soap is a good water softener and forms abundant suds with efficient cleansing properties. It makes lather formation faster.

(v) **Additive and Filling materials:** The binding materials improve soap texture and prevent the formation of precipitates in hard waters. The cleansing property of ordinary soap is also improved by adding certain binding materials like sodium silicate (5%), soda ash, trisodium phosphate, borax etc.

The weight of soap is increased by adding finely powdered insoluble abrasive materials such as talc, starch, quartz, sand, feldspar, glauber salt, pearl ash etc. without affecting the detergency. These materials are introduced in a soap during the finishing operations.

(vi) **Colouring matter:** Organic dyes and pigments are generally used for colouring bar and flake soap products. The colouring matter should be inert to alkali used. It should not affect the fragrance of the soap. Common colouring matters are methyl violet for violet shade, Bismark brown for brown, Rhodamine for red, zinc oxide for white, chrome green for green, cadmium yellow for yellow, methylene blue for blue, eosin for pink and vermilon for rose shade. Intermediate shades can be prepared by mixing the colouring materials.

(vii) **Some other materials added in soaps:** These materials are added in a soap during the mixing stage of the soap finishing and vary from soap to soap depending upon the properties required for the particular soap product.

(a) **Perfumes:** The essential oils imparting fragrance to the soap are known as perfumes. Natural perfumes are sandal wood oil, lemon grass oil, clove oil, etc. Synthetic perfumes are benzyl acetate (jasmine), phenyl ethyl alcohol (rose), terpeneol (lilac), benzoate (musk), etc.

(b) **Germicides:** Sulphur is added as a cure for dandruff and pimples, while mercuric iodide is added as a germicide in mercury soap. Antiseptic agents are added for medicated soaps.

(c) **Superfatting agents:** The materials such as lanolin or paraffin jelly are added to prevent the skin from becoming rough and dry. It also improves texture of the soap and prevents cracks on the soap when dry. Its 2% concentration is sufficient.

3.4 Chemical Reaction for Manufacture of Soap

- Soap is either made by hot process or cold process. Usually laundry soap and toilet or bath soaps are manufactured by hot process. Transparent and other special types of soap are produced by cold process. In most of the cases, soap obtained by hot process is settled or grained and separated from the spent layer containing the glycerol in the solution. This glycerol is recovered as a by-product of soap industry.

- Manufacture of various soap products involves the preparation of 'neat' soap either by saponification of oils and fats with alkalies or by direct neutralization of fatty acids and its processing. The saponification of oils and fats with aqueous alkalies gives a mixture of alkali soap and glycerol in the following manner:

$$
\begin{array}{ccc}
\underset{\text{Oil or Fat}}{\begin{array}{l} CH_2\!-\!O\!-\!COR \\ | \\ CH\!-\!O\!-\!COR \\ | \\ CH_2\!-\!O\!-\!COR \end{array}} + 3NaOH & \xrightarrow[250^{\circ}C]{\text{Saponification}} & \underset{\text{(Na soap)}}{3R\!-\!\overset{O}{\overset{||}{C}}\!-\!ONa} + \underset{\substack{\text{Glycerine} \\ \text{(by-product)}}}{\begin{array}{l} CH_2\!-\!OH \\ | \\ CH\!-\!OH \\ | \\ CH_2\!-\!OH \end{array}}
\end{array}
$$

- Soap making from fats and oils involves the following two important steps:

  (a) Preliminary processing of oils and fats and their blending in required proportions.

  (b) Preparation of neat soap by saponification processes.

  By-products of soap industry: The glycerine caught in the soap is removed by boiling with water and caustic soda. Then the lower water layer is removed which contains dissolved glycerine. The pure glycerine is obtained by redistilling above glycerine under reduced pressure and pulling away the water vapours until required concentration is obtained.

3.5 Types of Soap

- The main classes of soap are toilet and industrial soaps. The special types of soap products can be made as per demand, which are as follows:

  1. **Toilet soap:** The manufacture of the best quality toilet soaps requires the purest mixture of tallow and coconut oil in the ratios 80 : 20 or 90 : 10 respectively. It contains no fillers. It has about 10% moisture. For saponification, caustic soda (NaOH) is used, which makes a hard and stable soap. While caustic potash (KOH) produces a soft soap. The quality of soap depends upon the proportion of tallow oil used. Its manufacture from neat soap involves the following steps; drying, mixing with the perfumes and a dye, milling, pludding, pressing, stamping and wrapping.

     The good quality toilet soaps have the following important characteristics:

     (i)   Easy solubility in water with profuse lathering.

     (ii)   Persistance of the soap fragrance.

     (iii) Smooth glassy appearance without any cracks.

     (iv)   The colour of the soap should not stick to the skin or fabric.

  2. **Superfatted soap:** Superfatted toilet soaps are made by the addition of 1 to 6% of soft paraffin jelly or anhydrous lanolin or unsaponified oil in toilet soap base during milling process, which produce a soft cold-cream effect by leaving a residual film on the skin after washing. It is usually made from the mixture of tallow oil and coconut oil in ratios of 50 : 50 or 60 : 40. Some rosin is also added, the purpose of which is to make the finished soap sufficiently plastic for milling.

3. **Transparent soap:** These soaps can now be prepared in a number of ways. In the old method, the good quality soap is dissolved in alcohol by gentle heating and then 80% of the alcohol is transported into moulds. This method is good but expensive.

   Now-a-days, these soaps are usually made by semi-boiled method. Addition of alcohol, sugar, glycerine or castor oil to the hot soap inhibits the crystal growth during frame cooling and yields a glassy or transparent soap. Transparent soap contains glycerine which acts as a skin conditioner through moderation of the degreasing action of soap. It also maintains a thin film of moisture on the skin, so as to keep it smooth and flexible e.g. pears, savlon, etc.

4. **Medicated soap:** These toilet soaps contain small quantities of antibacterial or disinfecting agents like phenol, cresol, halogenated carbanilides, polybrominated salicylanilides. These agents are added during milling process. Antibacterial agents are effective in suppressing the growth of germ-positive skin bacteria responsible for body odour.

5. **Shaving soap and Shaving cream:** Shaving soaps are prepared by saponifying a mixture of best quality tallow and coconut oil, with small quantities of castor oil, lard oil, and lanolin with caustic potash (KOH) or caustic soda (NaOH) using full-boiled process. Small amounts of white paraffin and glycerine are added during milling process to improve soothing properties. This soap should be neutral in order to avoid irritation. The shaving soap must be capable of producing lather, that persists for long time.

   Shaving creams are formulated by saponifying a mixture of coconut oil and stearic acid with mixed solution of caustic potash (KOH). About 5-10% glycerol is added and 4-8% of stearic acid is left unneutralized to have the creamy and lasting lather. Shaving soaps and creams may also contain small amounts of antiseptic agents and menthol.

6. **Floating soap:** These soaps are prepared by bubbling air through the melted neat soap until the solid soap becomes lighter than water. It contains about 30% water. As the amount of air incorporated in soap increases, its volume also increases, which help to reduce soap weight. e.g. Le Cancy soap.

7. **Cleansing powders:** These soap products are manufactured in bar, paste or powder forms and contain finely powdered insoluble materials like talc, quartz, sand, china clay, feldspar etc. in addition to the filling agents (e.g. sodium silicate, sodium carbonate, sodium borate, etc.). Generally, these soap products contain 5-10% neat soap. These soap products are extensively used for domestic and industrial cleansing, such as cleaning of mechanic's hand, pots, floor tiles, walls, dishes, kitchen wares and tanks. Special scouring soaps are used in textile industry for scouring raw wool fibers.

8. **Shampoos:** Shampoos are hair cleaners, i.e. it cleans the hairs and the scalp, which when applied. After drying the shampoo makes the hairs easily combable, quick setting and attractive. It may be available as solution, paste or even powder. Shampoos should not irritate the skin and eyes. It should not be harmful to the hair or the skin. It should possess a very pleasant and aggreeable odour. It must be removing all dirt, dust and oiliness.

The common raw materials used for the manufacture of shampoos are:

(a)　A synthetic detergent, such as sodium or potassium lauryl sulphate, alkyl benzene, polyoxyethyl sulphonates.

(b)　Solubilising agent such as alcohol, urea, sodium toluene, sulphonate etc.

(c)　Amine-oxides, as foam stabilizers.

(d)　Disodium salt of EDTA as a chelating agent.

(e)　Formaldehyde as preservative.

(f)　Lanolin as hair softener.

(g)　Lemon juice, which is used as scum remover in case of soap shampoos.

• In addition to above raw materials, antidandruff agents (e.g. selenium sulphide) are also added. Antiseptics such as 3, 4, 4-trichloro-carbanilide are added against most skin damaging micro-organisms.

(B) DETERGENTS

3.6 Introduction

• Synthetic detergents are soap substitutes and were initially developed to avoid the short supply of soaps due to the shortage of edible oils and fats. A detergent may be regarded as a chemical formation, which consists of surface active agents or surfactants alongwith other subsidiary constituents such as fillers, builders, boosters etc. They have better wetting and cleansing properties compared to the soap. The washing or cleansing activity of detergents is not affected by hardness of water because of higher solubility of their calcium and magnesium ions. Due to this reason, synthetic detergents become very popular in a short course, for laundering.

• Soap-making involves the use of oils and fats which have potential food values, while the surfactants required for synthetic detergents are made from the petroleum products. Thus by producing more detergents, the oil and fats could be saved and this is a need today because of the increasing population. It can be used for washing delicate fibers like wool and silk. It is more active than soap in comparatively low concentration. It is excellent foaming agent. It has germicidal and bactericidal properties.

- Though the synthetic detergents have many advantages over soaps, they have following disadvantages:

    (i)   Many of them are not easily biodegradable as soap and hence cause water pollution.

    (ii) They are more toxic than soap.

    (iii) Antibacterial agents are not very effective when used in synthetic detergents, while soap makes them effective.

    (iv) They require the addition of soil-suspending agents while soap does not require it.

    (v)   Their recovery is very difficult as compared to that of soap when used in large amounts.

3.7 Meaning of the Terms

1. Surfactants:

Surfactants are nothing but the surface-active agents. 'Surface-active agent' is the most important ingredient of synthetic detergent products. Substances which lower the surface tension of water are commonly known as surface-active substances. Surface-active substances, when dissolved in water or dispersed in a liquid, wash a surface clean by removing oil in which dust particles are dispersed. The cleansing action of a surfactant depends upon its surface activity. It is a property which decreases the surface tension at the boundary surface between the two phases. The most commonly used surfactants in detergents are linear alkyl benzene sulphonates (LAS), sodium alkyl sulphonates, sodium stearyl sulphate, amide sulphonates etc.

In general, surfactants are organic compounds in which two dissimilar structural groups are water soluble and water insoluble. The composition, solubility properties, location and relative sizes of these dissimilar groups in relation to the overall molecular configuration determine the surface activity of the compound.

The substances denoted as surfactants consist of polar and non-polar type molecules and which have the following properties:

(i)   Solubility, at least in one phase of the liquid system,

(ii)   Amphipathic structure,

(iii) Orientation at interfaces,

(iv)   Adsorption at interfaces causes lowering of surface tension,

(v)   Functional properties such as a emulsifying, wetting, foaming, detergency, solubilizing and dispersing, which make the detergent as excellent cleaning agent.

2. Emulsion and Emulsifying agents:

The emulsion is defined as any dispersion of one liquid into the another liquid. When two immiscible liquids like water and oil are shaken together, the oily liquid is dispersed in fine droplets, but the emulsion is not stable. The liquids separate into two layers because of the aggregation of the fine droplets into bigger ones then ultimately form a separate layer.

In order to stabilize the emulsion, a third component is required called 'emulsifying or emulsifier' in the above system (mixture of two immiscible liquids). These agents (emulsifier) lower the interfacial surface tension, so that the emulsion is easily formed and also stabilize the emulsion by protecting the dispersed fine droplets of oil by forming a layer around them. The layer is formed by solubilizing the non-polar part of the surfactant in oil drop, while polar group remains in water, so that the amphipathic structure of surfactants make them an excellent emulsifying agent. Lather formation (foaming) is increased due to the lowering of water/air interfacial surface tension because of the adsorption of surfactant at the interface.

3. Wetting and Non-wetting agents:

In general, 'wetting' means the spreading of liquid on a surface with ease and this is attributed to a very small contact angle between the liquid and the solid surface, due to this, the liquid spreads over the solid surface easily. While, in case of non-wetting agents, the angle is greater than $90°$ and hence the liquid tends to ball up and run off the surface. The wetting action is generally accomplished by the use of surfactant additives which lower the interfacial surface tension.

Wetting agents (surfactants) typically consist of polar and non-polar type molecules (i.e. amphipathic structure). The polar portion of the molecule may be one of the functional groups of organic compounds containing oxygen (e.g. carboxylic acids, esters, ethers or alcohols), sulphur (e.g. sulphonic acid, their esters or sulphates) or even phosphorus, nitrogen and halogen, the groups may be or may not be ionic. The non-polar part or portion is usually hydrocarbon (aliphatic or aromatic).

4. Hydrophobic and Hydrophilic nature:

Anionic detergent is represented by a general formula as:

$R - O - SO_3^- Na^+$, where 'R' represents a long chain alkyl radical. Thus, anionic detergent consists of two parts:

$$CH_3-CH_2 + (CH_2)_n - \overset{}{\bigcirc} - O - SO_3Na$$

Hydrophobic   Hydrophilic
(water insoluble)   (water soluble)

The functional groups, which have a tendency to bind water are called **'hydrophilic'**. It means water loving or water liking or water attracting substance. These substances are water soluble. The hydrophilic functional group may be anionic (e.g. $-OSO_3^-$); cationic (e.g. $-\overset{+}{N}(CH_3)_3$, $C_2H_5\overset{+}{N}-$, etc.) or non-ionic $(-OCH_2CH_2)_n$ OH.

'Hydrophobic' means water hating or water disliking or water repelling substances. These are water insoluble and repel water. The hydrophobic portion of the compound is usually hydrocarbon containing 8-18 carbon atoms in a straight or slightly branched chain. In few cases, some carbon atoms may be replaced by a benzene ring e.g. $C_{12}H_{25}^-$, $C_5H_{19}^-$.

Anionic detergents dissociate into long chain anion which act as the hydrophilic end and the long carbon chain as the hydrophobic end. e.g. sulphated fatty alcohol, alkyl benzene sulphonates (ABS) etc. Cationic detergents are tetra alkyl ammonium salts with a long chain hydrocarbon part which acts as the hydrophobic end and cationic nitrogen constitutes the hydrophobic end.

5. **Amphipathic structures:**

If a molecule contains two dissimilar structural groups, e.g. water-soluble and water-insoluble, then such a molecule is known to have amphipathic structure. Common compounds of this class are soap and detergents.

The detergents containing both cationic as well as anionic groups are called amphoteric detergents. e.g. sodium lauryl sarcosinate or deriphat. It is used in the manufacture of tooth paste, shampoos, cosmetics etc.

3.8 Types (Classification) of Surfactants

- Surfactants are classified on the basis of their hydrophilic or solubilizing groups present in the molecule. It is classified into four categories: anionic, cationic, ampholytic and non-ionic surfactants.

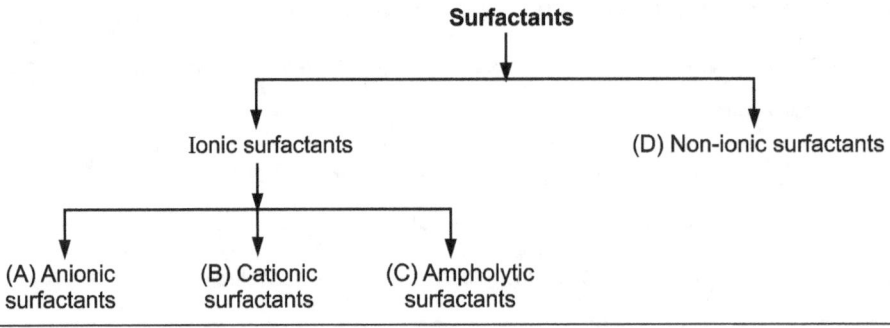

(A) Anionic surfactants:

The hydrophilic group in anionic surfactant is polar and negatively charged in aqueous solutions or dispersions. These are best for water absorbing fibres like cotton, wool and silk. The important anionic surfactants are as follows:

(i)   *Carboxylates:* e.g. soaps and amino carboxylates.

(ii)   *Sulphonates:* e.g. alkyl benzene sulphonates (ABS), linear alkyl benzene sulphonates, petroleum sulphonates etc.

(iii)   *Sulphates and sulphonated products:* e.g. fatty alcohol sulphates, ethylene oxide adduct sulphates.

(iv)   *Phosphate esters:* e.g. Na or K – alkyl phosphates.

The ionic environment associated with anionic surfactants influences the properties of their solutions.

(B) Cationic Surfactants:

The hydrophilic groups in cationic surfactants are amino or quaternary nitrogen. These amino groups or quaternary nitrogen bear a positive charge when dissolved in an aqueous medium. They act as wetting agents rather than detergents. They are used as softeners for textiles and paper. They can also be used as antibacterial algicidal agents. They are more expensive. They are antistatic agents and hence are used as finishes on synthetic fibers to avoid undesirable static charge. This class includes following compounds:

(i)   Amines containing oxygen: e.g. amine oxide, polyoxy ethylene, alkyl amines.

(ii)   Amines not containing oxygen: e.g. aliphatic mono, di and polyamines and resin derived amines.

(iii)   Amines having amide linkages.

(iv)   Amines having quaternary ammonium salt.

(C) Ampholytic (Amphoteric) Surfactants:

These surfactants contain both anionic and cationic groups (i.e. both acidic and basic hydrophilic groups). These ionic functions may be any one of the cationic or anionic groups i.e. they can behave as anionic or cationic according to whether the solution is in the basic or acidic pH range. They are used in cosmetics, shampoos, water emulsion paints and as corrosion inhibitors. They are also used as detergent santizers, emulsifying and wetting agents. A typical example of this class is N-fatty-β-aminopropionic esters. Sodium lauryl sarcosinate is used in tooth paste composition.

(D) Non-ionic Surfactants:

These surfactants bear essentially no charge when dissolved or dispersed in aqueous medium. The hydrophilic tendency in a non-ionic surfactant is due to the presence of oxygen molecule, which hydrates by hydrogen bonding to water molecule. Hydroxyl groups and ether linkages are the strongest hydrophilic groups in non-ionic surfactants. However, ester and amide linkages, which are also hydrophilic are present in non-ionic surfactants.

Non-ionic surfactants are more effective than other surfactants in removing soil at the lower temperatures in laundering synthetic fibers. They are also more effective for removing body oils. Some of the important non-ionic surfactants are as follows:

(i)   Ethylene oxide adducts: e.g. polyoxy ethylene surfactants, ethoxylated alkyl phenols and aliphatic alcohols, etc.

(ii)   Carboxylic esters and amides.

(iii) Alkylol amides and sorbitol compounds.

(iv)   Polymeric nonionics.

3.9 Raw Materials for Detergents

- The important raw materials required for the manufacture of detergents are:
  (a)   straight chain alkyl benzene,
  (b)   fatty acids and alcohols,
  (c)   detergent builders and
  (d)   additives.

These raw materials are obtained as follows:

(a) Straight chain alkyl benzenes:

- Detergents are made from phenyl substituted n-alkanes containing 11 to 14 carbon atoms. The straight chain paraffins or olefins needed are produced from petroleum or from ethylene.

  (I)   **From Petroleum fraction:** Paraffins or n-alkanes are separated from kerosene by adsorption using molecular sieves. Branched chain and cyclic alkanes have larger cross-sectional diameters than do the linear molecules, due to this sieve separation is possible. The separated n-paraffins are converted to benzene alkylates or cracked to olefins.

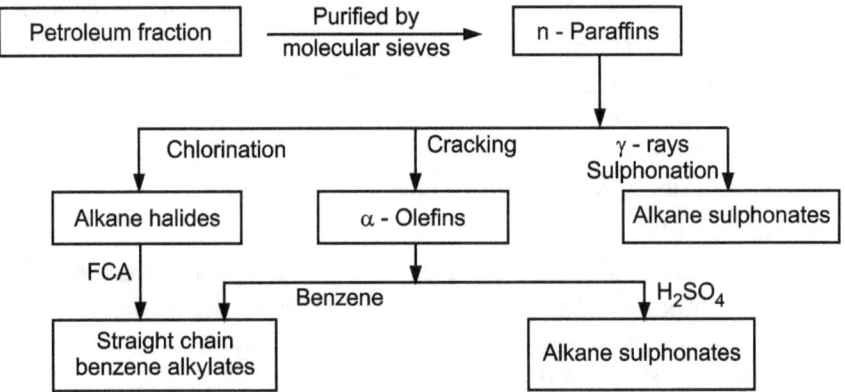

Fig. 3.1 (a): Simple paths to detergent compounds from petroleum fraction

(II) **From Ethylene:** Linear olefins are prepard by dehydrogenation of paraffins. In the first step, polymer of ethylene to α-olefins using an aluminium triethyl catalyst (Ziegler type), by cracking paraffin wax. Alpha-olefins or alkane halides can be used to alkylate benzene through the Friedel-Craft's reaction by using HF or AlF_3 as a catalyst.

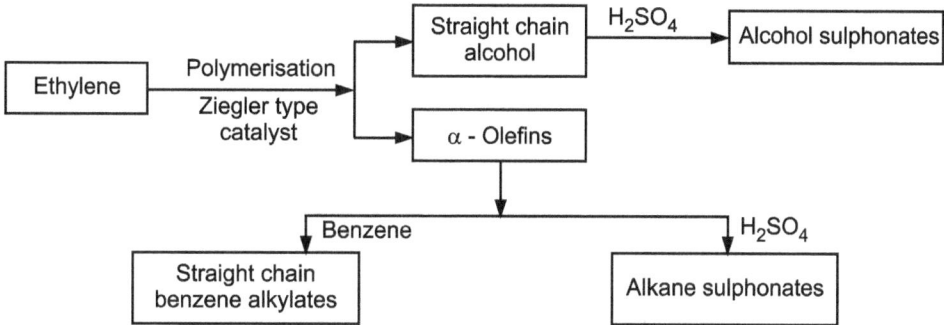

Fig. 3.1 (b): Simple paths to detergent compounds from ethylene

(b) Fatty acids and alcohols:

- Fatty acids and fatty alcohols are mainly consumed in the manufacture of soaps and detergents. Saturated fatty acids such as stearic acid as well as unsaturated fatty acids like oleic acids have been used in many industries as free acids or their salts. e.g. Magnesium stearates in face powders, Ca or Al soaps (insoluble) employed as water repellents in water proofing textiles and walls, and rosin soap consumed as a sizing for paper.

- Oils and fats have been used for the manufacture of fatty acids. Fatty acids are drawn off from the distillate receiver for further conversion to fatty acid salts. Fatty acids are purified by using the methods like, fractional distillation, pressing and solvent crystallization.

- Fatty alcohols are prepared by two important methods: Ziegler catalytic process and methyl ester hydrogenation process starting from α-olefins. The continuous hydrolysis of fats gives fatty acids, it may be hydrogenated to fatty alcohols. e.g. Gaseous ethylene is converted to higher, linear aluminium trialkyls by the action of aluminium triethyl (Zieglar catalyst).

$$Al\begin{matrix} CH_2-CH_3 \\ CH_2-CH_3 \\ CH_2-CH_3 \end{matrix} + CH_2{=}CH_2 \xrightarrow[\substack{1\text{-}15\ MPa \\ pressure}]{100\text{-}130°C} Al\begin{matrix} CH_2-CH_3 \\ CH_2-CH_2-CH_2-CH_3 \\ CH_2-CH_3 \end{matrix}$$

ethylene

(c) Detergent Builders:

- These include inorganic salts, such as sodium sulphate, sodium carbonates, sodium silicates and phosphates. They are called detergent builders because they increase the cleansing or washing activity of surfactants and thus make the detergent more effective.

Since detergents are highly concentrated and hence never be used in pure form, the surfactants are very expensive as compared to these builders. Hence, addition of these builders into synthetic detergents lowers the cost of the resulting product without affecting its wetting and detergent activities. On the other hand, these properties are improved by addition of builders.

(i) **Sodium sulphate:** The surfactant prepared by sulphonation or sulphitation processes always contain with it sodium sulphate and sodium sulphite to lesser extent. These salts improve the surface activity of surfactants when used in proper amounts. It also acts as a dehydrating agent for giving dry free flowing powders.

(ii) **Sodium silicate:** They are used in various ratios, $Na_2O : SiO_2$. Their function in detergents is to stop the corrosion action and maintain the soil particles in suspension to prevent redeposition.

(iii) **Sodium carbonate:** Sodium carbonate is also an important filling agent. It is inexpensive and has functions similar to those of sodium phosphates. Soda ash is most commonly used which provides high alkalinity and softness of hard water by precipitating Ca and Mg carbonates.

(iv) **Sodium phosphates:** These include sodium tripolyphosphates ($Na_5P_3O_{10}$) and tetra sodium pyrophosphate. They help to adjust the pH, soften the water, improve the soil removing power, and removal of water from detergent and accepting it as water of crystallization to yield a free-flowing powder.

(d) Additives:

These are the substances added to detergents for several purposes:

(i) **Bleaching agents:** Bleaching agents, such as sodium hydrosulphite or sodium hypochloride incorporated in some of the surfactants for removing colouring matters.

(ii) **Corrosion inhibitors:** Certain inhibitors are added in order to protect the metals, utensils, dishes and other materials from the action of detergent and water. e.g. sodium silicate, benzotriazole, etc.

(iii) **Opacifying agents:** These are water-soluble polymeric compounds used in the formulation of self-stable clear or creamy liquid syndets. On their addition these compounds opacify and increase viscosity of the resulting surfactant and it is possible to make a self-stable creamy liquid syndet.

(iv) **Optical brighteners:** These are colourless fluorescent dyes substantive to fabrics. Their function is to convert ultra-violet radiation into visible region thus masking the grayness developed inevitably in old garments. These brighteners are commonly used in synthetic detergent powders, ranging from 0.001 to 0.1%. It is used for fine fabric laundering in very small concentration. A striking visible improvement resulting from their use in very minor amounts made them very popular for all the medium to heavy duty detergent products.

(v) **Soil redeposition preventing agent:** Redeposition of soil on the cleaned surface occurs in washing operation because of the high soil load or due to the extensive dilution of the surfactants by the cleaning operation. Sodium carboxy methyl cellulose is extensively used in detergents to prevent soil redeposition and is more effective with cotton. For synthetic fibers, polymers such as polyvinyl pyrrolidone and polyvinyl alcohol are used for preventing soil redeposition.

(vi) **Enzymes:** Recently, certain enzymes are used in detergents for removing stains. These include proteolytic and amylolytic enzyme detergent additives. They are used in about 1000 to 1300 units per litre in the wash. Enzymes used for this purpose are α-amylase, alkaline protease, mexatase etc.

3.10 Washing Action of Soaps and Detergents

- Both soaps and detergents are functionally similar. They are dissolved or tend to dissolve in water and also in non-aqueous materials under certain conditions. In order to achieve this dual function, these compounds must have two distinct groups in their molecular structure.

3.10.1 Washing Action of Soap

- Soaps are the excellent emulsifying and frothing agents for the production of foam and emulsion between water and fatty acids. When a soap is dissolved in water, it has hydrophobic character of the hydrocarbon like tails. This fact happens due to:

  (i) Formation of oriented monolayers at the surface with the hydrocarbon tails pointing towards.

  (ii) The self aggregation of the soap molecules into the micelles in the body of solution. These phenomena are responsible for the dispersing and emulsifying powers which make soap solutions useful as cleaning agents and emulsifiers.

- The removal of dirt (i.e. mixture of oily material and solid particles), adhered to the surface, by soap solution proceeds according to the following equation:

  Surface – Dirt + Soap → Surface – Soap + Dirt – Soap

- This dirt itself is emulsified by the soap and carried away by moving water. The soap washing also removes other dirt like paint, soil, shoot and proteineous materials from the surface under treatment. This washing action of soap is due to the lowering of the interfacial surface tension of water, so that the dirt (oil) goes into the emulsion and the surface of fibre or the material becomes clean and wettable by water. The lowering of interfacial surface tension is due to the adsorption of soap at the interface.

- Soap is represented by a general formula, $R - COO^- Na^+$, where 'R' represents a long chain alkyl radical. Soap molecules contain two groups:

$$CH_3 - CH_2 - (CH_2)_n - CH_2 - COONa \qquad \text{(Na-soap)}$$

$$\underbrace{\qquad\qquad\qquad}_{\substack{\text{Hydrophobic} \\ \text{(water-insoluble)}}} \quad \underbrace{\qquad}_{\substack{\text{Hydrophilic} \\ \text{(water-soluble)}}}$$

- Hydrophilic means water loving or water liking or water attracting substance. Hydrophobic means water hating or water repelling substance.

- **Micelles:** Micelles are the aggregates of many small molecules or groups of atoms which are held together by secondary valencies i.e. by cohesive or van-der-Waals forces. Many inorganic colloids, emulsion soaps and detergents etc. generally form such micelles. Soap in water is colloidal, the particles are composed of a number of small molecules of sodium or potassium salts of fatty acids. However, the same soap is dissolved in alcohol as a single molecule. The micelles are usually less stable than macromolecules. The soap micelles are split even by dilution or heating of the soap solution.

3.10.2 Washing Action of the Detergent

- The cleansing action of the detergent (surfactants) depends upon the property of decreasing surface tension or interfacial tension at the boundary surface between two phases of matter (liquid-gas or liquid-liquid). The most important application of detergents is better wetting and cleansing action and no consumption by water, because of higher solubility of their Ca^{2+} and Mg^{2+} ions.

- Synthetic detergents are compounds which have a tendency to dissolve in water and in oils under certain conditions. It contains hydrophilic or water attracting groups on one end of the molecule, while hydrophobic or water repelling groups on the other end. The hydrophilic groups make the compound soluble in water, whereas hydrophobic groups make the compound oil soluble.

- When detergent ($R - OSO_3^- Na^+$) is added to water at the time of washing, it increases the wetting ability of water, so that it can easily penetrate the fabric and get to the location of the soil. The soil is removed by the process of wetting, emulsifying, dispersing or solubilizing the soil by the cleaning agent. Detergent molecule bearing aggregates of many small molecules or groups of atoms in water into spherical clusters which are held together by secondary valencies are called micelles. The hydrocarbon part (R) of the molecules gather together on the inside of the micelle and the polar groups (OSO_3^-) are on the outside. Dirts (oil soluble) are dissolved into the centre of the micelle attracted by the hydrocarbon groups. This process is known as solubilization.

- During washing with detergent soil removal, hydrophobic ends of the molecules are attracted to the soil particle and then the soil particle is surrounded by the hydrophobic ends. At the same time hydrophilic ends are pulling the soil particles away from the surface of cloths. Constituents of detergent maintain the dirt in stable solution or suspension.

- Cleaning action of detergent does not depend upon the solubility but on the ratio of molecular weight of the hydrophobic to that of hydrophilic part of the molecule. For example, detergent formed by the action of '10' molecules of ethylene oxide on lauryl alcohol is soluble in water and is a good detergent, but the same compound formed by the action of '5' molecules of ethylene oxide on lauryl alcohol is neither soluble in water nor a good detergent.

3.11 Comparison of Soaps and Detergents

	Soaps		Detergents
(i)	Soaps are the salts of long chain monocarboxylic acids i.e. Na or K salts of higher fatty acids.	(i)	Detergents are chemical formulations that consist of surface active agents and subsidiary, constituents such as filler, boosters, builders, etc.
(ii)	Soap making involves the use of oils and fats which have potential food values.	(ii)	The surfactants required for detergents are made from the petroleum products.
(iii)	The cleaning action of soap is reduced in hard water.	(iii)	The washing or cleaning activity of detergent is not affected by hardness of water.
(iv)	It is poor foaming agent.	(iv)	It is excellent foaming agent.
(v)	It cannot be used in acidic solution, due to formation of sticky precipitate getting adhered to the textile fibres.	(v)	It can be used in acidic solution and also for washing delicate fiber like wool and silk.
(vi)	It is less active and requires more concentration.	(vi)	It is more active and requires low concentration.
(vii)	It has no germicidal and bactericidal properties.	(vii)	It has germicidal and bactericidal properties.
(viii)	Its recovery is possible, when used in large amounts.	(viii)	Its recovery is very difficult as compared to soap when used in large amounts.
(ix)	It is biodegradable and hence not cause water pollution.	(ix)	It is not easily biodegradable and hence causes water pollution. i.e. it is more toxic than soap.

(C) COSMETICS

3.12 Introduction

- Cosmetic science is a very ancient science, it is changing as per the need of the society. The cosmetic consumption in India is growing at a very fast rate. Thus, the cosmeticology is focussed in the pharmaceutical industry. Cosmetics are also known as makeup or make-up. They are generally mixtures of chemical compounds, some being derived from natural sources and many being synthetics.

- Cosmetics is defined as an item intended to be rubbed, poured, sprinkled or sprayed on, introduced into, or otherwise applied to the human body or any part thereof for cleansing, beautifying, promoting attractiveness or altering the appearance, but soap is excluded from the definition. The world cosmetics is derived from the Greek, meaning 'technique of dress and ornament' and 'skilled in ordering or arranging'.

- On the basis of physical form, cosmetics are classified as:

  (a) Oils   :   Brilliantine, hair oils
  (b) Emulsions   :   Cold cream, cleansing cream, vanishing cream, all purpose cream, etc.
  (c) Suspensions   :   Liquid powder, cosmetic stockings.
  (d) Pastes   :   Toothpaste, deodorant paste.
  (e) Sticks   :   Lipstick, deodorant stick.
  (f) Jellies   :   Brilliantine jelly, wave set jelly.
  (g) Cakes   :   Rouge compacts, make-up compacts.
  (h) Powders   :   Face powder, tooth powder.
  (i) Solutions   :   After shave lotions, astringent lotions.

- On the basis of part of the organ where they are applied, cosmetics are classified as:

  [A] Cosmetics for Skin:
  (i)   Powders
  (ii) Creams
  (iii) Lotions
  (iv) Deodorants
  (v)   Suntan preparations
  (vi) Make-up
  (vii) Bath and cleansing preparations

  [B] Cosmetics for Hairs:
  (i)   Shampoos
  (ii) Hair tonics
  (iii) Hair dressings
  (iv) Shaving media
  (v)   Depilatories

[C]   Cosmetics for Nails:

(i)   Nail polishes and polish removers

(ii)   Maincure preparations

[D]   Cosmetics for Mouth:

(i)   Mouth washes

(ii)   Lipstick, lip gloss, lip liner, etc.

(iii)   Foundations.

3.13 Raw Materials for Cosmetics

- The raw materials required for synthesis of cosmetics are given as follows:

[1] Emulsifiers:

- An emulsifier is a substance that stabilizes an emulsion by increasing its kinetic stability, it is also known as emulant. Common emulsifiers used in cosmetics are surface active agents or surfactants. Emulsifiers will physically interact with oil and water, thus stabilizing the interface between the oil and water droplets in suspension. Many emulsifiers are used in pharmacy to prepare emulsion such as creams and lotions. These are the preparations which impart smoothness and a general sense of well-being to the skin, as determined by touch. Emulsion may also cause flattening of the surface countours of the skin, plumping of individual corneocytes and general smoothing and diminishing of facial lines.

- Common examples include emulsifying wax, cetearyl alcohol, polysorbate 20, hydrocarbon oils, silicone oils, vegetable oils and fats, fatty acids and alcohols. The choice is determined by personal preference, data on personal skin irritation, the degree of greasiness and apparent residual film on the skin. 'Moisturing' is useful property claimed for cosmetic creams and it is most widely used. Water is the only material which will plasticize the outer dead layers of the epidermis to maintain a soft, smooth skin.

[2] Lipid Components:

- Lipids are a group of naturally occurring molecules that include fats, waxes, sterols, fat-soluble vitamins, monoglycerides, phospholipids, etc. The main biological functions of lipids are storing energy, signaling and acting as structural components of cell membranes. Lipids have applications in the food and cosmetic industries. Lipids may be defined as hydrophobic or amphiphilic small molecules. The term lipid is sometimes used as synonym for fats. Fats are a subgroup of lipids called triglycerides. Unsaponifiables are components of an oily mixture that fails to form soap, these unsaponifiable constituents are an important consideration when selecting oil mixtures for the manufacturer of soaps. Unsaponifiables can be beneficial to make cosmetics because they may have properties such as moisturization, conditioning, vitamins, texture of skin etc. The proportion of unsaponifiable components is carefully controlled to produce good quality cosmetics.

[3] Humectants:

- Humectants are those substances used to keep thing moist, it is opposite to a desiccant. Humectants are used so as to prevent drying of skin. It is often a molecule with several hydrophilic groups, like hydroxyl, amines, carboxylate groups, etc. They are used in many products, including food, cosmetics, medicines and pesticides. A humectant attracts and retains the moisture in the air nearby via absorption, drawing the water vapour on the skin surface.

- In pharmaceuticals and cosmetics, humectants can be used in topical forms to increase the solubility of chemical compounds (active ingredients) which help to penetrate skin and its activity time. This hydrating property can also be needed to counteract a dehydrating active ingredient e.g. soaps, alcohols, corticoide, etc. Therefore humectants are commonly used in cosmetic and personal products that make moisturization of hairs and skin. Initially glycerine (50% solution) was used as humectants, but now 70% sorbitol syrup is used as it is less expensive than glycerine. Propylene glycol may also be used as a humectant.

[4] Colours (Dyes and Pigments):

- All the colours we see around us is a gift of organic molecules called dyes. A dye is a coloured organic compound or mixture that may be used for colouring the surface. A substance possessing following properties is known as a dye:

  (i)   The substance must be coloured.

  (ii)   The substance must be able to produce colour when dispersed in or reacted with other materials by process which, atleast temporarily attach with substrate like hair or skin. Some dyes cannot dye animal and vegetable fibres directly, but require the presence of a medium of third substance, called mordants. Dye should have an attractive appearance, smooth surface of uniform colour, should be retained during shelf life, should not excude oil and become brittle over the range of temperatures. It should be safe both dermatologically and if ingested should be easy to apply, reasonably permanent film of stable colour. For example, congo red, indigo, zinc and magnesium stearate, iron oxides, carnauba wax, rose alcohols and esters.

- Pigments are various organic and inorganic soluble substances that are used widely in surface coatings to impart colour to skin, opaqueness or other desirable properties to the hair or skin. Pigments are almost always applied in an aggregated or crystalline-insoluble form. Examples are white lead, cobalt blue, chrome yellow, red lead, chrome green etc. An ideal pigment is chemically inert, free of soluble salts, insoluble in all media used, and is unaffected by normal temperature.

  o   **Staining dyes:** For example, water soluble eosin and other halogenated derivatives of fluorescein, tetrabromo fluorescein.

  o   **Pigments:** Titanium dioxides, calcium lakes, barium lakes.

[5] Preservatives and Antioxidants:

- The preservative is a substance that is added to products such as food, pharmaceuticals, paints, cosmetics, etc. to prevent decomposition by microbial growth or by undesirable chemical changes. In general, prevention is implemented in two ways, chemical and physical. Chemical preservation is achieved by adding chemical compounds in products, while physical preservation entails refrigeration and drying. They are used in foods, cosmetics and many other products. Preservatives reduce the risk of skin infections, decrease microbial spoilage and preserve fresh attributes and quality. Some physical techniques for preservation include dehydration, UV-C radiation, freeze drying, etc. Chemical preservation and physical preservation are usually combined for improving the skin surface.

- The oxidation process spoils most food, those with high fat content. Fats from skin quickly turn rancid when exposed to oxygen. Antioxidants prevent or inhibit the oxidation process. The most common antioxidant additives are ascorbic acid (vitamin C) and ascorbates. A variety of agents are added to deactivate metal ions that otherwise catalyze the oxidation of fats present in skin. Common agents like disodium EDTA, citric acid, tartaric acid and lecithin are used to deactive the metal ions.

3.14 Cosmetics for Skin

[1] Types and Problems of Skin:

- The skin is the outer part of our body. Moist, clear, growing skin is a sign of good health. Skin is the largest organ in the human body. For an average adult human, the skin surface area is between 1.5-2.0 square metres. Skin has mesodermal cells, pigmentation or melamin which absorb some of the potentially dangerous UV radiations from sunlight. Skin is composed of three primary layers:

    (i)   Epidermis: Which provides waterproofing and serve as a barrier to infection.

    (ii) Dermis: Which serves as a location for the appendages of skin.

    (iii) Hypodermis: Which is subcutaneous adipose layer.

- If your skin is itching, breaking out or acting weird, get an overview of symptoms and types of skin condition. These are two basic types of dry skin. The first is due to prolonged exposure to low humidity and air movements, which modifies the normal hydration gradient of the stratum corneum. The second is due to physical or chemical changes in the skin due to processes such as ageing, continual degreasing. Parabeans can cause skin irritation and contact dermatitis in individual with parabean allergies, a small percentage of the general population. Sun protection is the best way to avoid sunburn, even on cloudy days. Cellulite is normal fat beneath the skin. The fat appears bumpy because it pushes against the connective tissue beneath skin. Blisters come in all sizes. Some are painful, red or itchy. Peritis or itchy skin, can be caused by dry skin.

[2] Key ingredients of skin cleansing:

- The following key ingredients are present in skin cleansing cosmetic products:

    (i) Glycerine: It prevents excessive drying out of the cream, which takes place, the product is of the oil in water type within the external phase, while sufficient glycerine prevent rolling of the skin.

    (ii) Alkalies: Potassium hydroxide, sodium hydroxide, potassium carbonate, aqueous ammonia, triethanolamine borax. Potassium hydroxide is most generally used because it makes a cream of fine texture and excellent consistency without excessive hardness.

    (iii) Preservatives: If the cream contains substances likely to deteriorate under bacterial or fungal action. For example, methyl, propyl and butyl hydroxy benzoate, phenyl mercuric nitrate, bronopol, etc.

    (iv) Perfumes: Organic compounds either as they come or dissolved in alcohol or a perfume solvent.

[3] Toners:

- Toners are used after cleansing the skin to freshen it up and remove any traces or cleanser, mask or makeup, as well as to help restore the skins at natural pH. They are usually applied to a cotton pad and wiped over the skin, but can be sprayed onto the skin from a spray bottle. Toners normally contain alcohol, water and herbal extracts or other chemicals depending upon the skin type. Toners containing alcohols are quite astringent and usually applied for oily skins. Dry or normal skin should be treated with alcohol-free toners. Witch hazel solution is a popular toner for all skin types. Many toners contain salicylic acid and benzoyl peroxide. These type of toners are applied for oily skin as well as acne-prone skin.

[4] Moisturizers:

- Most beneficial property of cosmetic creams is moisturizing the skin. The water is the only material which will plasticize the outer dead layers of the epidermis to maintain a soft, smooth skin. If water is lost more rapidly from the stratum corneum then it is received from the lower layers of the epidermis, the skin becomes dehydrated and loses its flexibility, oil alone will not restore flexibility. The approach to restoring water to dry skin has taken three different routes-occlusion, humectancy and restoration of deficient materials which may be combined.

- Occlusive substances e.g. non-water permeable substances such as mineral and vegetable oils, lanolin and silicones. Cold cream is one of the oldest cosmetics used for cooling sensation caused by evaporation of water in the cream after it is applied to the skin. Cold creams may be oil in water or water in oil. Cold creams consist of waxes and preservatives like methyl or propyl parahydroxy benzoate 0.15% are added to the formulation. Night and massage creams are designed to be left on the skin for several hours or to remain mobile on the skin even after rubbing. The occlusive layers of these creams slow the rate of trans-epidermal water loss, thus having moisturizing effect also makes the skin surface feel smooth, be the action of lubricating surface. Vitamin D, A, E and H are oil soluble and essential for skin health.

[5] Protective Sunscreen:

- Exposure to sunlight can have both beneficial and harmful effects on the human body, depending on the length and the frequency of exposure, the intensity of the sunlight and sensitivity of the individual. Short term effect temporary damage of the epidermis, slight erythema to painful burns, fever and nausea and sometimes itching, swelling of the skin. The sun-screen are the substances which prevent or minimize the harmful effect of the solar radiation or to assist in tanning the skin without any painful effects. Sunscreen consists of sunburn preventive agents and sustaining agents. For example, p-amino benzoic acid and its derivatives, salicylates, cinnamic acid derivatives, stilbene, quinine, tannic acid and its derivatives.

[6] Talcum powder:

- The substances which impart a smooth finish to the skin, making minor visible imperfections and any shine due to moisture or grease are known as talcum powders.
- Covering powder is used to conceal various defects of the facial skin, to cover more area e.g. titanium dioxide, zinc oxide, kaolin, magnesium oxide.
- Following are some desired properties of face powder:
    (i) **Absorbency:** These agents eliminate shiny skin in certain facial areas by absorbing sebaceous secretions and perspiration e.g. colloidal kaolin, micro-crystalline cellulose, magnesium carbonate.
    (ii) **Adhesiveness:** To cling powder well to the face. e.g. talc, zinc and magnesium stearate.
    (iii) **Slip:** To increase the flow and ease for spreadability, these substances are added e.g. talc, magnesium stearate.
    (iv) **Colour:** Iron oxides, inorganic and organic pigments.
    (v) **Perfume:** Increases the cosmetic acceptability, alcoholic solution of floral bouquets.
    (vi) **Bloom:** Requirement as per fashion trend. e.g. chalk, rice starch, powdered silk.

[7] Bleaching Products:

- These are agents which lighten the skin colour used for makeup, protection of skin against ultraviolet radiation. The lightening of the skin colour may be reducing pigmentation, decolourize the melanin present. Subscreening agent in a skin lightening preparation which prevents reoxidation by UV light the leuco or reduced form of melanin.

- Bleaching agents are as follows:

    (i) Opaque covering agents: Titanium dioxide, zinc oxide, kaolin, talc etc.

    (ii) Oxidising agents: Creams containing hydrogen peroxide, sodium hydrochlorite solution.

    (iii) Mercury compounds: Red mercuric oxide, mercurous chloride.

    (iv) Hydroquinone.

    (v) Catechol and its derivatives.

    (vi) Natural ways: Materials used - cucumber juice, lemon juice, butter milk, crushed strawberries and fresh horseradish.

[8] Nourishing:

- The skin is the outer reflection of your inner health. Moist, clear, growing skin is a sign of good diet while dry, pale, scaly or oily skin may result when your diet is not upto mark. Just every nutrient has a role in maintaining healthy skin. Vitamin C helps build collagen, the 'scaffolding' between the tissues of our body. Deficiency of vitamin C can cause bruising, loss of skin strength and elasticity and poor healing of cuts and scraps. Just one glass of orange juice or a bowl of strawberries supplies vitamin 'C' you need. Healthy skin also needs the vitamin 'B' found in whole grains, milk and wheat germ. Vitamin 'A' in dark orange or green vegetables and fruits, eggs and livers, maintain epithelial tissues, thus helping to prevent premature wrinkling. Vitamin 'D' in milk might help curb symptoms of psoriasis. Zinc in meat, seafood and legumes aid in the healing of cuts and scrapes. Water keeps the skin moist and regulates normal functions of oil glands. The list of nutrients that benefit the skin are almost endless.

3.15 Hair Care

- Hair care is overall term for parts of hygiene and cosmetology involving the hair on the human head. Hair care will differ according to ones hair type and according to various processes that can be applied to hair. All hair is not the same; hair is a manifestation of human diversity. Hair care mention may be made of processes and services which impact hair on head and other parts of the body. This includes men's and women's facial, public and other body hair, which may be coloured, trimmed, shaved, plucked or removed with treatments such as waxing, sugaring and threading. These services are offered in salons, barbershops and day spas and products are available commercially for home use.

1. Classification of hair care products:

- The products which are intended to promote certain favourable conditions of hair and reduce or eliminate properties of hair which are regarded as undesirable are called as hair care products.

- Hair care products include shampoos, hair creams, conditioners, hair oils, hair tonics, etc. It may be classified into two groups:

  (i)   Those which work by purely **physical** mechanisms e.g. shampoos, hair sprays, etc.

  (ii) Those which bring about **chemical** changes in hair e.g. waving, sting preparations, permanent dyes, etc.

2. Ingredients in hair care products:

- The ingredients present in hair care products are SD alcohols, butyl ether, water, benzyl benzoate, fragrance, dihydroabietyl alcohol, yellow 6 aluminium lake, etc. Exact ingredients of hair tonic vary based on the specific product. The primary ingredient in hair tonic is usually mineral oil or liquid petroleum jelly. Hair tonic gives hair a glossier look. If too much hair tonic is used, it may look greasy. Most hair tonics are liquids and they can be used to style hair as they hold the hair in place. Hair tonic can improve hair healthy by adding moisture to the hair and scalp, which reduces split ends. The moisture makes good choice for people with dry or fine hair. Hair products like mousses and styling gels also took place of hair tonics. Hair tonics is smooth, which makes it a good choice for scalp massages. It can also be used for facial hair health and styling. Some hair tonics have different fragrances, such as rosemary mint or sweet almond. Some contains sun screen and others may promote growth and thickness of hairs.

- Some more commonly used ingredients in hair care products and their purpose are as follows:

  (i)   Ammonium lauryl sulphate: This is a high-foam surfactant that makes a good base for cleansers because they disrupt hydrogen bonding in water.

  (ii) Behentrimonium chloride: This is wax like organic compound used as an antistatic agent and disinfectant, it is commonly used in conditioners, hair dye, etc.

  (iii) Benzyl alcohol: This is colourless liquid and has a mild pleasant aromatic odour. It is generally used as a solvent for inks, paints and epoxy resin coatings.

  (iv) Citric acid: This is a mild fruit acid commonly used in hair products for its ability to open the cuticle layer and allow deeper penetration of other products which are beneficial to the hair.

  (v) Lanolins: This substance is secretion of wool-bearing mammals such as sheep. It is used in conditioners to coat and seal the hair against damage.

  (vi) Resorcinol: This is obtained on fusing many resins with knott. It is used to create diazo dyes and used as an antiseptic and disinfectant agents.

[3] Special additives for conditioners and scalp health:

- Following additives are useful as hair conditioning and scalp health.

  1. Conditioners: Conditioners smooth, soften texturize and restore the protective sheath on hair. The agents used as conditioners are lanolin, mineral oil, polypeptides, herbal additives, egg derivatives and some synthetic resins.

2. **Viscosity modifiers:** Various thickeners used are 1-4% w/w ammonium and sodium chloride, alginates, karaya gun, tragacanth, carboxymethyl cellulose, hydroxyethyl cellulose and carboxyvinyl polymers.

3. **Opacifying and clarifying agents:** Opacity and opalescence is provided by finely dispersed zinc oxide, titanium oxide, glycerol monostearates and palmitates, magnesium, calcium or zinc salts of stearic acid, latexes, magnesium aluminium silicate, etc.

4. **Preservatives:** Milder surfactants are not effective against bacteria. Natural additives make shampoos prone to microbial attacks. Therefore, preservatives like hydroxybenzoate esters, quaternary ammonium surfactants, formaldehyde etc.

5. **Sequestering agents:** These are required to prevent the formation and deposition of calcium and magnesium soaps onto the hair, while rinsing with hard water. EDTA and pyrophosphates are generally used.

[4] Hair colourants:

*   Hair colouring is the practice of changing the colour of hair. Hair colouring can be done professionally by a hair dresser or independently at home. Today hair colouring is immensely popular in women dying their hair. The three main classes of hair colourants are temporary, semi-permanent and gradual colourants.

    (i)   **Temporary colourants:** Temporary colourant is available in various forms including rinses, shampoos, gels, sprays and foams. The temporary hair colours are typically brighter and more vibrant than other two colourants. It is always used to colour hair for special occasion such as costume parties. The pigment molecules cannot penetrate the cuticle layer. The colour particles remain adsorbed to the hair shaft and easily removed with a single shampooing.

    (ii) **Semi-permanent colourants:** Semi-permanent colourants has smaller molecules than temporary colours. These dyes only partially penetrate the hair shaft. These colours may be removed by 4-5 shampooing with repeated washing. Semi-permanent colours contain very low levels of developer, peroxide or ammonia and are therefore safer for damaged or fragile hair. The final colour of each strand of hair will depend on its original colour, so there will be subtle variations in shade across the whole head. Semi-permanent colour cannot be lighter than air.

    (iii) **Gradual colourants:** These colourants generally contain ammonia and must be mixed with developer or oxidizing agent in order to permanently change hair colour. Ammonia in gradual hair colour is used to open the cuticle layer, so that the developer and colour molecules together penetrate into the cortex. The concentration of oxidizing agent and developers vary in colours. Dark hair need 2-3 shades, lighter may need higher developer. Timing may vary with permanent hair colouring but typically 30-40 minutes are required for maximum gray coverage.

[5] The plant materials (herbs) used in hair cosmetics:

- There are many natural ways to colour the hair instead of having to use colour that contains several chemicals. A lot of the natural hair colouring can be used simply at home. The use of herbs such as henna, castor oil, sandalwood and turmeric for skin care. Women are obsessed with looking beautiful. So, they use various beauty products that have herbs to look charming and young. Indian herbs and its significance are popular that have worldwide. Herbal cosmetics have growing demand in the world market and is an invaluable gift of nature. Herbal formulations always have attracted considerable attention because of their good activity and lesser or nil side effects. Herbs and species have been used in maintaining and enhancing human beauty. Indian women have long used henna to colour the hair, palms and soles and natural oils and perfumes are used for their bodies. Herbal beauty treatments were carried out in royal palaces of India to heighten sensal appeal and maintain general hygiene.

- For dry hair, treatment used is coconut oil, sunflower oil, oleo, etc. In anti-aging treatment used golden root (roseroot), carrot, ginko. In dandruff treatment used common herbs including neem, kapoor and henna, hirda, behada and amalaki, magic nut, rosary pea, sweet flag, cashmere tree and mandor.

- Some essential oils are also extracted from herbs. These oils are volatile and liquid aroma compounds from natural sources usually plants. The essential oils contain mainly volatiles as terpenoids, benzenoids, fatty acid derivatives and alcohols. Essential oils can be used in several ways for cosmetic purpose like inhalation, baths, massage, steam treatments, room fragrance, etc. These oils are generally extracted from rose, eucalyptus citronella, etc. herbs.

Exercises

(A) Answer the following:

1. What are the advantages and disadvantages of detergents?
2. What are soaps? Give the raw materials required for soap manufacture.
3. What are surfactants? How are they classified?
4. Describe the manufacture of detergents with the help of flow-sheet diagram.
5. What is meant by saponification process?
6. Explain in brief:
    (i) Cleaning powders
    (ii) Shaving soap and shaving cream
    (iii) Medicated soap
    (iv) Shampoos
    (v) Cosmetics for skin
    (vi) Hair care

7. Discuss the manufacture of 'Neat-soap' from fatty acids/oils and fats.

8. Write notes on:
    (i)   Washing action of soap
    (ii)   Washing action of detergent
    (iii)   Detergent builders
    (iv)   Additives
    (v)   Transparent soap
    (vi)   Floating soap
    (vii)   Preservatives and Antioxidants

9. Explain the following:
    (i)   Wetting and non-wetting agents
    (ii)   Emulsion and emulsifying agents
    (iii)   Hydrophobic and hydrophilic nature
    (iv)   Amphipathic structure
    (v)   Micelle formation
    (vi)   Toilet soap
    (vii)   Emulsifiers

(B) Multiple Choice Questions (MCQs):

(i)   The hydrophilic group in soap is _____

        (a) –COONa   (b) –OSO_3Na (c) –$CONH_3$ (d) –NH_2

(ii)   The important raw material for the manufacture of detergent is _____

        (a) oils and fats **(b) alkyl benzene**   (c) ethylene   (d) NaCl

(iii)   The weight of soap is increased by addition of _____

        (a) alkyl benzene sulphonate (b) starch **(c) fats and oils**

        (d) sodium hydroxide

(iv)   The cleaning capacity of ordinary soap is improved by adding _____

        (a) sodium silicate (b) sodium chloride (c) polyethylene **(d) talc**

(v)   The antibacterial agent added in medicated soap is _____

        (a) aldehyde **(b) phenol** (c) amide (d) toluene

(vi)   The stabilizers used in shampoos are _____

        (a) amine halides (b) amine carbonates **(c) amine oxides**

        (d) amine sulphate

(vii)   The superfatting agent used in soap manufacture is _____

        (a) E.D.T.A. (b) lemon juice (c) acetic acid **(d) lanolin**

(viii) The important by-product in soap industry is _____

(a) lanolin (b) acetic acid **(c) glycerol** (d) rosin

(ix) Humectants are those substances used in cosmetics _____

(a) to dry the skin **(b) to keep skin moist**   (c) to lighten the colour of skin (d) impart smooth finishing to the skin

(x) Ammonium lauryl sulphate used in hair care products are called _____

(a) solvents   (b) antiseptic agents (c) nourishing agent **(d) cleansers**

■■■

Chapter 4...

Dyes, Paints and Pigments

Contents ...

(A) DYES

4.1   Introduction
4.2   Qualities of a Good Dye
4.3   Dye Intermediates
4.4   Classification of Dyes
    4.4.1   Classification of Dyes According to Chemical Constitution
    4.4.2   Classification of Dyes According to Mode of Application
4.5   Theory of Colour
    4.5.1   Chromophore
    4.5.2   Auxochrome (Greek, auxin = to increase; chroma = colour)
4.6   Structures and Applications of Some Dyes
    4.6.1   Nitro Dyes
    4.6.2   Nitroso Dye
    4.6.3   Azo Dyes
        4.6.3.1 Acid Azo Dye
        4.6.3.2   Basic Azo Dyes
        4.6.3.3   Direct or Substantive Azo Dyes
    4.6.4   Phthaleins
    4.6.5   Xanthene Dyes
    4.6.6   Rhodamines
    4.6.7   Thiazine Dyes
    4.6.8   Anthraquinone Dyes
    4.6.9   Indigoids
    4.6.10 Thioindigoid Dyes
    4.6.11 Cyanine Dyes
        4.6.11.1 Phthalocyanines
4.7   Vat Dyes
4.8   Heterocyclic Dyes

(B) PAINTS

4.9   Introduction
4.10 Classification of Paints
4.11 Methods of Applying Paints

(C) PIGMENTS

4.12 Introduction
4.13 Classification of Pigments
4.14 Physical Properties and Uses of Pigments
•   Exercises

(A) DYES

4.1 Introduction

- All beautiful colours we see around us is a gift of organic molecules called dyes. Life is colourfull because of dyes. A dye is a coloured organic compound or mixture that may be used for colouring the surface. The substances such as textile fibre and hence clothes, papers, plastics, leather, metal sheets etc. may be coloured with the help of dye. *A dye may be defined as a 'coloured compound which is capable of (either directly or with the help of mordant) imparting permanent colour to the substrate'.* Some dyes cannot dye animal and vegetable fibers directly, but require the presence of a medium of third substance, called **mordants.**

- In other words, dyes are substances capable of colouring fabrics in such a manner that the colour cannot be removed by rubbing or washing. It should also be noted that every coloured substance is not a dye. For example, azobenzene is of orange red colour, but it is not a dye, because it is not capable of colouring the fiber.

4.2 Qualities of a Good Dye

- All coloured substances are not dyes. A coloured compound possessing following properties is a dye.

  (i)   It must have an attractive and suitable colour.

  (ii) It must be able to attach itself to the material like cloth etc. from the solution. There must be a chemical or physical union between the dye and the substrate.

  (iii) Dye must be soluble in a suitable solvent and should form a stable dispersion in the solvent.

  (iv) The pick-up of the dye from the medium by a substance to be dyed (substrate) should be good. That is, the substrate must have affinity for a particular dye and must be able to absorb it from the solution.

  (v)   Dye applied on to the surface must be fast to washing, dry cleaning, heat, light etc.

4.3 Dye Intermediates

- The raw materials used for the manufacture of dyes are mainly aromatic compounds, such as benzene, toluene, naphthalene, anthracene, phenol, pyridine, carbazole, pyrene etc. These raw materials are known as **primaries** and exclusively obtained from the distillation of coal tar. In recent years, **petroleum** and **natural gas** have become important sources of primaries such as benzene, toluene, naphthalene, xylene etc. Aromatic hydrocarbons in recent years have also been obtained from other sources such as water gas, methane, and olefines by catalytic processes.

- A large number of **inorganic compounds** have also been used in dye industry to serve various purposes. These materials include sulphuric acid, oleum, nitric acid, acetic acid, caustic soda, hydrochloric acid, chlorine, bromine, sodium chloride, sodium nitrite, sodium carbonate, sodium sulphate, sodium hydrosulphite, sodium sulphide, sodium dichromate, manganese dioxide, aluminium chloride etc.

- The primaries of dyes are never directly used in the synthesis of dyes. They are first converted into a large number of derivatives, which are in turn made into dyes. **The derivatives or derivates are generally known as dye intermediates, because they act as intermediate between the primaries and the final dye.**

- A large number of important reactions such as nitration, oxidation, halogenation, sulphonation, reduction, condensation etc. have been used in the production of intermediates. These reactions give rise to be formation of substituted hydrocarbons which are functional in nature (They contain functional groups which undergo further chemical reactions to produce dye).

- Sulphonation, nitration, amination by reduction, halogenation, dehydration, Friedel-Craft's reaction etc. are the most important and common unit processes which are involved in the synthesis of dye.

- Aliphatic compounds, aromatic compounds and heterocyclic compounds are the three main types of intermediates needed for the manufacture of dyes.

- Acetyl chloride and other acid chlorides are used in many organic reactions such as Friedel Craft's reaction for the production of intermediates.

- Aldehydes and ketones are generally used in the manufacture of ranges of intermediates. Paraformaldehyde, acetaldehyde, benzaldehyde, methyl isopropyl ketone etc. are used for this purpose.

- In addition, some other aliphatic compounds such as urea, ethylene oxide, acetonitrile, thiourea, acrylic acid, dimethyl sulphate, acrylonitrile etc. have also been used in the manufacture of intermediates and dyes.

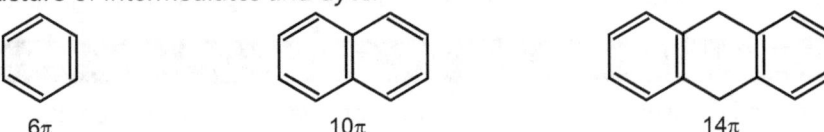

6π 10π 14π

- The **aromatic dye intermediates** are commonly prepared from benzene, naphthalene and anthraquinone. Biphenyl, acenaphthene, benzanthrone, pyrene, perylene etc. have also been used in making aromatic dye intermediates, but less frequently.

- The reactivity of aromatic compounds depends mainly upon the availability of π electron cloud on the system. The increase in the π electron cloud follows the order: **Benzene (6π) < Naphthalene (10π) < Anthracene (14π).**

4.4 Classification of Dyes

- Dyes can be classified by number of methods. Large number of dyes have been synthesized. Hence their classification is also a difficult task. Useful classification can be made on the basis of:

  (a) Chemical constitution of dyes and

  (b) On the basis of their mode of application.

4.4.1 Classification of Dyes According to Chemical Constitution

- In this method, dyes are classified into various classes on the basis of what chromophoric group is present in the molecule. The main classes are:

  (i) **Nitro dyes:** These dyes contain nitro group as a chromophore. Generally, they are nitro derivatives of phenols. For example, picric acid.

  (ii) **Azo dyes:** Chromophore is $-N=N-$ (azo) group and common auxochromes are $-NH_2$, $-NR_2$, $-OH$ etc. For example, congo red.

  (iii) **Nitroso dyes:** In these dyes, nitroso group is a chromophore and hydroxyl group is generally auxochrome at the ortho position. For example, fast printing green.

  (iv) **Phthalein dyes:** These are dihydroxy triphenyl methane derivatives with carboxyl or sulphonic acid group ortho to central carbon atom in the third phenyl ring. For example, phenolphthalein.

  (v) **Diphenyl methane dyes:** These contain NH_2, NR_2 or $-OH$ group into para position of benzene ring of triphenyl methane. For example, crystal violet.

  (vi) **Xanthene dyes:** These are derivatives of xanthene. $-NH_2$, $-OH$ etc. group is introduced into dibenzo - 1,4 pyran (xanthene). For example, fluorescein.

  (vii) **Heterocyclic dyes:** These contain heterocyclic rings. For example, safranin-T.

  (viii) **Anthraquinone dyes:** These are derivatives of anthraquinone and related polycyclic aromatic quinones. The chromophore is $>C=O$, while auxochrome may be $-OH$, $-NH_2$ etc. For example, alizarin.

  (ix) **Indigo and thioindigoid dyes:** Indigo is oldest known dye. It occurs in plant of indigofera group. When $-NH$ group of the indigo is replaced by sulphur atom, thioindigoes are obtained. For example, indigotin, indigosol-o.

  (x) **Sulphur dyes:** Sulphur dyes are coloured solids having complex structures. They are prepared by heating various organic compounds with sodium polysulphide.

  (xi) **Phthalocyanine dyes:** These are metal complexes of isoindoles. For example, copper phthalocyanine.

  (xii) **Diphenyl amine dyes:** These are the derivatives of diphenyl amine containing $-NH_2$ as a chromophore and $-OH$ as a auxochrome.

4.4.2 Classification of Dyes According to Mode of Application

- This classification is practically useful for dyers. Dyes are classified according to their mode of application. Important classes are given below:

   (i)   **Acid dyes:** Acid dyes are useful to dye animal fibers having basic groups such as wool, silk etc. These are sodium salts of sulphonic acids and nitrophenols. For example, picric acid, naphthol yellow, orange-II.

   (ii)   **Basic dyes:** These dyes have basic amino group. The zinc salt or hydrochloric salt of these are used for dying. Animal fibres like wool or silk can be directly dyed but for cotton mordant like tannin is required. For example, magenta, crystal violet etc.

   (iii)   **Direct dyes:** These dyes directly attach to fibre without any mordant. They contain sulphonic acid group but it is not used as a means of attachment to the fiber. These dye wool, silk and cotton also. For example, congo red, zambeski black D.

   (iv)   **Mordant or Adjective dyes:** These contain two or more acidic or basic groups. These dyes do not attach directly to animal or vegetable fiber. They require mordant or adjective for attachment. For acidic dyes, metal hydroxides are used as mordant while for basic dyes tannic acid is used. Mordant material binds the dye to fibre. For example, alizarin (acidic dye) is applied with aluminium hydroxide as a mordant.

   (v)   **Vat dyes:** For application of these dyes, large wooden tank called vat are used. The reduced form of these dyes is colourless and soluble. This form is called leuco compound. The cloth to be dyed is immersed in the vat containing dissolved leuco compound (reduced form of dye). The reduced dye is absorbed by the fabric. The original insoluble coloured dye is obtained by oxidation with air or chemical. For example, indigo, anthraquinone etc.

   (vi)   **Developed dyes:** These dyes are developed on the surface to be dyed. For example, the cloth is first soaked in the solution of diazonium salt and then in the solution of phenol or amine. The coupling takes place on the surface of cloth giving a colour.

   (vii)   **Disperse dye:** These are water insoluble dyes which are dispersed by using emulsifying agent before the application to synthetic fibres.

   (viii)   **Organic pigments:** These are not used for dying fibre but are used in printing and textile in combination with a resin binder. They are also used in paints, varnishes etc.

   (ix)   **Food dyes:** They are used as edible colours. These are selected and tested for harmless effects. These dyes are used in colouring foods, candles, cosmetics and confectionaries.

4.5 Theory of Colour

- In 1876, Witt stated that, colour of an inorganic compound is due to the presence of certain unsaturated groups, to which he called chromophores. A compound containing chromophore is called as **chromogen**.

4.5.1 Chromophore

- (**Chroma** means **colour**, **phores** mean **bearing group**). It is a group which is responsible for imparting colour to a substance.

- Some examples of chromophoric groups are as follows:

$-N=O$	Nitroso group	$\diagdown C=S$	Thiocarbonyl
$-N\mathord{\overset{O}{\underset{O}{\lessgtr}}}$	Nitro	$-N=N-NH$	Azoamine
$-N=N-$	Azo	$-N=N-O$	Azoxy
$-CH=N-$	Azomethine	$\diagdown C=O$	Carbonyl

4.5.2 Auxochrome (Greek, **auxin** = **to increase**; **chroma** = **colour**)

- According to Witt, certain groups present in chromogen, do not impart colour but increase the intensity (deepen) of the colour. Such groups are called '**auxochromes**'. Auxochromes are the saturated groups which do not produce colour but deepen the colour of chromogen.

- For example, benzene is colourless, while aniline is yellow in colour. Auxochrome may be either acidic or basic.

- **Acidic auxochromes:** SO_3H, $-COOH$, $-OH$, $-Cl$.

- **Basic auxochromes:** NH_2, $-NHR$, $-NHR_2$.

4.6 Structures and Applications of Some Dyes

4.6.1 Nitro Dyes

- These dyes are characterized by the presence of $-NO_2$ groups as chromophore. These are polynitroderivatives of phenols, containing atleast one nitro group in the ortho or para position to hydroxyl ($-OH$) group. For example, picric acid, martius yellow etc.

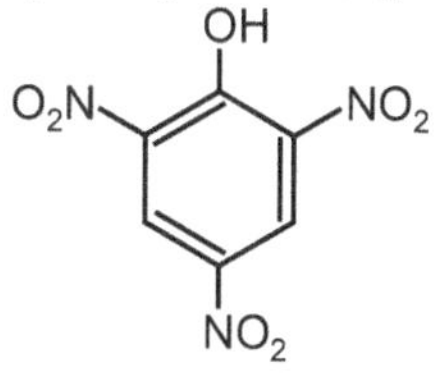

Picric acid 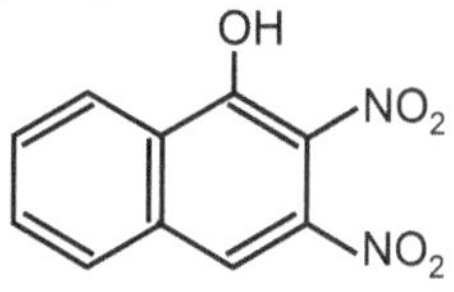   Martius yellow

- Picric acid is used to dye silk and wool yellow, but the colour is fugitive.
- Other example is Naphthol yellow S, which is cheap dye for wool and silk in an acid bath and give pure yellow shades. It is non-poisonous and so used as food colour. The structure of Naphthol yellow S is

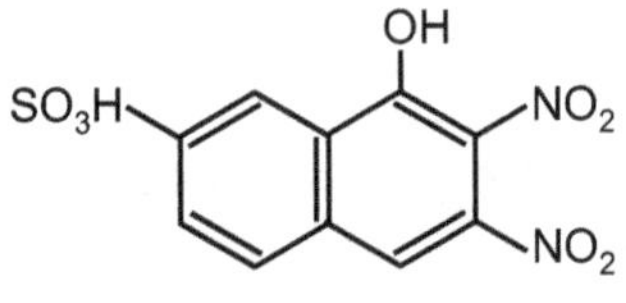

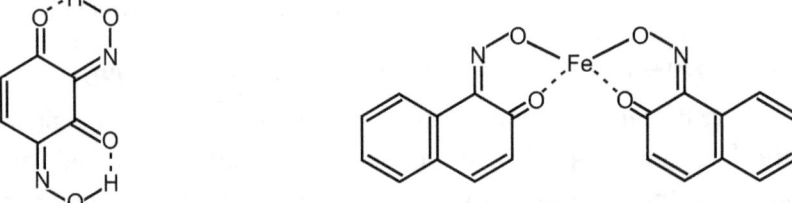

Naphthol Yellow S

4.6.2 Nitroso Dye

- In these dyes, chromophore is $-NO_2$ or $= N-OH$. In other words, these dyes are characterized by the presence of nitroso group as chromophore and phenolic group as auxochrome in the ortho position with respect to each other. These dyes are generally employed in dyeing and calico printing. For example, fast green O, Naphthol green Y (gives green lake, known as **fast printing green** with ferrous sulphate).

Fast Green O   Fast Printing Green

4.6.3 Azo Dyes

- Azo dyes include practically all classes of dyestuffs, such as acid dyes, basic dyes, direct or substantial dyes, mordant or adjective dyes, ingrain or naphthol dyes etc.
- The azo dye class represents the largest and most important group of dyes and includes many hundreds of commercial dyes of various applications. The azo chromophore ($- N = N -$) forms part of the conjugated system and joins two or more aromatic rings.

4.6.3.1 Acid Azo Dye

- Acid azo dyes are characterized by the presence of one or more acidic groups like $- SO_3H$, $- COOH$, $- OH$ (phenolic) etc.
- Methyl orange (orange-II) is para-dimethyl amino azobenzene para-sulphonic acid. It is an acidic azo dye.

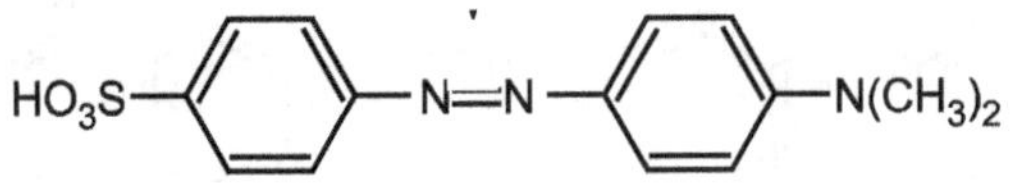

Methyl orange

The dye is isolated as its sodium salt.

Uses:

(i)   Methyl orange is not an important dye. It imparts orange colour to silk and wool but colour is not fast to light and washing. Methyl red is used as an indicator in acid alkali titration.

(ii) Its sodium salt is used as indicator in the acid-base titration. It shows yellow colour in alkali and red in acidic solution. The change in colour with medium is due to change in the structure as shown below:

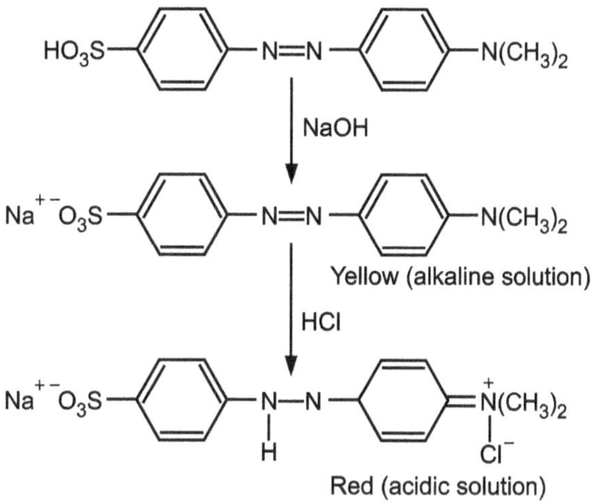

Yellow (alkaline solution)

Red (acidic solution)

- Following are the other examples of acid dye:

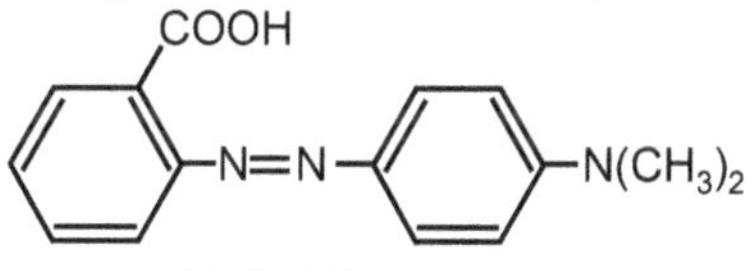

Methyl Red

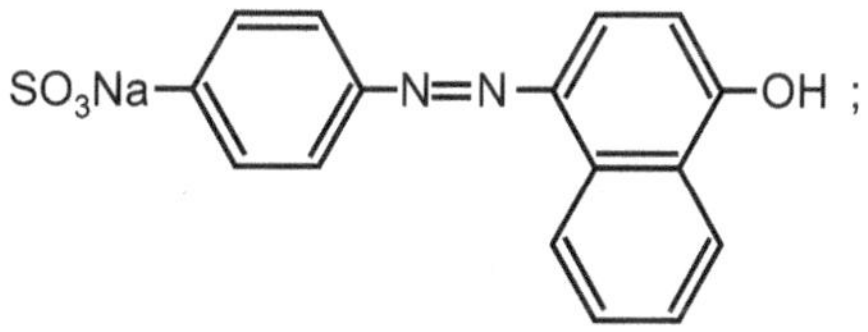

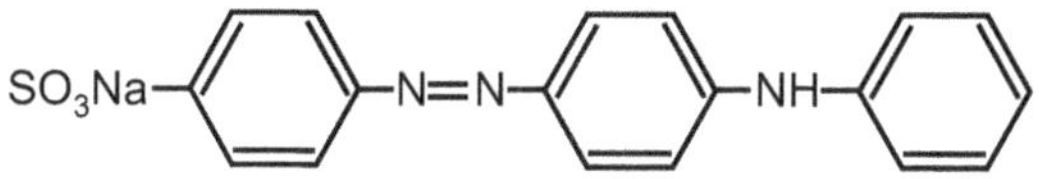

Orange I

Orange IV

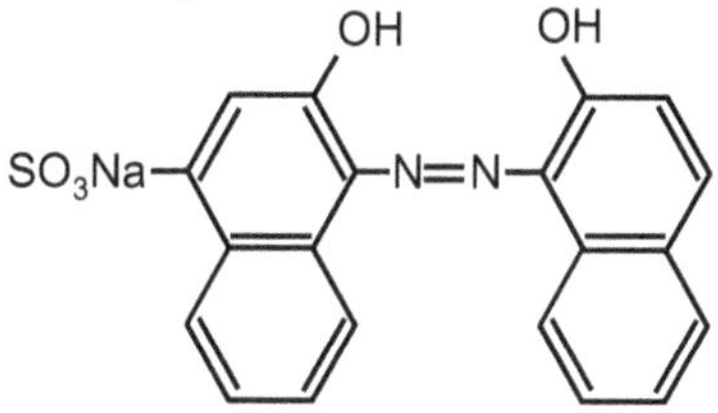

Chrome Blue Black R

4.6.3.2 Basic Azo Dyes

- These dyes contain amino or substituted amino groups $-NH_2$, $-NHR$ or NR_2 as auxochromes. The number of basic dyes are relatively low, and they are not of great importance in industries. Following are few examples of basic azo dyes:

(i) 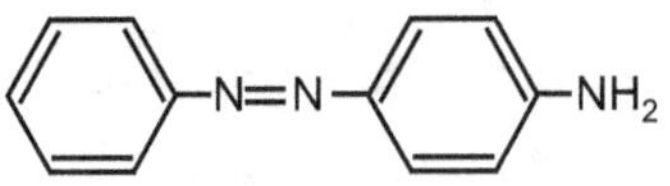 [Aniline Yellow structure: benzene ring—N≡N—benzene ring—NH$_2$]

(ii) [Chrysoidine structure: benzene ring—N≡N—benzene ring with NH$_2$ and NH$_2$]

Aniline Yellow
(p-aminoazo benzene)

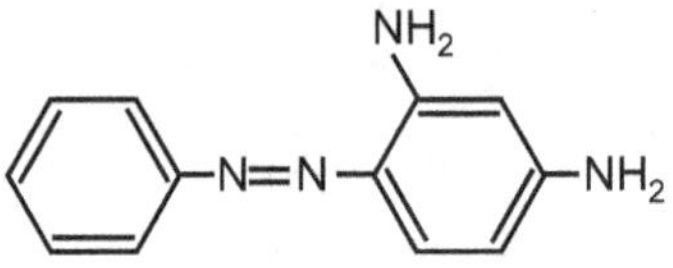

Chrysoidine
(2,4-diaminoazo benzene)

Aniline yellow is rarely used a dye, because it is readily affected by acids. Chrysoidine is an orange dye and used for dying silk, wool, cotton, leather and paper. It dyes wool and silk directly and cotton mordanted with tannic acid.

4.6.3.3 Direct or Substantive Azo Dyes

- The acidic or basic azo dyes dye directly the proteinous fibres such as wool, silk and leather, but they require mordant for dying cellulose fibres. Direct or substantive azo dyes represent the largest single subgroup of azo dyes, which can also dye cellulose fibres directly i.e. without a mordant.

- Congo red is most important example of azo dye, capable of dying cotton directly. It is also used as an indicator to distinguish between organic acid and inorganic (mineral) acid.

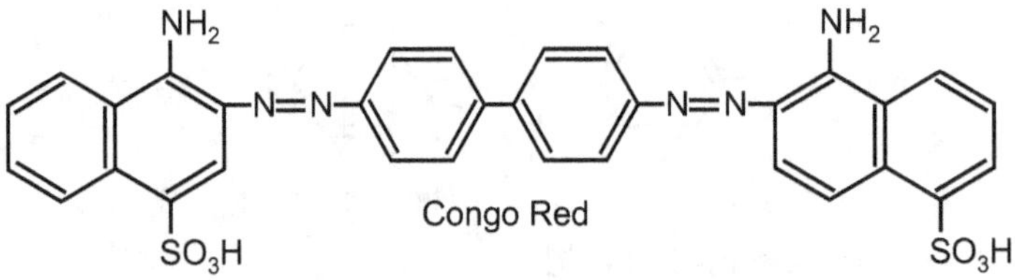

[Congo Red structure]

Congo Red

4.6.4 Phthaleins

- Phenolphthalein is phthalein type of dye. It is synthesized from phthalic anhydride. First phthalic anhydride is prepared from phthalic acid by heat treatment. These dyes may also be regarded as the derivatives of triphenyl methane. For example, phenolphthalein.

It is a colourless crystalline solid, insoluble in water but soluble in ethyl alcohol giving colourless solution.

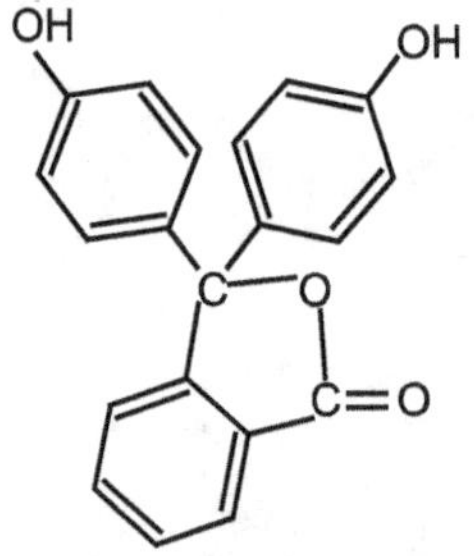

[Phenolphthalein structure]

Phenolphthalein

Uses:

1. It is not famous as a dye but it is best used as a acid-base indicator. It is colourless in acidic solution but form pink colour with alkali. The change in colour is due to change in structure (benzonoid form to quinonoid form). Both these forms are shown below:

2. It is also used as a laxative in medicines.

Colourless (acidic) Benzonoid form   Pink (alkaline) Quinonoid form

4.6.5 Xanthene Dyes

• These dyes are derivatives of xanthene and are quite related to phthalein dye. Fluorescein is xanthene dye. It is prepared from phthalic anhydride and resorcinol. Phthalic anhydride is prepared from phthalic acid and heated with resorcinol (1 : 2) at 200°C. The reaction taking place is

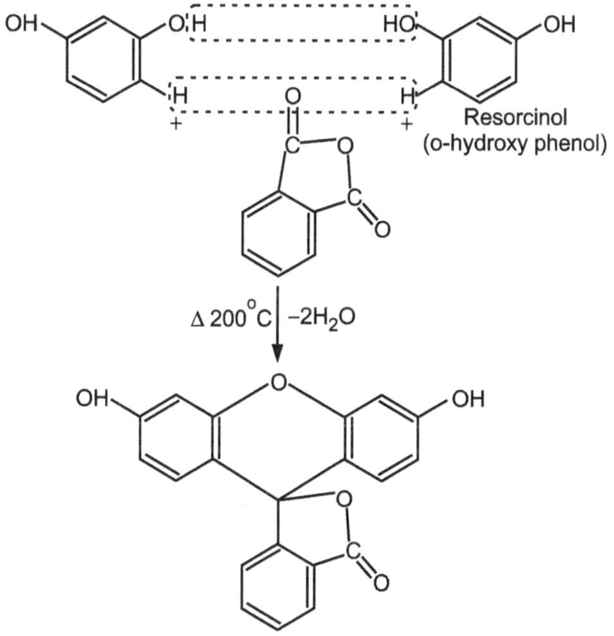

Resorcinol
(o-hydroxy phenol)

Δ 200°C $\mid$ −2H$_2$O

Fluorescein

It is a fluorescent dye. It is red coloured water insoluble dye.

Uses:

1. Its sodium salt is used to dye wool and silk.

2. It is used as a marker during accidents as well as tracing underground currents in sea and rivers.

- Tetrabromofluorescein or **Eosine** is another important example of xanthene dye which is used for wool and silk with a tin or alum mordant.

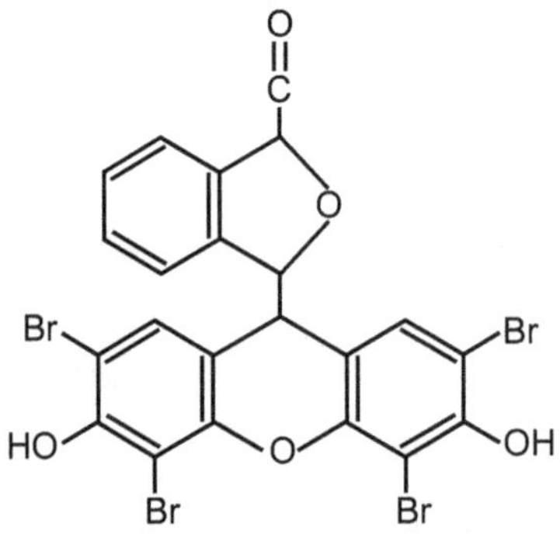

Eosine

4.6.6 Rhodamines

- Basic violet 10 (Rhodamine B) is a dye for bast fibers, mordanted cotton, leather And paper. Its salts with certain acids and acid dyes provide pigments and solvent dyes.
- Basic violet 10 is prepared by condensing phthalic anhydride with m-diethyl aminophenol and treating with hydrochloric acid. This is the general preparative route for rhodamines.

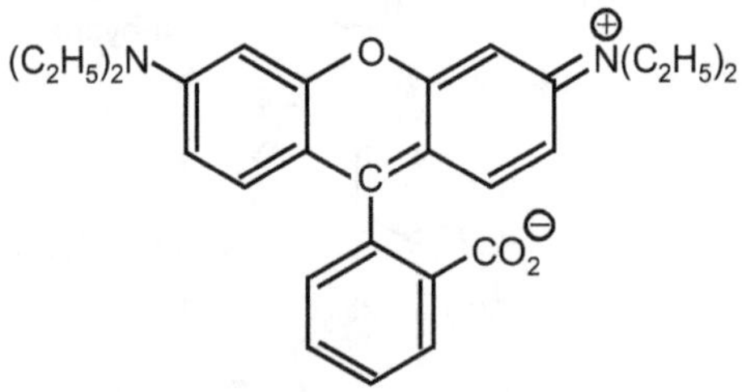

Basic violet 10

4.6.7 Thiazine Dyes

- **Methylene blue** is an important member of this class. It is prepared by the oxidation of a mixture of dimethyl aniline and p-aminodimethyl aniline with potassium dichromate in the presence of sodium thiosulphate.

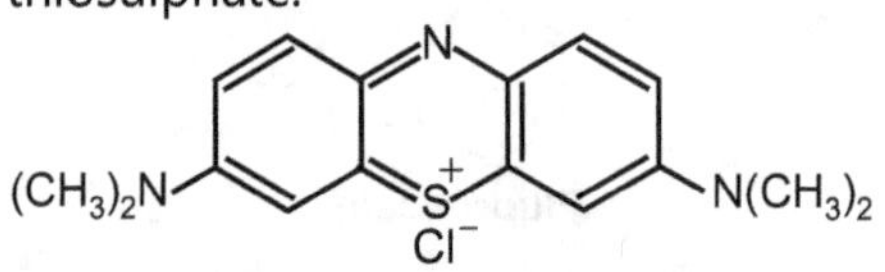

Methylene Blue

- It is also a dye which is used in calico printing, as an indicator and in medicine.

4.6.8 Anthraquinone Dyes

- These dyes contain chromophores $= C = O$ and $= C = C -$ arranged in anthraquinone complex. They are mordant dyes, vat dyes, acid dyes etc.

- **Alizarin** is an anthraquinone mordant type dye. Chemically it is 1, 2 dihydroxy anthraquinone. It is synthesized in following two steps:

(a) In the first step, anthraquinone is prepared from phthalic anhydride and benzene in the presence of $AlCl_3$ as follows:

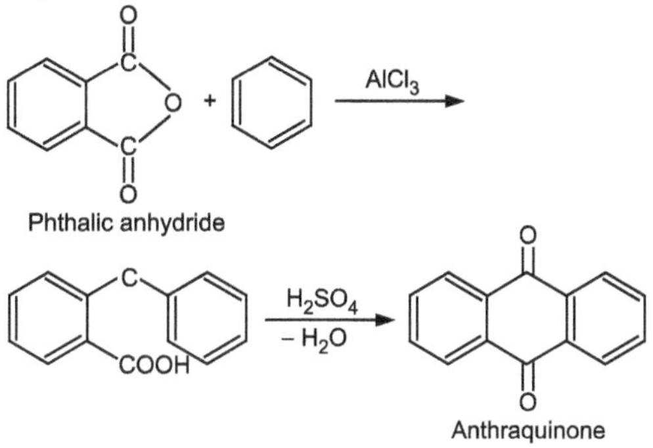

Phthalic anhydride

Anthraquinone

(b) In this step, anthroquinone is treated with fuming sulphuric acid to give anthraquinone 4-sulphonic acid. This on fusion with NaOH and $KClO_3$ at 180-200°C under pressure and further treatment with HCl gives alizarin. The series of reactions taking place are as given below:

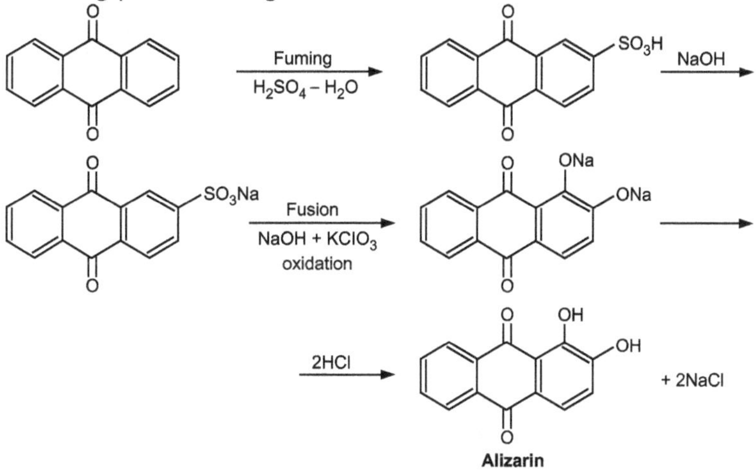

Alizarin

(i) It produces turky red colour to wool when applied with aluminium hydroxide mordant.

(ii) Calcium salt of it is bluish red coloured powder which is used as a pigment.

(iii) It combines with metallic hydroxides to form coloured insoluble compounds called lakes.

4.6.9 Indigoids

- Indigo blue or indigotin is the oldest and one of the most important **vat type dye.**
- It can be prepared by variety of methods. Following are the important commercial methods:

    (a)   **Manufacture of Indigo from Anthranilic acid:** First anthranilic acid is prepared from naphthalene. The reactions taking place are:

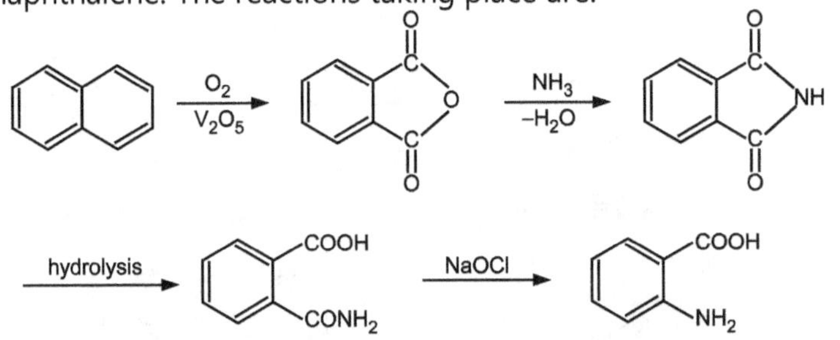

Anthranilic acid is heated with chloroacetic acid to give phenyl glycine-o carboxylic acid, which is then fused with mixture of KOH and sodamide to undergo ring closer and decarboxylation to give indoxyl.

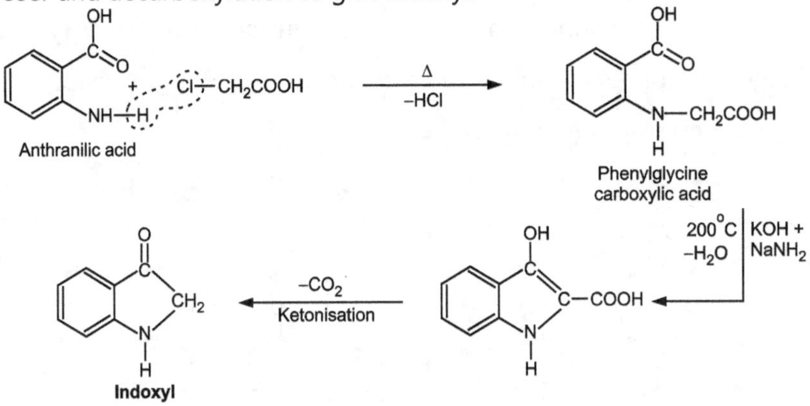

Indoxyl undergoes air oxidation to give indigo as follows:

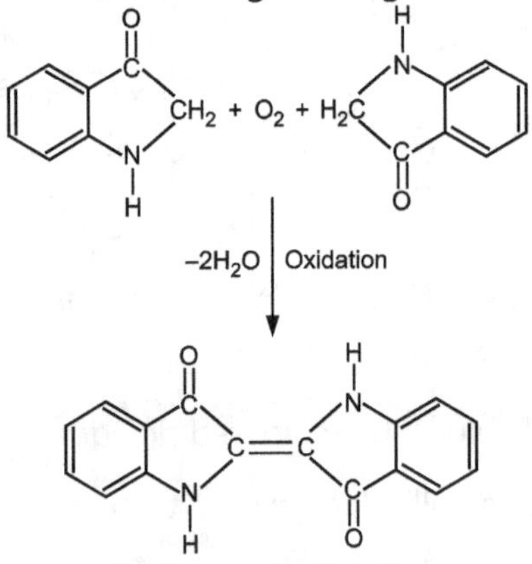

Indigo or Indigotin

(b) **Manufacture of Indigo from Aniline:** Aniline when heated with chloroacetic acid gives phenyl glycine.

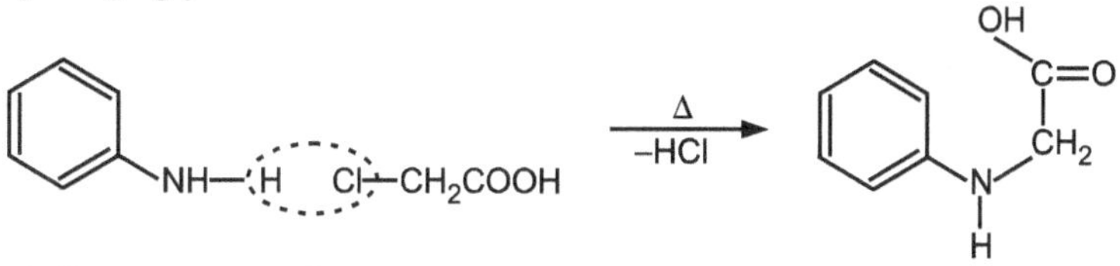

| Aniline | Chloroacetic acid | Phenyl glycine |

Phenyl glycine is fused with KOH and sodamide to give indoxyl.

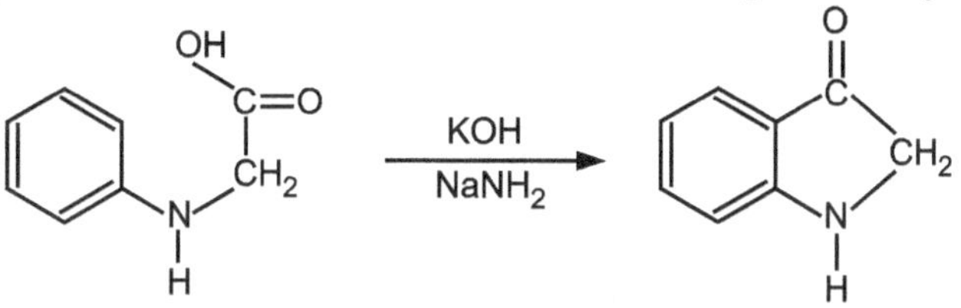

| Phenyl glycine | **Indoxyl** |

Indoxyl on air oxidation gives indigo as shown in the previous synthesis.

Uses:

1. Navy blue shades can be obtained on clothes made from cotton wool, rayon that are used to make uniforms.

2. It is used for printing purposes (calico or similar fabric).

3. Its leuco compound called indigo white can be made by dissolving indigo in alkaline hyposulphite solution.

$$\text{Indigo} \xrightarrow[\text{NaOH}]{\text{Na}_2\text{S}_2\text{O}_4} \text{Indigo white} \xrightarrow[\text{oxidation}]{\text{air}} \text{Indigo}$$

4.6.10 Thioindigoid Dyes

- Vat Red 41 (Thioindigo) is made by the reaction of thiosalicylic acid with chloroacetic acid, followed by fusion with caustic soda and oxidation by air.

- Vat Red 41 is dull bluish red on cotton. On polyester fibres, it produces bright pink shades. Many of its derivatives are of great commercial importance on cotton. e.g. Vat Orange 5, Vat Red 41 and Vat Orange 5 structures are shown below.

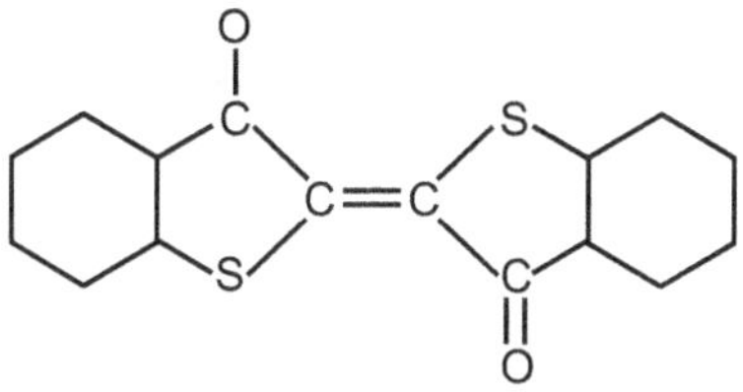

| Vat Red 41 | Vat Orange 5 |

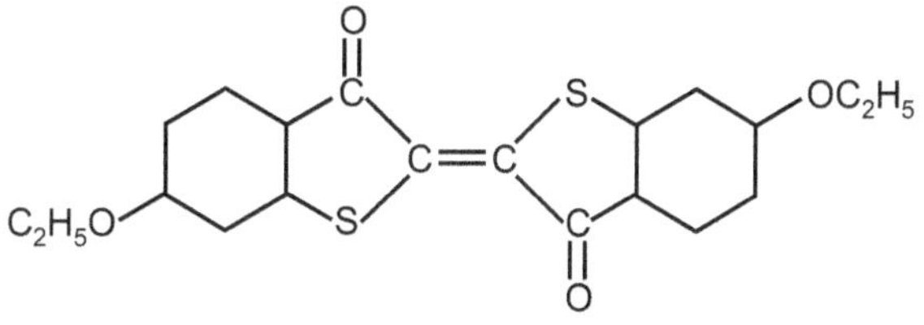

4.6.11 Cyanine Dyes

- Cyanine dyes are molecules containing polymethine bridge between two nitrogen atoms with a delocalized charge.

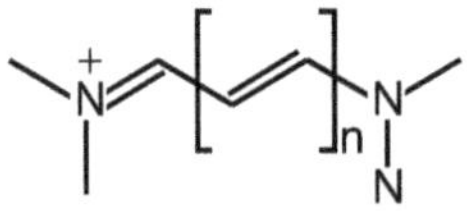

$n = 1, 2, 3$ ....

- A number of cyanine dyes have been used for life science applications.

- There are two varieties of cyanine dyes: non-sulfonated cyanines and sulfonated cyanines. Both these cyanines can be used for labelling of biomolecules such as DNA, proteins, antibodies, peptides, nucleic acid probes and any other kind of other biomolecules to be used in a variety of fluorescene techniques.

- Available non-sulfonated dyes include Cy3, Cy5 and Cy7.

- Cy stands for 'Cyanine' and first digit identifies the number of carbon atoms between the indolenine groups.

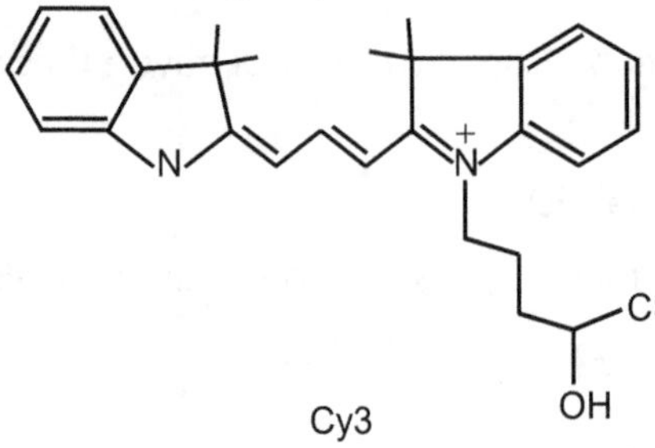

Cy3

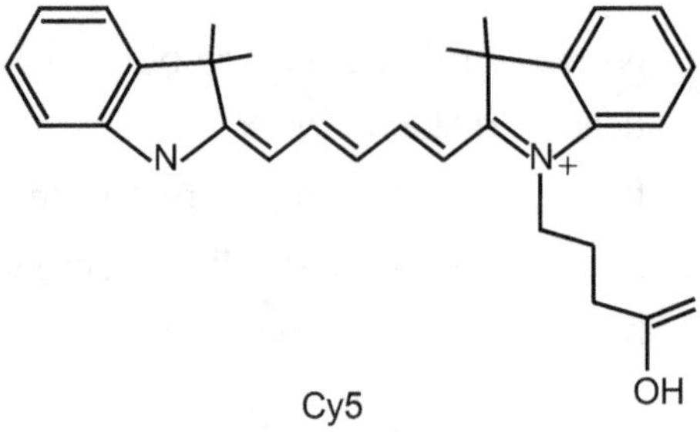

Cy5

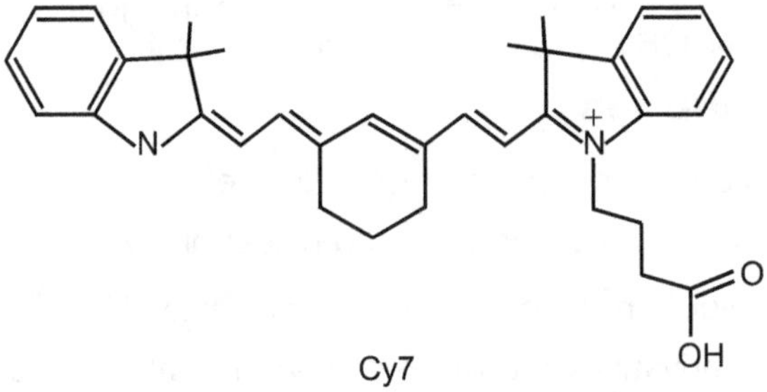

Cy7

4.6.11.1 Phthalocyanines

- The Phthalocyanines constitute an important class of synthetic pigments and dyes. The parent compound is Pigment Blue 16 (phthalocyanine). One of the method of preparation involves the fusion of phthalonitrile with cyclohexamine in an inert solvent. The two central hydrogen atoms can be replaced by metals such as copper, nickel, iron and cobalt, e.g. Pigment Blue 15.

- Pigment Blue 15 (copper phthalocyanine) is made by the fusion of phthalonitrile with copper metal or a copper salt. An alternate method involves the fusion of phthalic anhydride with urea and copper salt in the presence of molybdenum catalyst.

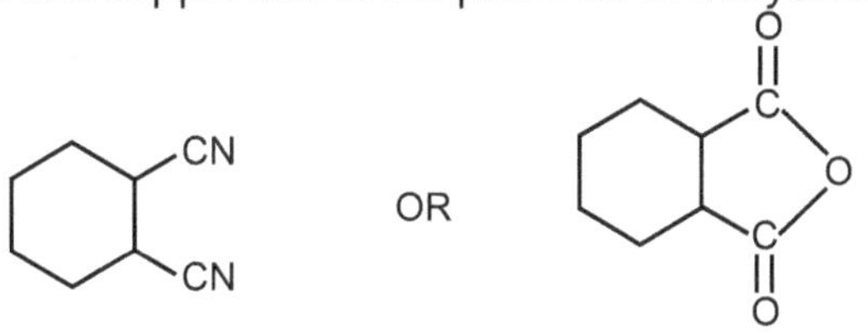

Phthalonitrile   OR   Phthalic anhydride

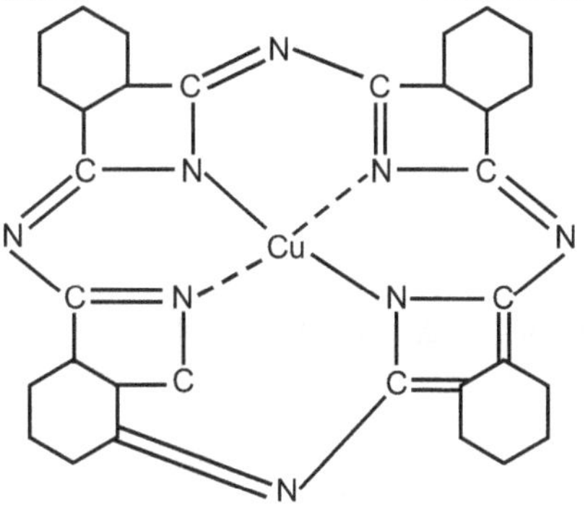

- A number of phthalocyanine derivatives can be made by replacing the hydrogen atoms on the benzene rings. For example, Pigment Green 7, Vat Blue 29, Direct Blue 86.

Applications:
- Direct Blue 86 produces very bright blue green shades on cotton, viscose and paper.
- Blue 25, spirit soluble derivative of copper pthalocyanine is useful for inks, lacquers and stains.

4.7 Vat Dyes

- These dyes are insoluble in water, but their reduced form is soluble in an alkali solution and as a result, leuco vat is obtained. Hence these dyes are utilized in their reduced form.
- The reduced form of the dye is obtained by treating the dye compound with a reducing agent like sodium hydrosulphate $Na_2S_2O_4$ in a large vat. The reduced dye becomes soluble in alkali forming sodium salt. **This process of reduction and solubilization is known as vating.**
- Vat dyes are widely applied to cotton, but least applied to wool and silk as these fibres are sensitive to alkalies. Indigo and anthraquinone vat dyes are good examples of this class.
- In actual process, **vat dyeing** is carried out by a continuous process (also refer page 4.5) in which cotton cloth from a roll is conveyed over a system of rollers into a solution of reduced dye. The impregnated cloth is then conveyed into a chamber, where proper fixation of the leuco compound to the impregnated fabric is carried out by steaming process. The fabric is next passed into a oxidising bath, containing chromate and acetic acid and finally to the soaping, rinsing and drying baths.

4.8 Heterocyclic Dyes

- These contain heterocyclic rings. The development of new structure of azo dyes has been a subject of interest and many novel structures of these dyes are useful in the commercial application to polyester, polyamide or polycyclic as well as their blends with other fibres. The general structure of heterocyclic dye is as follows:

R = Various naphthols

- These dyes mostly give pink, red and yellow shades on nylon and polyester fibres having very good to excellent washing fastness, rubbing, fastness etc. These dyes have better exhaustion on nylon than polyester.

(B) PAINTS

4.9 Introduction

- Paints are stable mechanical mixtures of one or more pigments ('Pigments', we will see in part C). The purpose of paint may be protective or decorative or both. The paint is applied on a metal or wood surface to give it protective coating.
- The paint is applied by **brushing, dipping, spraying or roller coating**. Some of the various drying oils that have been used in making paints are linseed oil, tung oil, castor oil, tall oil, etc. Linseed oil is widely used. Boiled linseed oil is usually used instead of unboiled oil, because the former develops a good drying power. The drying time may be reduced by adding driers to the paint.
- Thinners are also added to paints. Drier promotes the processes of film formation and hardening. Thinners maintain the uniformity of the film.
- In general, the paints are known for their gloss, adhesion and chemical and mechanical properties and are suitable for interior decoration as well as painting.

4.10 Classification of Paints

- The important varieties of paints are emulsion paints, latex paints, metallic paints, epoxide resin paints, oil paints, water paints or distempers etc.
- On the basis of their applications, paints can be classified as:
    - **(i)** **Exterior House Paints:** These paints generally have constituents such as **pigments** (ZnO, TiO_2, white lead etc.), **extenders** (talc, barytes, clay etc.), **vehicle** (e.g. boiled linseed oil) and **thinners**. Coloured pigments are also added in varying amounts for a light tint.
    - **(ii)** **Interior Wall Paints:** These paints are prepared by **mixing pigments** (e.g. white and coloured pigments), **vehicle** (e.g. varnish or bodied linseed oil) and **resins**.

(iii) **Fire Resistant Paints:** These paints consist of borax, zinc borate, ammonium phosphate, synthetic resins etc. as antifire chemicals. These paints impart a protective action on the article being coated through easy fusion of the pigments and other paint ingredients giving off fumes on heating, that do not support combustion.

(iv) **Chemical Resistant Paints:** These paints consist mainly of baked oleoresinous varnishes, chlorinated rubber compositions, bituminous varnishes and phenolic dispersions as chemical resistant materials in paint formulations.

(v) **Luminous Paints:** These paints consist of phosphorescent paint compositions such as **pigments** (sulphides of Ca, Cd and Zn dispersed in spirit varnish), **vehicle** (chlorinated rubber, styrol etc.) and **sensitizer** for activation in U.V. region.

(vi) **Marine Paints:** This is also known as **antifouling paint** and can be prepared by mixing various ingredients such as **pigments** (ZnO and Venetian red), **resin** (shellac), driers (Mn lineolate), **vehicle** (coal tar), **diluent** (pine oil), **toxic components** (cuprous oxide and mercuric oxide) and small amount of **Bees wax**.

(vii) **Emulsion Paints:** These paints contain an emulsion of alkyds, phenol form aldehyde etc. (vehicle) in water pigments and extenders are also added to get other desirable properties. These paints are highly durable, impermeable to dirt, resistant to washing, rapidly drying, contain water as a thinner and can be easily cleaned.

(viii) **Latex Paints:** These paints usually contain (a) a **protein dispersion** that can be prepared by stirring soyabean proteins or casein in aqueous ammonia solution for about an hour at room temperature (b) **Pigments** such as ZnS, TiO_2 etc. dispersed in water, (c) **Extenders** such as clay, talc, $MgSiO_3$, $BaSO_4$ etc. (d) Preservatives such as penta chlorophenol, (e) **Antifoaming agent** as pine oil, (f) Plasticizer such as tributyl phosphate (g) **Latex** prepared from a butadiene styrene copolymer in water. All these ingredients are well stirred in water, screened, again stirred and packed.

   (a) Aluminium Paints: These paints are used as heat reflecting paints and consist of pigment (aluminium powder) and vehicle (spirit varnishes) and cellulose nitrate lacquers.

   (b) Metal Paints: These are coatings applied on the metal surfaces or bodies for protection and decoration. These coatings may be of **barrier type** or **galvanic type**. In **barrier type**, a protective barrier is formed between the surface coated and its surroundings. These consist of pigment, vehicle, anticorrosive agents (e.g. zinc or chrome yellow), resins (e.g. alkyds, epoxy, polyamides, chlorinated rubbers and silicones) etc.

   Alkyds resist weathering of metals, epoxy and polyamides form tough film resistant to chemicals, chlorinated rubbers resist action of soaps, detergents and strong chemicals and silicons are added as heat resistant and water repellents.

In **galvanic type**, protection is provided by self undergoing of galvanic corrosion. Zinc coating (Galvanisation) on steel is an example of this class. Before applying metal paints it is important to clean thoroughly the surface to be coated. Moreover, paint should be applied over a primer such as red lead by a high pressure spray gun.

(c) **Cement Paints:** These paints are prepared by mixing white cement with colouring matter or pigments, hydrated lime and fine sand as inert filter. **Cement paints** are available in the form of powder of a particular colour. The dispersion medium may be water or an oil depending upon the purpose of coating. In case of stone or brick structure, the dispersion medium is water, but boiled linseed oil is used as the dispersion medium if the purpose of coating is corrugated metal surface. Before applying cement paint, a primer coat consisting of a dilute solution of sodium silicate and zinc sulphate is necessary. Cement paints have marked water proofing capacity, give a stable and decorative film and do not require fresh application even in four to five years, if coated even on rough surface.

(d) **Distempers:** Distempers are water paints consisting of pigments which may be white as well as coloured (e.g. Reinmann's green), extenders (e.g. chalk powder, talc), binders (e.g. casien or glue) and dispersion medium water. These water paints have good covering power, easy applicability, and smooth, pleasent looking durable film. The major disadvantage of these is the porous nature of the film which is not moisture proof.

4.11 Methods of Applying Paints

- There are so many methods of applying paints on the surface. In every method now-a-days new technologies are used.

- The important methods are as given below:

(a) **Hand Painting or Brushing:** A surface may be painted by taking the paint on a brush of a well selected variety with fine bristles and applying straight away on the surface, with or without any primer coat, already applied. In order to have stable, uniform and glossy finish, more than one coat is necessary. Brushes are available as per the type paint to be applied.

(b) **Spraying:** In this method, paint is sprayed on the surface by using spray gun. Spraying is advantageous because it paints uniformly and takes much less time. The main disadvantage of spraying is that some paint is lost due to its jet injection and consequent excessive spread, beyond the article to be painted. Moreover, the sprayed paint spoils the atmosphere too. To overcome these disadvantages, spraying is done in special booths fitted with exhaust fans and paint may be recovered from the exhaust fans in many cases. Spraying technique is generally used for painting articles such as furniture, refrigerators, automobiles etc. In recent years, spraying is done in a **high voltage electrostatic field**. In this method, the article to be sprayed is made anode of a high tension electrostatic field. Spray of the paint from a spray gun is directed towards the article. As a result, article is uniformly painted on all corners and edges. Hence areas which are not directly covered by the spray gun also get evenly coated with the paint. The system, working largely on the principle of electrical precipitators also prevent fog and other problems during painting.

(c) Dipping: In this method the article to be coated is dipped in a body of the paint taken in a tank, taken out and held above the surface of the paint for some time for drainage of the excess paint and dried. For example, enamelled wire is coated by enamel by dipping the wire in the paint, the wire is passed through ovens for **baking** the coating over the wire. The tears and beads formed by dipping are stopped by controlling the speed at which the wire is passed through the paint. Tear and bead formation can also be avoided by making the wire an electrode of high voltage electrostatic field which repels the excess of paint material. The disadvantages of dipping process are non-uniform coating of paint and formation of tears and beads here and there over coated surface.

(d) Roller Coating: This technique consists in applying the paint on a sheet metal or flat sheet during its slow motion through a pair of rubber coated rollers which are also provided with arrangement for the painting materials to dribble through at regular rates. This process is rapid and imparts a durable uniform finish and flat sheets. Sheet metals for containers and metal signs are coated by paints by this technique.

(e) Tumbling: This technique is applicable for small articles, particularly made of wood. The article and the required quantity of the paint to be applied are taken in a barrel. The latter is closed and then rotated for a specified period. The article, during tumbling, receives a uniform deposit of paint, which form a firm setting on the surface, is given mild **baking, as a post tumbling operation**. The articles are dried on drying trays.

(C) PIGMENTS

4.12 Introduction

- The pigment industry is usually regarded as associated with paints, but in fact it is a separate industry which should be considered by itself, because a large number of pigments is mined or manufactured for the commercial preparation of paints. **Pigments** are various organic and inorganic insoluble substances, which are widely used in surface coatings. They are also employed in the ink, plastic, rubber, ceramic, paper and linoleum industries to impart colour. About 70 years back, white lead [$2PbCO_3 + Pb(OH)_2$], zinc oxide (ZnO) and lithopone ($ZnS + BaSO_4$) were the principal white pigments used.

Coloured pigments consisted of Prussian blue, lead chromates, various iron oxides and a few lake colours. (**A lake** may be regarded as an organic dye on an inorganic absorbent, such as clay).

- Now we find a large number of pigments. **Titanium dioxide** is one of the most important of the white pigments. **Carbon black, graphite and lamp black** are the chief black pigments, chromium oxide (Cr_2O_3) and Guignet's green (hydrated chromium oxide, $Cr_2O(OH)_4$ give brilliant green colours. **Chrome yellows** are the most popular yellow pigments. Chromate pigments, such as strontium chromate and barium chromate are also yellow pigments. Organic pigments (metal phthalocyanides) are finding an increasingly important place as durable pigments.

- After independence in 1947, the production of various pigments, such as titanium dioxide, ultramarine blue, chrome pigments, phthalocyanide blue, Prussian blue, zinc chrome basic lead sulphate and metallic pigments, such as aluminium paste has already been started in India.

- Pigments are generally incorporated into paints to affect properties associated with appearance such as colour, opacity, gloss, metallic look and depth. In addition, pigments commonly are used to protect the substrate against corrosion, attack by microbes and to retard flammability. Other desirable properties can be obtained by the addition of pigments. For example, pigments can be used in paints to control flow and levelling as well as spray viscosity or brushability, depending upon the type of system. In addition, pigments are added to paint to control the cost of the raw material.

4.13 Classification of Pigments

- Pigments are classified into two main categories:
  - (a) Inorganic pigments
  - (b) Organic pigments
- Inorganic pigments generally hide better than organic pigments when dispersed in paint. Inorganic pigments impart flowability to paint because they do not tend to swell in presence of common paint solvents. In addition inorganic pigments do not bleed in organic solvents and they afford excellent colour permanence. Inorganic pigments are thermally stable and generally impart heat resistance to the coating.
- Organic pigments are insoluble solids and thus differentiated from dyes, which are coloured organic compounds that are soluble in the media in which they are used. Pigments require binder in order to be used as colorants. Organic pigments that are insoluble in their pure form are referred to as **"toners"**. Organic pigments that require precipitation by an inorganic base such as a metal to be insoluble are referred as **"lakes"**. Organic pigments have greater decorative value than inorganic pigments.

4.14 Physical Properties and Uses of Pigments

- Some important pigments, their properties and uses are listed in the following Table 4.1.

Table 4.1: Pigments, their properties and uses

Sr. No.	Pigment	Properties	Uses
1.	White lead (2 $PbCO_3 \cdot Pb(OH)_2$)	• High specific gravity. • High refractive index. • High hiding powder. • Readily mix with oil to form smooth paste, which on drying produces a tough and elastic film. • Low heat resisting power.	• Used for manufacture of paints. • High covering power due to its high refractive index.
2.	Zinc oxide (ZnO)	• Brilliantly white having excellent texture. • Opacity and refractive index is slightly smaller than white lead. • It causes no decolourisation even in contact with CO_2 gas and causes no chalk formation. • Oil absorption capacity is very high.	• It is also used as white paint. • Its covering power is greater than white lead. • It is opaque to UV light and therefore protects the vehicle. • No chalking.
3.	Lithophone ($BaSO_4$ + ZnS)	• Brilliantly white. • Good hiding power.	• Used for cold water paints. • Floor coverings and oil cloth industry.
4.	Titanium dioxide (TiO_2)	• It is whitest of white pigments. • High opacity. • High hiding power. • Low specific gravity, therefore high oil absorbing capacity. • Its spreading power is double than that of white lead. • Chemically stable. • Little or no tendency of chalking.	• Ready application in paints, paper, textile and other industries.

contd. ...

5.	Red lead (Pb_3O_4)	• Bright to lead powder with high specific gravity. • Excellent covering power. • Its brightness is not affected by light but get affected by acid fumes. • High corrosion inhibiting properties. • Increases the drying process, if spread in linseed oil.	• Used as primary coat for structural steel. • Used for imparting red colour to glass for making bangles.
6.	Synthetic iron oxide (Fe_2O_3)	• Brilliant colour. • High covering power. • High tinting strength.	• Used in domestic paints, enamels, floor paints.
7.	Chrome green (Cr_2O_3)	• Higher oil absorption than other green pigments. • Lack of brilliancy and opacity.	• Used as green pigment known as 'chrome green'.
8.	Chromium oxide	• Permanent green pigment. • Good covering power. • High corrosion inhibition capacity.	• Used as paint for metal surfaces. • Non fading green for washable distempers.

Exercises

(A) Answer the following:

1. What are dyes? What is their importance?
2. What are the characteristics of a good dye?
3. What do you mean by complimentary colour?
4. Define and explain the term Dye.
5. How dyes are classified according to their chemical constitution?
6. What do you mean by:
   (a) Vat dyes (b) Mordant dyes (c) Direct dyes (d) Developed dyes
7. Give structure and applications of following dyes:
   (a) Methyl orange (b) Azo dye (c) Indigo (d) Thioindoxyl (e) Phenolphthalein (f) Fluorescein (g) Alizarin
8. What are the uses of: (a) Indigo   (b) Phenolphthalein   (c) Fluorescein (d) Phthalocyanines

9. What are paints?
10. List different methods for application of paints.
11. Give the classification of paints.
12. What are cement dyes?
13. What are distempers?
14. What do you mean by pigments?
15. What are the uses of pigments?
16. Classify the pigments.
17. Give the properties and uses of following pigments: (i) Lead oxide (ii) Zinc oxide (iii) Lithophone (iv) Titanium dioxide (v) Red lead (vi) Synthetic iron oxide.

(B) Multiple Choice Questions (MCQs):

(i)   The dyes which contain nitro group as a chromophore are called _____.
      (a) Azo dyes **(b) Nitro dyes** (c) Phthalein dyes (d) Xanthene dyes

(ii) Azo dye contains _____ chromophore.
      (a) –N = N– (b) NO_2 (c) –OH (d) – NH_2

(iii) The compound containing chromophore is called _____.
      (a) auxochrome **(b) chromogen** (c) paint (d) pigment

(iv) Picric acid is an example of _____.
      (a) azo dye (b) nitroso dye **(c) nitro dye** (d) none of these

(v)   Fast Green O is _____.
      (a) azo dye **(b) nitroso dye** (c) nitro dye (d) none of these

(vi) Congo Red is _____.
      (a) acid azo dye (b) basic azo dye **(c) direct azo dye** (d) none of these

(vii) Fluorescein is _____.
      (a) xanthene dye (b) azo dye (c) nitro dye (d) none of these

(viii) White lead is an example of _____.
      (a) dye (b) paint **(c) pigment** (d) chromogen

(ix) Methyl orange is ____ dye.
      (a) acid azo (b) azo (c) phthalein (d) triphenyl methane

(x)   The group which increases the intensity of colour is known as ____.
      (a) chromophore **(b) auxochrome** (c) functional group (d) none of these

(xi) Dyes containing polymethine bridge between two nitrogen atoms are called ____.
      (a) azo dyes (b) nitro dyes (c) nitroso dyes (d) cyanine dyes

(xii) Acid azo dyes contain ____.
      (a) **–COOH group** (b) NO_2 group (d) –NH_2 group (d) –NHR or NR_2 group

Chapter **5**...

Chemistry of Pharmaceutical Industries

Contents ...

5.1   General Aspects of Drug Action
    5.1.1   Introduction
    5.1.2   Classification of Drugs
    5.1.3   Nomenclature
    5.1.4   Structure-Activity Relationship (SAR)
    5.1.5   Action of Drugs
    5.1.6   Factors Affecting Drug Action
    5.1.7   Metabolism of Drugs
    5.1.8   Methods of Production
    5.1.9   Pharmacological Activity
5.2   Meaning of Terms
    5.2.1   Prescriptions
    5.2.2   Doses
    5.2.3   Analgesics
    5.2.4   Antipyretics
    5.2.5   Diuretics
    5.2.6   Anesthetics
    5.2.7   Antibiotics
    5.2.8   Anti-inflammatory
    5.2.9   Anti-viral
    5.2.10   Tranquilizer
    5.2.11   Anti-ulcer
    5.2.12   Anti-allergic and Bronchodilators
    5.2.13   Cardiovascular
    5.2.14   Cold Preparations
    5.2.15   Anti-Hypertensive
    5.2.16   Cough Preparation
    5.2.17   Anti-Neoplastic
    5.2.18   Sedatives and Hypnotics
    5.2.19   Steroidal
    5.2.20   Contraceptive
    5.2.21   Histamine and Antihistamine
5.3   Synthesis and Uses
    5.3.1   Paracetamol (p-Acetyl Aminophenol)
    5.3.2   Aspirin (Acetyl Salicylic Acid)
    5.2.3   Sulphanilamide (p-Amino Benzene Sulphonamide)
•   Exercises

5.1 General Aspects of Drug Action

5.1.1 Introduction

- **The pharmaceutical industry is an important component of health care systems throughout the world.** The word drug is derived from the French word 'drogue' which means 'dry herb'. Drug is in the broadest of terms, a chemical substance that has known biological effects on humans or other animals. In pharmacology, drug is a chemical substance used in the treatment, cure, prevention or diagnosis of disease or used to otherwise enhance physical or mental well being. Drug is a substance with abnormal effect on certain body functions. According to World Health Organization (WHO), a drug may be defined as *'any substance or product which is used for modifying or exploring physiological systems or pathological states for the benefits of the recipient'.*

- Pharmaceutical industry includes manufacturing, development, marketing and distribution of drug products including quality assurance of these activities. Pharmaceutical chemists design, develop, analyze and evaluate new and better drugs for health care industry. Pharmaceutical companies may deal in generic or brand medications and medical devices. In India pharmaceutical industry is a success story of providing employment for millions and ensuring that essential drugs at affordable prices are available to vast population of this country.

5.1.2 Classification of Drugs

- Drugs are classified into two ways:

  (a) On the basis of their chemical structures

  (b) On the basis of their therapeutic actions.

  (a) **On the basis of chemical structure:** It is suitable for studying their chemical properties, synthesis and so on but not their therapeutic action.

  (b) **On the basis of therapeutic action:** This classification is not giving the information about chemistry of various groups of drugs.

- Limitations of two types of classification compromise these two systems, first drugs are divided according to their therapeutic actions and then subdivided according to their chemical structure.

- According to their therapeutic actions, the drugs are classified into two types.

  (a) **Pharmacodynamic agents or Functional drugs:** These are the drugs which act on various functions of a body. The drugs which stimulate or depress various functions of the body so as to provide relief from the symptoms of discomfort are known as functional drugs. These agents are used in the case of non-infectious diseases to correct abnormal functions of a body. The functional drugs may be further classified into following types:

1. Analgesics and antipyretics
2. Diuretics
3. Cardiovascular agents
4. Local anesthetic
5. Antihistamine
6. Tranquilizer
7. Cholinergic and anti-cholinergic agents
8. Hypoglycemic agents
9. Anti-depressants

(b) **Chemotherapeutic agents or drugs:** The drugs which are used in the treatment of infectious diseases are called chemotherapeutic agents. The drugs are designed to kill the invading organisms without harmful further upon the host. These are the drugs that primarily remove the cause of disease. The chemotherapeutic drugs may be further classified into following types.

1. Anti-septic
2. Antibiotics
3. Antibacterial
4. Anti-malarial
5. Antifungal
6. Organometallic compounds
7. Anti-neoplastic
8. Anti-protozoals
9. Anti-tuberculosis
10. Anti-inflammatory drugs.

5.1.3 Nomenclature

- Pharmaceutical drugs have four types of names:

    1. **Chemical name:** It is given IUPAC name of the compound. It is the scientific name based on molecular structure of the drug. These names are typically long and very complex and difficult to remember. This name is not suitable for routine use by medical professionals or common people. This name is useful for the discovery of new compounds.

2. **Generic names or Nonproprietary names:** Generic name actually designate a family relationship among drugs e.g. Benzodiazepines include a number of drugs like diazepam, nitrazepam, flurazepam etc. Medical professionals choose the non-proprietary name for its simplicity.

3. **Brand names or Trade names or Proprietary names**: It is shorter, simpler, easier to remember and most frequently used. A drug can have several trade names.

4. **Code name:** Code name is the first name that is given to a drug by the pharmaceutical manufacturers. It may be abbreviation, number or both combinations. For example, Ciprofloxacin has the code name Bay-o-9867, where Bay comes from the name of famous pharmaceutical company that produced it, BAYER. It is little or pharmaceutical example of drug nomenclature.

   o **Code name:** Bay-o-9867

   o **Chemical name:** 1-Cyclopropyl-6-fluoro-4-oxo-7-(1-piperazinyl)-1,4-dihydro-3-quinolinecarboxylic acid

   o **Non-proprietary name:** Ciprofloxacin

   o **Trade names:** Baycip, Ciloxan, Ciflox, Ciplox, Cipro, CiproXR, CiproXL, Ciproxin etc.

5.1.4 Structure-Activity Relationship (SAR)

• The structure-activity relationship is the relationship between the chemical structure and biological or physiological activity of chemicals. The compounds are often classed together because they have structural characteristics in common including shape, size, stereochemical arrangement and distribution of functional groups. Other factors contributing to structure-activity relationship include chemical activity, electronic effects, resonance and inductive effects. The analysis of SAR enables the determination of chemical groups responsible for evoking a target biological effect in the organism. SARs are based on the notation of structural "similarity". Similar compounds have similar activity. The principle is assumed, but in the reality it is not always true. Structure-property correlations refer to all statistical mathematical methods used to correlate any structure to any other property (Chemical or biological), using statistical regression and pattern recognition is known as quantitative structure-activity relationship (QSAR). Medicinal chemists use the techniques of chemical synthesis and computational drug design to insert new chemical groups into the biomedical compound and test the modifications for their biological effects.

5.1.5 Action of Drugs

• The action of drugs on human body is called pharmacodynamics and what body does with drug is called pharmacokinetics. The drugs that enter the human body tend to stimulate certain receptors, ion channels, act on enzymes or transporter proteins. As a result, they cause the human body to react in specific way. There are two different ways of drug action: (1) Drug stimulates and activates the receptors are called agonists. Drug bind effectively to their receptor must be capable of producing an effect in the targeted area and (2) Drug stops the agonists from stimulating the receptors are called antagonist. Drugs that block receptors must bind effectively but have little or no intrinsic activity because their function is to prevent an agonist from interacting with it receptors.

- Once the receptors are activated, they either trigger a particular response directly on the body or they trigger the release hormones or other endogenous drugs in the body to stimulate a particular response.

- Drugs affect only the rate at which the existing biological functions proceed. Drugs can speed up or slow down the biochemical reactions that cause muscles to contract, kidney cells to regulate the volume of water and salts retained or eliminated by the body, glands to secrete substances and nerves to transmit messages.

- **Potency of Drug:** Potency means strength of drug. It is measure of how much a drug is required in order to produce a particular effect. Therefore, only a small dosage of high potency of drug is required to induce a large response.

5.1.6 Factors Affecting Drug Action

- Following factors affect drug action:

    (i)   Body size

    (ii)   Pregnancy: If possible to avoid giving any drug during pregnancy.

    (iii) Lactation.

    (iv)   Age: Pediatric and geriatric.

    (v)   Genetic factors.

    (vi)   Disease states: Kidney and liver.

    (vii) Routes of drug administration.

    (viii) Environmental factors.

    (ix)   Psychological factors.

    (x)   Tolerance and resistance.

- Variations in drug response due to many reasons:

    Differences in age, weight, genetics, and gender are factors that influence the differences in response to medication among people. Children metabolize certain drugs more rapidly than adults. Metabolism rate increases between 1 to 12 years. After 12 years metabolism rates decline with age to a normal adult level. Adults experience a decrease in many physiological functions after age 30 years. Decreases in affects on drug activity are gradual.

1. Difference in pharmacokinetic handling of drugs – variability in plasma concentration.
2. Receptor number or state difference
3. Other host and environmental factors.

• Knowledge can guide the choice of appropriate drug and dose for an individual patient.

5.1.7 Metabolism of Drugs

• Drug metabolism is the process by which the body breaks down and converts medication into active chemical substances. The primary site of drug metabolism is the liver, the organ that plays a major role in metabolism, digestion, and detoxification and elimination substance from the body. Enzymes in liver are responsible for chemically changing drug components into substances known as metabolites. Metabolites are then bound to other substances for excretion through the lungs or body fluids such as saliva, sweat, breast milk and urine. It is also known as xenobiotic metabolism. It is the biochemical modification of pharmaceutical substances by living organisms, usually through specialized enzymatic system. Drug metabolism converts lipophilic chemical compounds into more readily excreted hydrophilic products. The rate of metabolism determines the duration and intensity of drug's pharmacological action.

5.1.8 Methods of Production

• The production of drug can be included in a series of unit operations, such as milling, granulation, filtration, compounding, blending, drying, coating, tablet pressing etc.

• Formulation development evaluate drug for uniformity, stability and other factors. After evaluation, solution must be developed to deliver drug in its required form such as solid, semisolid, controlled release or immediate, tablet, capsule and many other variations.

• In the production of drug milling is necessary process to reduce particle size in drug powder because of many reasons such as increasing homogeneity, dosage uniformity, increasing bioavailability and solubility.

• Granulation process is opposite of milling. In these process, small particles are converted to larger particles called granules. This process is carried out because granulation prevents remixing of components in the mixture, improve flow characteristics of powders and improve compaction properties of tablet formation.

5.1.9 Pharmacological Activity

• Each biologically active compound possesses number of biological activities. Its specificity of action is always relative and is defined by the peculiarities of object, dose, route etc. Pharmacological activity describes the beneficial or adverse effects of drug on living matter. Pharmacological activity plays an important role since it suggests uses of compounds in the medicinal applications. However, chemical compounds may show some adverse and toxic effects which may prevent their use in medical practice.

5.2 Meaning of Terms

5.2.1 Prescriptions

• Prescription is a written direction by registered medicinal practitioner to a patient to be issued with medicine or treatment. The symbol 'R' or 'Rx' is used for prescription.

5.2.2 Doses

• Dose means specific quantity of medicine prescribed to be taken at one time or at stated intervals. Medicines are available in different forms such as liquid, tablet, capsule and suppository. These form of the product written on the prescription in order to avoid confusion.

• The quantity of drug to be taken, timing of administration, routes of administration and dosage forms should be written on the prescription to avoid any confusion.

Calculations of doses:

Fried's Rule:

$$\text{Approximate child dose} = \frac{\text{Age in months}}{150} \times \text{Adult dose}$$

Yong's Rule:

$$\frac{\text{Age of child (Yr)}}{\text{Age} + 12} \times \text{Adult dose} = \text{Approximate child dose}$$

5.2.3 Analgesics

• The drug which is relieving pain by acting on central nervous system without loss of consciousness is called as analgesic drug. It is also called as painkiller. It provides mainly pain relief. The commonly used analgesic drugs are Aspirin, Paracetamol, and Ibuprofen etc.

• Besides their therapeutic use, analgesics have several drug classes:

(a) Opioids (or narcotic analgesics): Which play a major role in the relief of acute pain and in the management of moderate to severe chronic pain e.g. Morphine and Codeine.

(b) NSAIDs (Non-steroidal Anti Inflammatory Drugs) and acetaminophen: Which are the most widely used analgesic drugs for relieving mild to moderate pain and reducing fever e.g. Piroxicam, Meloxicam, Aspirin.

(c) Triptans (the antimigraine medications): Which are specifically designed and targeted for acute and abortive treatment of migraine and cluster headaches; and

(d) Analgeses adjuvants: It is a new emerging class of analgesics that include tricyclic antidepressants such as amitriptyline, anticonvulsants such as gabapentin and pregabalin, and topical analgesics such as lidocaine patches that can be used to treat neuropathic pains.

5.2.4 Antipyretics

- It is Greek word anti means against and pyreticus means pertaining to fever. The drug which is bringing down the elevated body temperature to normal body temperature is called as antipyretics. The commonly used antipyretics are Paracetamol, Aspirin, Ibuprofen etc.

5.2.5 Diuretics

- The substance which promotes the production of urine. The drug which increases the volume of urine produced by promoting the excretion of salt and water from the kidneys is called diuretics. Diuretics are used to reduce the edema. These drugs are commonly used in treatment of hypertension. The common types of diuretics are: (a) Thiazide diuretics, (b) Potassium-sparing diuretics and (c) Loop-acting diuretics. The commonly used diuretics are Hydrochlorothiazide, Chlorthalidone, Metolazone etc.

5.2.6 Anesthetics

- Anesthesia means lack of sensation. Insensitivity to pain is induced by the administration of gases or the injection of drugs before surgical operation. Types of anesthesia are (a) General anesthesia, (b) Local anesthesia and (c) Regional anesthesia. The drugs used to create condition of anesthesia are called as anesthetics. The commonly used anesthetics are Marcaine, Polocaine, Benzocaine, Procaine, Orthocaine etc.

5.2.7 Antibiotics

- The substances which are produced by or derived from living cells and which are available in small amount of substance are capable of inhibiting the life processes or destroying the microorganisms such as bacteria, viruses, fungi, algae etc. The activity of antibiotics are specific i.e. it is found to be effective against certain types of microorganisms. Commonly used antibiotics are Streptomycin, Penicillin, Amoxicillin, Chloromycetin etc.

5.2.8 Anti-inflammatory

- The drugs which are used to treatment that reduces inflammation, swelling, tenderness, fever and pain. The drugs acting on arthritis and rheumatic diseases are called as anti-inflammatory agents. They also have analgesic and antipyretic property. These are of two types (a) steroidal and (b) non-steroidal anti-inflammatory drugs. Commonly used non-steroidal drugs are Naproxen, Indomethacin, Oxaprozin, etc. and steroidal drugs are Cortisone, Hydrocortisone, Dexamethasone etc.

5.2.9 Anti-viral

- The drugs which are used to treat viral infections are called as anti-viral drugs. Like antibiotics for bacteria, specific anti-virals are used for specific viruses. Unlike most antibiotics, antiviral drugs do not destroy their target pathogen; instead they inhibit their development.

  (a) Anti-HIV agent's examples retrovir, tenofovir etc.

  (b) Protease Inhibitors examples saquinavir, ritonovir etc.

  (c) Anti-herpes and anti –CMV agent's example cidofovir.

5.2.10 Tranquilizer

- It is used in the treatment of mental disorder. The drug is used to reduce anxiety, tension, fear, agitation and related states of mental disturbances. These drugs are of two types (a) antipsychotic drugs are classed as major tranquilizer, for example: chlorpromazine, diphenylbutyl piperidine, etc. are used as antipsychotics and (b) anxiolytic drugs are classed to minor tranquillizer, for example, benzodiazepines. Medications like Alprazolam, Diazepam, Lorazepam and Clonazepam are commonly used as anti-anxiety medications.

5.2.11 Anti-ulcer

- Anti-ulcer drugs are used to treat ulcers in the stomach and upper part of small intestine. Recurrent gastric and duodenal ulcers are caused by Helicobacter pylori infections.

- Peptic ulcer is erosion in the lining of the stomach or the first part of the small intestine, on area called duodenum. Peptic ulcer is a broad term for an ulcer occurring in the esophagus, stomach or duodenum within the upper GI tract. Ulcers develop when there is an imbalance between mucosal defensive factors and aggressive factors.

- Amoxicillin, Metraonidazole, Clarithromycin, Tetracycline etc. are used as anti-ulcer drugs.

5.2.12 Anti-allergic and Bronchodilators

- Anti-allergic drugs are used to prevent and treat allergic conditions and allergic reactions.

- Anti-allergic drugs include diphenhydramine, certirizine, chlorpheniramine maleate, etc.

- Bronchodilator agent is a substance that relaxes contractions of smooth muscle of the bronchioles to improve ventilation to lungs. Pharmacologic bronchodilators are used to improve aeration in asthma. These are the medicines that act on respiratory tract and they expand the tubes that carry air to lungs. Commonly used bronchodilators include albuterol, terbutaline, pirbuterol, epinephrine, salmeterol etc.

5.2.13 Cardiovascular

- It is a class of diseases in controlling cardiovascular that involve the heart or blood vessels. The agents used in the treatment of angina, cardiac arrhythmias, hypertension, erectile dysfunction, hyperlipidemias, and disorders of blood coagulation. Cardiovascular disease includes coronary artery diseases such as angina and myocardial infarction or known as heart attack. Other cardiovascular diseases are stroke, hypertensive heart disease, rheumatic heart disease, congenital heart disease etc. Cardiovascular agents represent a group of drugs which have direct action on the heart or other parts of the vascular system so that they modify the total output of the heart or the distribution of blood to certain parts of circulatory system. Different types of cardiovascular drugs are available, for example, diuretics, anticoagulants antiplatelet, beta blockers, vasodilators, calcium channel blockers, etc. For pharmacists it is to be necessary that they understand the pathophysiology of cardiovascular diseases and the agents used to treat these syndromes. The bases for advances in the control of heart disease have been (a) a better understanding of the disease state, (b) the development of effective therapeutic agents, and (c) innovative medical intervention techniques to treat problems of the cardiovascular system. The drugs are used for their action on the heart or other parts of the vascular system, to modify the total output of the heart or the distribution of blood to the circulatory system.

5.2.14 Cold Preparations

- It is mainly used for the treatment of symptoms of a cold. It is generally in a combination of a nasal decongestant. For example, phenyl propanolamine, paracetamol etc. It can be defined by a certain set of signs of symptoms such as nasal discharge, nasal congestion/ obstruction, sore, throat headache, cough, sneezing etc.

5.2.15 Anti-Hypertensive

- It is a class of drugs that are used to treat hypertension (high blood pressure). Hypertension is a consequence of many diseases. Hemodynamically, blood pressure is a function of the amount of blood pumped by the heart and the ease with which the blood flows through the peripheral vasculature (i.e., resistance to blood flows by peripheral blood vessels). Diseases of components of the central and peripheral nervous systems, which regulate blood pressure and abnormalities of the hormonal system, and diseases of the kidney and peripheral vascular network, which affect blood volume, can create a hypertensive state in humans. Hypertension is generally defined as mild when the diastolic pressure is between 90 and 104 mm Hg, moderate when it is 105 to 114 mm Hg, and severe when it is above 115 mm Hg.

- **Primary (essential) hypertension** is the most common form of hypertension. Although advances have been made in the identification and control of primary hypertension, the etiology of this form of hypertension has not yet been resolved.

- **Renal hypertension** can be created by experimentally causing renal artery stenosis in animals. Renal artery stenosis also may occur in pathological conditions of the kidney, such as nephritis, renal artery thrombosis, renal artery infarctions, or other conditions that restrict blood flow through the renal artery. Hypertension may also originate from pathological states in the CNS, such as malignancies.

- Tumors in the adrenal medulla that cause release of large amounts of catecholamines create a hypertensive condition known as pheochromocytoma. Excessive secretion of aldosterone by the adrenal cortex, often because of adenomas, also produces hypertensive disorders.

- Arterial blood pressure is regulated by several physiological factors, such as heart rate, stroke volume, peripheral vascular network resistance, blood vessel elasticity, blood volume, and viscosity of blood. Endogenous chemicals also play an important part in the regulation of arterial blood pressure. The peripheral vascular system is influenced greatly by the sympathetic–parasympathetic balance of the autonomic nervous system, the control of which originates in the CNS. Enhanced adrenergic activity is a principal contributor to primary (essential) hypertension.

- Antihypertensive therapy is used to prevent the complications of high blood pressure such as stroke and myocardial infarction. Hypertension is a disease characterized by elevated blood pressure. A drug used in the treatment of hypertension act by reducing the cardiac output and/or reducing the total peripheral resistance. The drugs commonly used in the treatment of hypertension are clonidine hydrochloride, methyl dopa, diazoxide etc.

5.2.16 Cough Preparation

- Cough is uncomfortable and irritating, interfering with day time activities and sleep. Coughing is a reflex response to any irritation in the respiratory tract. Most coughs are due to having a cold which are caused by viral infections. The infection results in congestion or excess mucus in the respiratory passages and this triggers the cough response. Sometimes excess mucus/phlegm can be coughed up but with some coughs this mucus/phlegm is too sticky to be coughed out easy.

Coughs are of three types:
   (a) **Productive coughs:** These type of cough describes the phlegm or mucus that collects in the airways that people feel they want to cough to clear their breathing.
   (b) **Non-productive coughs** are dry, and
   (c) **Barking coughs** with a tickle that can keep people awake at night.

- There are three types of medicines available for the relief of coughs.
   (i) **Cough suppressants:** These are usually used to alleviate the symptoms of a dry, tickly, irritating cough. They can provide useful relief, particularly at night when sleep is disturbed. The ingredients which do this are **Pholcodine, Dextromethorphan** and **Codeine** which work at the cough centre in the brain to suppress the cough reflex.

(ii) Demulcent cough preparations: It is worked by coating the throat, protecting against irritants, and so reducing the stimulus to cough. These include syrups and products with glycerine, often with flavourings like honey and lemon, traditional herbal medicinal products, and cough lozenges which contain a variety of ingredients some of which also ease the pain of a sore throat.

(iii) Expectorants: These drugs help loosen sticky mucus, thinning it so people can cough up the mucus or phlegm. People will still cough but the cough will push out the irritating phlegm. **Guaifenesin** and **ipecacuanha** are both expectorants. Some medicines contain a combination of ingredients to treat the most common symptoms of a cold.

- In addition to the cough ingredient, these products may also contain:
  - **Painkillers (analgesics)** such as paracetamol is to relieve pain and help bring down a temperature.
  - **Decongestants** (pseudoephedrine or phenylephrine) to relieve congestion in the nasal passages by constricting swollen blood vessels in the nasal lining and reducing mucus secretion.
  - **Antihistamines** (diphenhydramine, promethazine or triprolidine) to 'dry up' a runny nose, reducing mucus secretions, sneezing and itching. Sedating antihistamines such as diphenhydramine can also help people sleep at night. Antihistamines are also used in allergy products.

5.2.17 Anti-Neoplastic

- It is also called as anticancer drug. Cancer is a tumor, which means an unusual amount of growth of tissue due to unlimited and uncontrolled repeated growth of some cell. Anti-neoplastic agents travel in the body and destroy cancer cells. Anti-neoplastic agents use, metabolism, and adverse effect profiles for the alkylating agents, antibiotics, natural products, anti-metabolites, and tyrosine kinase (TK) inhibitors used in the treatment of cancer.

- Radio therapy and surgery, chemotherapeutic agents are used in the treatment of cancer which are called as anti-neoplastic agents.

5.2.18 Sedatives and Hypnotics

- Sedative and hypnotic drug products are a class of drugs used to induce and/or maintain sleep. It is also called as sleep disorder drug.

  (a) Sedative: It is a central nervous system depressant that should reduce anxiety and exert a calming effect with little or no effect on motor or mental function. e.g. Paraldehyde, butyl chloral hydrate, carbomal etc.

(b) **Hypnotic drug** should produce drowsiness and encourage the onset and maintenance of a state of sleep that as far as possible resembles the natural sleep state e.g. Trichloro ethanol, chloral hydrate, sulphonal etc.

5.2.19 Steroidal

- It is the organic compound that contains four rings joined together. It is characteristic property of arrangement of 17 carbon atom in a four ring structure. Six carbon atoms of three rings such as A, B and C and forth one is five member ring D. Another property is to attach eight carbon atom to D ring and one or two methyl groups attached to point of fused ring.

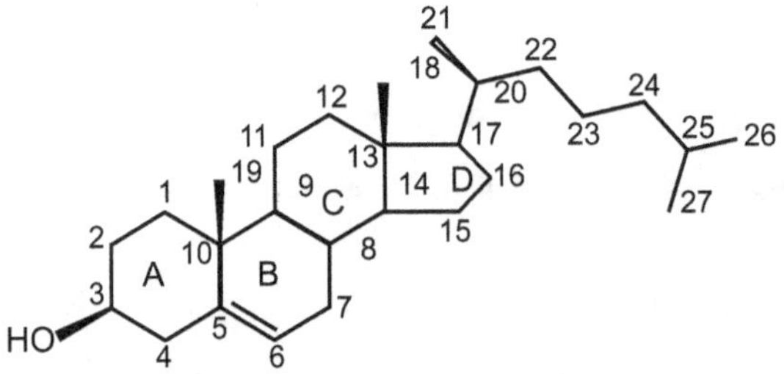

- Examples of steroids include cholesterol, sex hormone estradiol and testosterone and anti-inflammatory drug dexamethasone.
- Steroidal drugs are quick acting but have serious side effects. Generally, these drugs boost the physiological systems in the body and hence increase the ability of body to fight against the conditions of disease.

5.2.20 Contraceptive

- It is used to prevent unwanted pregnancy. It is used for birth control. Hormonal contraceptives consist of one or more synthetic female sex hormones. These sex hormones prevent pregnancy by blocking the normal process of ovulation. They may also alter the lining of the uterus so that it is unable to support a fertilized egg and they change the mucus in the cervix so that it is hard for the sperm to travel, hence conception is less likely should ovulation to occur.
- To control population, Northindrone and Mesotranole drugs are used for making birth control pills. Generally, these are the tablets (pills) taken regularly as per prescribed schedule.
- Contraceptives are used in the form of creams, jellies or aerosol foams to protect against pregnancy.

5.2.21 Histamine and Antihistamine

Histamine:

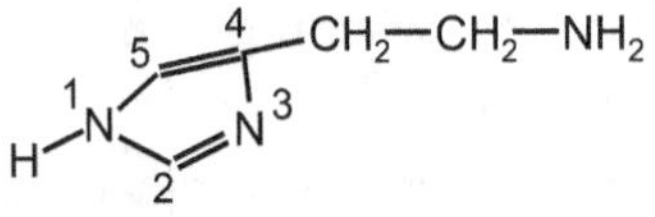

- Histamine or imidazolylethylamine is an enzyme that is expressed in many mammalian tissues including gastric mucosa parietal cells, mast cells, and basophils and the central nervous system (CNS). Histamine plays an important role in human physiology including regulation of the cardiovascular system, smooth muscle, exocrine glands, the immune system, and central nerve function. It is also involved in embryonic development, the proliferation and differentiation of cells, hematopoiesis, inflammation, and wound healing. Histamine exerts its diverse biologic effects through four types of receptors. The involvement of histamine in the mediation of immune and hypersensitivity reactions and the regulation of gastric acid secretion have led to the development of important drug classes useful in the treatment of symptoms associated with allergic and gastric hyper secretary disorders. The source of histamine in our body is the decarboxylation of histidine amino acid.

  It is major role in many allergic reactions, dilating blood vessels and making the vessel walls abnormally permeable. Histamine is part of the body's natural allergic response to substances such as pollens, dust etc.

- **Antihistamines** are the drugs which are preventing the release of histamine from certain cells thereby blocking the allergic reaction.

  Selected antihistamines are Lodoxamide, Tromethamine, Cromolyn Sodium, Brompheniramine, Chlorpheniramine, Dexchlorpheniramine, Triprolidine, Phenindamine etc.

5.3. Synthesis and Uses

5.3.1 Paracetamol (P-acetyl Aminophenol)

Class: It is analgesic and Antipyretic Functional Drugs:

Structure:

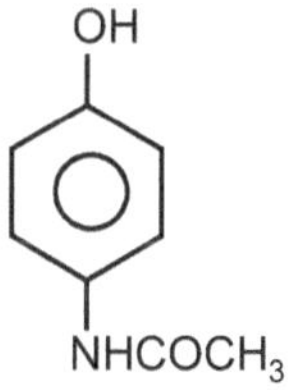

OH

NHCOCH$_3$
Paracetamol

Synthesis: It is prepared from phenol or p-hydroxy acetophenone as starting materials.

(a) Synthesis of Paracetamol from Phenol: Nitration of phenol using dil. nitric acid gives p-nitrophenol. The reduction of p-nitrophenol using Sn/HCl and subsequent acetylation by glacial acetic acid or acetic anhydride gives paracetamol.

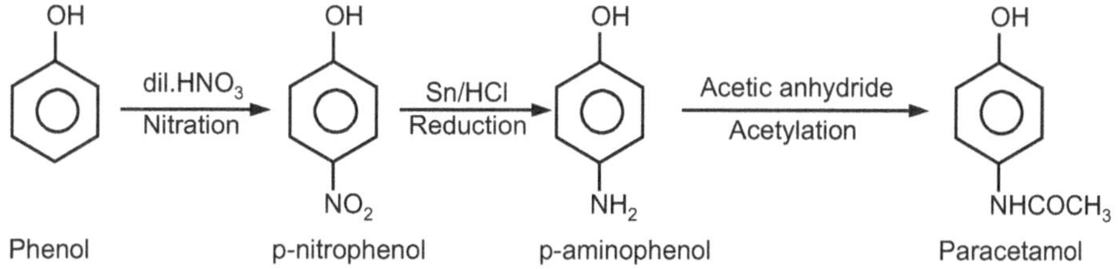

| Phenol | $\xrightarrow[\text{Nitration}]{\text{dil.HNO}_3}$ p-nitrophenol | $\xrightarrow[\text{Reduction}]{\text{Sn/HCl}}$ p-aminophenol | $\xrightarrow[\text{Acetylation}]{\text{Acetic anhydride}}$ Paracetamol |

(b) Synthesis of paracetamol from p-hydroxy acetophenone: p-hydroxy acetophenone reacts with hydrazine to give p-hydroxy acetophenone hydrazone. This molecule undergoes rearrangement to give paracetamol.

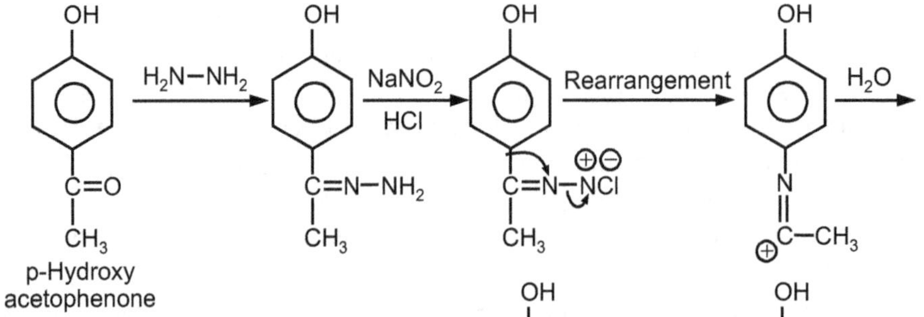

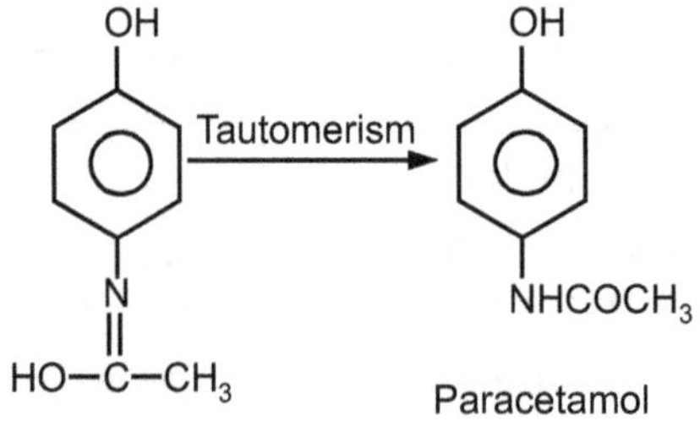

Uses:

(a) It is used as an analgesic and antipyretic drug.

(b) It can relieve headache, arthritis and muscular pains.

(c) Less side effect and less toxic than aspirin

5.3.2 Aspirin (Acetyl Salicylic Acid)

Class: Analgesic and antipyretic functional drug

Structure:

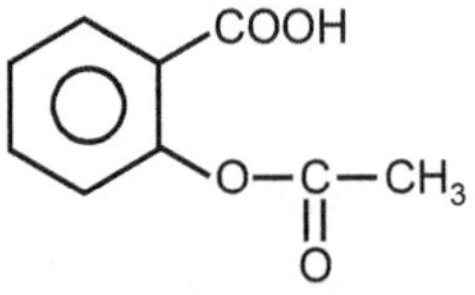

Aspirin

Synthesis: Synthesis of aspirin from salicylic acid

Salicylic acid when treated with acetic anhydride and small amount concentrated H_2SO_4 it gives aspirin.

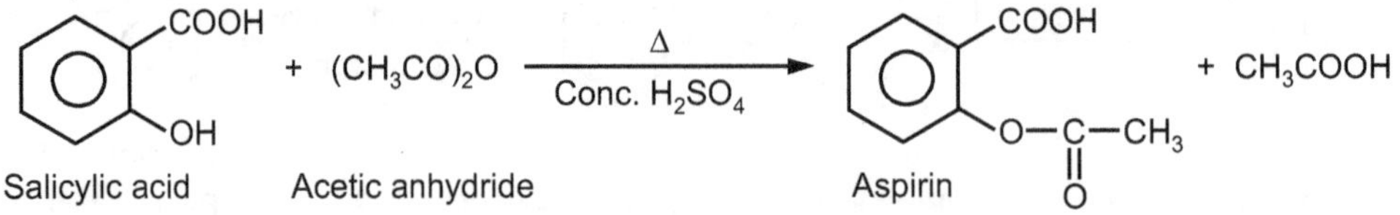

Uses:

(a) It is used as analgesic and antipyretic drugs.

(b) It is used for the treatment of heart disease.

Side effects:

(a) Lowering of blood pressure, intense thirst, nausea and vomiting,

(b) It may cause ulcers in the stomach and cause bleeding

(c) Rashes on skin due to allergic reaction.

5.2.3 Sulphanilamide (p-Amino Benzene Sulphonamide)

Class: Antibacterial drug or sulpha drug (Chemotherapeutic drug).

Structure:

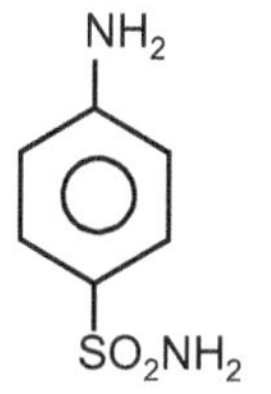

Sulphanilamide

Synthesis:

(a) Synthesis of sulphanilamide from acetanilide: In the first step when acetanilide is treated with excess chlorosulphonic acid, it gives p-acetamido benzene sulphonyl chloride. In the second step by treating aqueous ammonia to form p-acetamidobenzenesulphonamide.

Acetanilide   Chlorosulphonic acid   p-acetaidobenzenesulphonyl chloride   Sulphanilamide

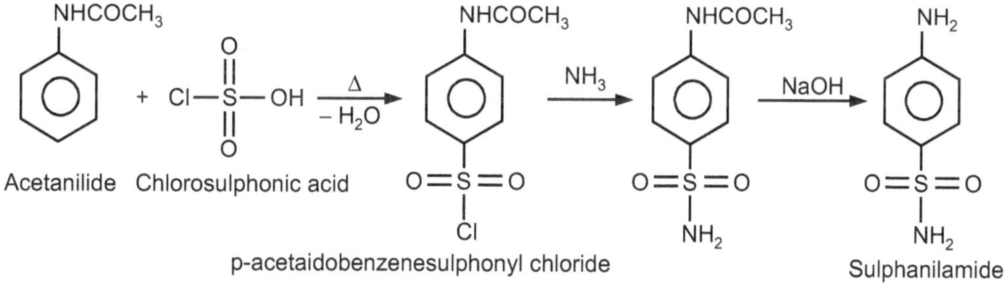

(b) Synthesis of sulphanilamide from p-chlorobenzenesulphonyl chloride: p-chlorobenzene sulphonyl chloride is treated with ammonia in the presence of copper catalyst to form sulphanilamide.

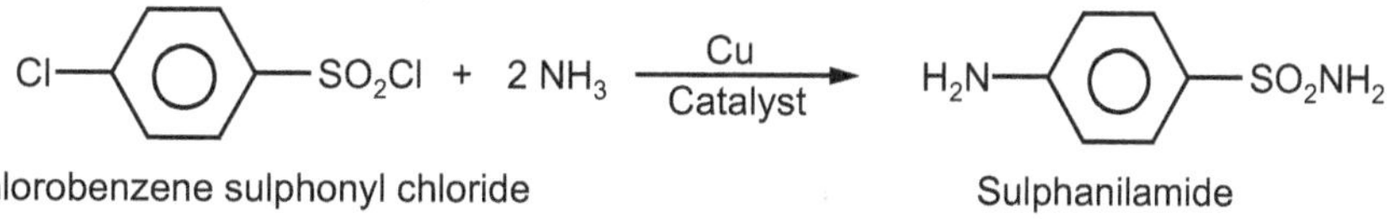

p-chlorobenzene sulphonyl chloride   Sulphanilamide

Uses:

(i)   It is used as a antibacterial drug.

(ii)   It is very important in the control of cocci infections such as streptococci, gonococci and pneumococci.

(iii) It is used as a starting material for the preparation of orange colored dye namely prontosil.

Exercises

(A) Answer the following:

1.   Answer the following terms with suitable examples:

(1) Antibiotics, (2) Tranquillizers, (3) Anesthetics, (4) Analgesic, (5) Antipyretic, (6) Diuretic, (7) Anti-Inflammatory, (8) Anti-viral, (9) Antiulcer, (10) Anti-allergic and Bronchodilators, (11) Cardiovascular, (12) Cold preparations, (13) Anti-hypertensive, (14) Cough Preparation, (15) Anti-neoplastic, (16) Sedative (17) Hypnotics, (18) Steroidal, (19) Contraceptive, (20) Histamine and Antihistamine.

2.   Define the following terms: (i) Chemotherapeutic agents, (ii) Functional drugs.

3.   What do you mean by drug? Give the classification of drugs.

4.   Explain the synthesis and uses of following drugs: (1) Paracetamol, (2) Aspirin, (3) Sulphanilamide.

5.   What is drug? Give the nomenclature of drug.

6.   What are the factors affecting drug action?

7.   Write notes on:

(a)   Structure - activity relationship

(b)   Action of drugs

(c)   Metabolism of drugs

(d)   Pharmacological activity

8.   What are prescriptions?

9.   What are doses?

10.   What are sulpha drugs? Give the synthesis and uses of sulphanilamide.

11.   What are antipyretics? Give the synthesis and uses of paracetamol.

12.   What are analgesics? Give the synthesis and uses of aspirin.

(B) Multiple Choice Questions (MCQs):

(i)   Antineoplastic is used for ....

(a) Cancer, (b) HIV, (c) arthritis, (d) Plastic surgery

(ii)   Antipyretic drugs give relief from ......

(a) Elevated body temperature, (b) pain, (c) cough, (d) HIV

(iii)   Ulcer disease related to .... part of body

(a) Head, (b) leg, (c) chest, **(d) stomach**

(iv)   Diuretics drugs are related to ....

(a) Heart disease, (b) cold, (c) blood circulation, **(d) kidney functions.**

(v)   Bronchodilators are used to cure ....

(a) Cough, (b) arthritis, **(c) asthma,** (d) heart disease

(vi)   Aspirin belongs to a class ....

(a) Functional drugs, (b) antiseptic, (c) chemotherapeutic drugs, (d) diuretics

(vii)   The substances that increase the output of urine by kidneys are called ....

(a) Antipyretics, **(b) Diuretics,** (c) Antibiotics, (d) Tranquilizers

(viii) The drugs which are employed in the treatment of mental disorder are called ....

(a) Analgesics, (b) Contraceptives, (c) Antibiotics, **(d) Tranquilizers**

(ix)   The drug which is used to treat high blood pressure is called ....

(a) Anti-hypertensive, (b) Antihistamine, (c) Anesthetic, (d) Anti-inflammatory

(x)   The drug used to stop life process or destroy the micro-organism is called ....

(a) Antiseptic, **(b) Antibiotic,** (c) Anti-fungal, (d) Anti-ulcer

(C) State True or False:

(i)   Paracetamol belongs to a class of chemotherapeutic drug.

(ii)   Sulphanilamide is a functional drugs.

(iii) Steroidal drugs are known for their serious side effects

(iv) Contraceptive drugs used for birth control

(v) Analgesic is a pain relieving by acting on central nervous system without loss of consciousness.

Ans.: (i) - False, (ii) - False, (iii) - True, (iv) - True, (v) - True

■■■

Chapter 6...

Pollution Prevention and Waste Management

Contents ...

6.1 Introduction

6.2 Importance of Waste Management

6.3 Atom Economy

6.4 Terms Involved in Waste Minimization

    6.4.1 Source Reduction and Waste Reduction

    6.4.2 Recycling and Reuse

    6.4.3 Biological Reprocessing (Product Changes)

    6.4.4 Energy Recovery

    6.4.5 Avoidance and Reduction Methods (Source Control)

6.5 Assessment Procedure

6.6 Types of Wastes

6.7 Treatment and Disposal of Industrial Waste

6.8 Treatment of Waste or Effluents with Organic Impurities

    6.8.1 What is Organic Waste?

    6.8.2 Waste Volumes and Contribution

    6.8.3 Organic Wastes Degradation by Aerobic and Anaerobic Biology

    6.8.4 Recycling and Reuse

6.9 Treatment of Waste with Inorganic Impurities

    6.9.1 Disposal of Waste

    6.9.2 Recyclables

6.10 The Nature, Effect and Treatment of Some Important Chemical Wastes

    6.10.1 Pulp and Paper Industries

        6.10.1.1 Chemical Processes

        6.10.1.2 Advanced Treatment by Chemical Oxidation of Pulp and Paper Effluent from a Plant Manufacturing Hardboard from Waste Paper

    6.10.2 Soap and Detergent Industry

        6.10.2.1 The Removal of Phosphate from Waste Water

    6.10.3 Food Industry

• Exercises

6.1 Introduction

- Environmental pollution is an undesirable change in the physical, chemical or biological characteristics of our air, land and water that may or will harmfully affect living conditions and cultural assets or that may or will waste or deteriorate our raw material sources. Though the pollution problems are faced almost in all the countries of the world, particularly highly developed countries are most affected. In India also we are facing pollution problems in big cities like Mumbai, Kolkatta, Delhi, Kanpur and others. Industrial activities produce a large number of wide range of waste products which are usually added into water streams.

- The normal approach of pollution prevention policy is to study pollution prevention and through this industry can achieve better environmental protection and thereby increased industrial efficiency, profitability and competitiveness. The pollution prevention can be achieved by modifying manufacturing processes. Pollution prevention can help to solve complex problems like global warming, solid waste, garbage, etc. Air and water pollution control equipment removes harmful substances but produce harmful solid and hazardous wastes. These are then disposed off in landfills. Some of these landfills have been connected to ground and water contamination. Pollution prevention can also make good economic sense.

- Waste management is the process and the policy of reducing the amount of waste produced by a person or a society. Waste management involves efforts to minimize resource and energy use during manufacture. For the same commercial output, usually the fewer materials are used, the less waste is produced. Waste management usually requires knowledge of the production process and detailed knowledge of the composition of the waste. Most communities use an integrated approach to waste management, meaning they use a variety of ways to handle the trash produced by their citizens. Some of these include pollution prevention, landfilling, recycling, composting, waste reduction, waste-to-energy plants, hazardous waste disposal, and litter prevention and control.

6.2 Importance of Waste Management

- Waste is any substance that is unwanted or any undesired material left over after the completion of a process. Urban India is likely to face a massive waste disposal problem in the coming years. A closer look at the current and future scenarios reveals that, unless waste is treated in an efficient manner, we will be facing gargantuan problems by the next decade. To approach this kind of menace, we should fight at all fronts. The most important process of waste management is getting the general public involved in all the processes.

- The waste minimization must be a policy of company. This policy must include span the range from inventory management through equipment and process modification to reuse. Thus, waste minimization becomes an integral part of company's operations.
- There are number of concepts about waste management which vary in their usage between countries. Some of the most general, widely recommended concepts are as follows:

(a) Inventory management and improved operations

(i) To keep records of all trace raw materials.

(ii) There should be purchase of minimum toxic and more non-toxic production materials.

(iii) Regularly arrange employee training program.

(iv) Taking management feedback and it should be implemented for improvement in industrial operations.

(v) Improve material receiving, storage and handling practices.

(b) Modification of equipments:

(i) Install equipments that produce minimum waste.

(ii) Modify equipments to improve recovery or recycling.

(iii) Improve operating efficiency of the equipment which helps to produce less waste.

(iv) Maintain a strict preventive maintenance program of equipments.

(c) Production process changes:

(i) Separate wastes by types for their recovery.

(ii) Remove leaks and spills.

(iii) Substitute non-hazardous raw materials for hazardous materials.

(iv) Reformulate end products to be less hazardous.

(v) Optimize raw materials and types of reactions.

(d) Recycling and reuse:

(i) Exchange waste between industry i.e. waste of one industry may be a raw material for other industry.

(ii) Recycle on-site and off-site waste for reuse.

(iii) Install closed-loop systems.

(iv) Pollution can be reduced to a greater extent by reuse and recycling wastes.

6.3 Atom Economy

- Atom economy (atom efficiency) describes the conversion efficiency of a chemical process in terms of all atoms involved. In an ideal chemical process, the amount of starting materials or reactants equals the amount of all products generated (see stoichiometry) and no atom is wasted. Recent developments like high raw material (such as petrochemicals) costs and increased sensitivity to environmental concerns have made atom economical approaches more popular. Atom economy is an important concept of green chemistry philosophy.

- Atom economy can be written as:

$$\text{Percent atom economy} = \frac{\text{Molecular weight of desired product}}{\text{Molecular weight of all reactants}} \times 100$$

- Note that atom economy can be poor even when chemical yield is near 100%, see for instance the Cannizzaro's reaction. If the desired product has an enantiomer the reaction needs to be sufficiently stereoselective even when atom economy is 100%. A Diels-Alder reaction is an example of a potentially very atom efficient reaction that also can be chemo-, regio-, diastereo- and enantioselective. Catalytic hydrogenation comes the closest to being an ideal reaction that is extensively practiced both industrially and academically. The Gabriel synthesis of amines is an example of extremely low atom economy, as stoichiometric quantities of phthalic acid derivatives are formed. In most cases, the atom economy of the Gabriel synthesis is <<50%.

- Atom economy can be improved upon by careful selection of starting materials and a catalyst system. Atom economy is just one way to evaluate a chemical process. Other criteria can include energy consumption, pollutants released and price.

- It is fundamental in chemical reactions of the form

$$A + B \rightarrow C + D$$

that two products are necessarily generated though product C may have been the desired one. That being the case, D is considered a byproduct. As it is a significant goal of green chemistry to maximize the efficiency of the reactants and minimize the production of waste, D must either be found to have use, be eliminated or be as insignificant and innocuous as possible. With the new equation of the form

$$A + B \rightarrow C$$

the first step in making chemical manufacturing more efficient is the use of reactions that resemble simple addition reactions with the only other additions being catalytic materials.

6.4 Terms Involved in Waste Minimization

- The waste minimization techniques involved source reduction and on-site/off-site recycling.

- Following are some important terms involved in waste minimization.

6.4.1 Source Reduction and Waste Reduction

- The reduction or elimination of waste production at the source, i.e. waste generation takes place within a chemical process itself. This waste reduction includes process modification, feedstock changes, improved household management and in process recycle.

- In industrial manufacturing process to minimize the generation of hazardous waste it must be carried out by regular maintenance of the machinery in the factory. According to OTA (Office Technology Assessment), actions taken against to waste generating activity, like waste recycling or treatment of wastes, or concentration of hazardous content are not considered as waste reduction.

6.4.2 Recycling and Reuse

- Recycling is one of those methods. It is an excellent way to reduce the amount of trash or garbage going into a landfill and, at the same time, conserve natural resources.

- Today, recycling programs focus on three key elements: collecting materials; reprocessing or re-making materials; and selling the re-made materials. Most countries have recycling programs in place. Newspaper, glass, metal, and plastic are the most common materials collected and recycled. These materials are generally reprocessed into the same items and used again to make new products. Certain items, such as plastic soda bottles, may be made into plastic toys, or carpeting, or even clothing.

- A steel car body may end up in its "second life" as a steel bridge. In addition to more commonly recycled items, like motor oil, anti-freeze, scrap metal (from appliances), tires, all sorts of paper and magazines, and other forms of plastic. By taking these items out of the waste "stream," communities are helping the state achieve its goal of 25% reduction in wastes statewide.

- The most common consumer products recycled include aluminium beverage cans, steel food and aerosol cans, HDPE and PET bottles, glass bottles and jars, paperboard cartons, newspapers, magazines, and corrugated fiberboard boxes. PVC, LDPE, PP, and PS are also recyclable, although these are not commonly collected. These items are usually composed of a single type of material, making them relatively easy to recycle into new products. The recycling of complex products (such as computers and electronic equipment) is more difficult, due to the additional dismantling and separation required.

6.4.3 Biological Reprocessing (Product Changes)

- Waste materials that are organic in nature, such as plant material, food scraps, and paper products, can be recycled using biological composting and digestion processes to decompose the organic matter. The resulting organic material is then recycled as mulch or compost for agricultural or landscaping purposes. In addition, waste gas from the process (such as methane) can be captured and used for generating electricity and heat (CHP/cogeneration) maximizing efficiencies. The intention of biological processing in waste management is to control and accelerate the natural process of decomposition of organic matter.

- There are a large variety of composting and digestion methods and technologies varying in complexity from simple home compost heaps, to small town scale batch digesters, industrial-scale enclosed-vessel digestion of mixed domestic waste. Methods of biological decomposition are differentiated as being aerobic or anaerobic methods, though hybrids of the two methods also exist.

- Anaerobic digestion of the organic fraction of Municipal Solid Waste has been found to be in a number of LCA analysis studies to be more environmentally effective, than landfill, incineration or pyrolysis. The resulting biogas (methane) though must be used for cogeneration (electricity and heat preferably on or close to the site of production) and can be used with a little upgrading in gas combustion engines or turbines. With further upgrading to synthetic natural gas it can be injected into the natural gas network or further refined to hydrogen for use in stationary cogeneration fuel cells. Its use in fuel cells eliminates the pollution from products of combustion (SO_x, NO_x, particulates, dioxin, furans, PAHs...).

6.4.4 Energy Recovery

- The energy content of waste products can be obtained directly by using them as a direct combustion fuel, or indirectly by processing them into another type of fuel. Recycling through thermal treatment ranges from using waste as a fuel source for cooking or heating, to anaerobic digestion and the use of the gas fuel (see above), to fuel for boilers to generate steam and electricity in a turbine. Pyrolysis and gasification are two related forms of thermal treatment where waste materials are heated to high temperatures with limited oxygen availability. The process usually occurs in a sealed vessel under high pressure. Pyrolysis of solid waste converts the material into solid, liquid and gas products. The liquid and gas can be burnt to produce energy or refined into other chemical products (chemical refinery). The solid residue (char) can be further refined into products such as activated carbon. Gasification and advanced Plasma arc gasification are used to convert organic materials directly into a synthetic gas (syngas) composed of carbon monoxide and hydrogen. The gas is then burnt to produce electricity and steam. An alternative to pyrolysis is high temperature and pressure, supercritical water decomposition (hydrothermal monophasic oxidation).

6.4.5 Avoidance and Reduction Methods (Source Control)

- An important method of waste management is the prevention of waste material being created, also known as waste reduction. Methods of avoidance include reuse of second-hand products, repairing broken items instead of buying new, designing products to be refillable or reusable (such as cotton instead of plastic shopping bags), encouraging consumers to avoid using disposable products (such as disposable cutlery), removing any food/liquid remains from cans, packaging, and designing products that use less material to achieve the same purpose (for example, lightweighing of beverage cans).

6.5 Assessment Procedure

- To be able to identify waste minimization opportunities in a given facility or process, it is necessary to use a systematic approach that takes into consideration all of the important factors.

- The Waste Minimization Assessment Procedure (WMAP) is required for systematic approach. Assessment Procedure (WMAP) represents such an approach. One part of a larger waste minimization programme that is required of hazardous waste generators, the procedure involves a step-by-step approach to (1) understand the facility's waste and processes, (2) identify options for reducing waste, and (3) determine which of the option exhibit sufficient technical and economic feasibility to justify implementation. Naturally, it is necessary to modify the procedure to fit the specific needs of individual companies. Thus, it should be viewed as a source of ideas and concepts, rather than a vigorous prescription of how to do assessment.

- The waste minimization procedure consists of four phases:

  1. Planning and organization (Schedule and set-up).
  2. Assessment phase (Evaluation).
  3. Feasibility analysis (Practicability).
  4. Implementation (Execution).

1. **Planning and Organization**

   The success of waste minimization programme depends on careful planning and organization. There should be strong management commitment from the very beginning. For these a selection of qualified staff is critical.

2. **Assessment Phase**

   The assessment phase serves to identify the best options for minimizing waste through a thorough understanding of the waste-generating processes, waste streams, and operating procedures. Therefore, the initial tasks in the assessment phase include collecting information about the facility's waste streams, processes, and operations.

Information about the facility's waste streams can come from a variety of sources, such as hazardous waste manifests, biennial reports, environmental audits, emission inventories, waste assays, and permits. Mass balance should be developed for each of the important waste-generating operations to identify sources and gain a better understanding of the wastes' origins.

(a) **Collect facility data:** In addition to data about waste streams, other information is needed to fully understand the facility's operations, including the following items:

- Process, equipment and facility design information.
- Raw material production information.
- Operating cost information.
- Policy and organizational information.

Ideally, assessment should be conducted on all of the waste-generating operations in a plant. However, in larger plants this often is not practical considering the limited resources available.

(b) **Prioritizes and selects targets:** In these cases, a program task force should prioritize the streams. Important criteria to consider in prioritizing waste streams and/or facility areas include the following.

- Compliance with current environmental regulations.
- Disposal cost and/or volume of the waste.
- Hazardous nature of the waste, and other safety consideration.
- Potential for (and case of) minimization.
- Potential for removing production or waste treatment nottlenecks.
- Available budget and expertise for the waste minimization assessment program.

A practical consideration in determining which waste streams to select is to find those that can be reduced with minimum economic or production impact. A successfully implemented waste minimization project will ensure the acceptance of further waste minimization efforts within the organization.

(c) **Select personnel teams:** The assessment team must include people who are familiar with the area of the facility to be assessed (e.g. first line operators and the production supervisors are recommended). These people may or may not already be on the assessment program task force. (In a large facility, the task force should have a broad understanding of the facility's operations, whereas the assessment team should have a specific understanding of the areas to be assessed). It may be advisable to include people from other parts of the facility that regularly interact with the areas to be assessed.

(d) **Collects and Reviews data:** Although collecting and reviewing data is important in the assessment, the assessment team must be familiar with the actual operation at the site. Therefore, the assessment team should visit the site during various stages or cycles of an operation. If all of the assessment team members work at the facility (or are located relatively closeby) it is easy for the team members to visit the site. However if some members are from outside the facility, it is recommended that a formal site inspection be carried out.

(e) **Inspects site and characterizes waste:** A formal inspection can address many questions raised by data collected earlier in the assessment phase. An inspection can also confirm whether the facility is operating in the way it was originally intended to operate. An inspection concentrates on understanding how the wastes are generated.

The following guidelines will help in organizing an effective site inspection.

- Prepare an agenda in advance.
- Schedule the inspection to coincide with the particular operation of interest.
- Interview operators, foremen, and supervisors, and access the operating personnel's awareness of the waste generation aspects of the operation.
- Observe the housekeeping aspects of the operation.
- Assess the overall cleanliness of the site.
- Review the organizational structure and the level of coordination of waste-related activities between the assessed facility area and other related areas.
- Assess the administrative controls.

(f) **Generates and develops options:** Identifying potential option requires the expertise of the assessment team members, much of whose knowledge comes from their education and on-the-job experience. Other sources of background information on potential options include the following:

- Trade associations.
- Published literature.
- Environmental conferences and exhibits
- Equipment vendors.
- Plant personnel (especially the operators)
- Federal state and local government environmental agencies.
- Consultants and/or employees from other facilities.

(g) **Screens and selects options:** A successful assessment will result in the proposal of many waste minimization options, so it is necessary to identify those options that offer a real possibility of minimizing waste and reducing costs. The purpose of the screening step is to eliminate those options that are perceived to be impractical. The screening of options may be achieved through our informal decision made by the assessment team, or a weighted sum method that combines relative weight of such factors as operating cost, reduction, capital cost requirement, and reduction in the waste hazard.

3. Feasibility analysis

The waste minimization options that are successfully screened in the assessment phase then undergo a more detailed feasibility analysis. Most important, the feasibility analysis consists of three steps; technical evaluation, economic evaluation and implementing option selection.

All affected groups in the facilities should contribute to review the results of the technical evaluation. If the option calls for a change in production methods, its effects on the quality of the final product must be determined. Only those projects that are judged to be feasible and practical in the technical evaluation go on to an economic evaluation.

Waste minimization projects need to show a saving in operating costs to be economically effective. Operating costs and saving typically associated with waste minimization projects include the following:

(i) Reduce waste treatment, disposal and reporting costs.

(ii) Raw material cost saving.

(iii) Insurance and liability savings.

(iv) Increased costs (or savings) associated with product quality.

(v) Decreased (or increased) utilities, operating and maintenance costs.

Once the capital and operating costs saving have been determined, a project's profitability can be determined by using profitability measures.

An important consideration of waste minimization projects is their potential to reduce the toxicity of a waste stream and thereby to reduce the environmental risk.

The product of the feasibility analysis is a report that presents technical and economic information concerning the feasibility of each option. It also contains the recommendations to implement the options. The report should include project cost and performance information.

4. Implementation

Implementation of the waste minimization project requires management's commitment to overcome the natural resistance to change that occurs within an organization. Once the project is implemented and is operating, it is important to evaluate its performance. Is it performing as expected? If not, should it be modified or is its use still beneficial? What other potential options were identified during the implementation and operation of this option?

The waste minimization program should be viewed as a continuing one. As waste minimization option is implemented, the task force should continue to look for new opportunities, assess other waste streams and consider options that were not persuade earlier. The ultimate goal is to reduce the toxicity and volume of wastes to the minimum extend practical.

6.6 Types of Wastes

- Generally, there are different types of wastes generated by the construction and operation of any development. With this in mind, it is important to devise proper mechanisms to sort and categorize the solid waste. In sorting solid waste the development intends to create a differential system, assigning each class of solid waste to a different treatment category.

- The four broad categories of solid waste are:

  1. Construction and field waste
  2. Domestic waste
  3. International waste
  4. Commercial waste
  5. Industrial waste
     (a) Process waste
     (b) Chemical waste

6.7 Treatment and Disposal of Industrial Waste

- The industrial wastes may be broadly grouped as organic effluent, inorganic effluent and chemical effluent present. The treatments used for industrial wastes are similar to sewage treatments. The method of treatment and disposal of industrial waste are classified into three steps:

  (i) Preliminary or Mechanical treatment: The removal of wastes such as rags, waste paper, grit, oil, grease etc. from industrial waste water is known as preliminary treatment or pretreatment. The preliminary treatments consisting of the processes of:

  (a) Screening
  (b) Grinding, Cutting and Shreding
  (c) Grit chambers
  (d) Pre-aeration
  (e) Sedimentation
  (f) Chemical treatment for neutralization, coagulation, precipitation, oxidation and reduction of industrial waste.

(ii) **Secondary or Biological treatment:** The method of biological treatment involved in removal of solid wastes with the help of living organisms is called as secondary treatment. The secondary treatments include the aerobic decomposition methods like trickling filters, activated sludge, oxidation ponds, aerated lagoons and oxidation ditch. The anaerobic treatments include anaerobic lagoons and anaerobic digestion. The most important role of secondary treatment is to transform the remaining organic matter into stable form by either oxidation or nitrification.

(iii) **Tertiary treatment or Advanced biological, chemical and physical treatment:** Purification of waste water by modern biological, chemical and physical techniques and also the recycling of the waste water is known as tertiary treatment.

Anaerobic digestion has been successfully applied in the treatment of organic wastes such as meat, milk, tannery etc. In this treatment, methane is obtained as a byproduct and it can be used as a fuel.

It is possible to prefer a suitable method for a particular effluent in industrial waste treatment due to the uniform quality of industrial waste.

For the purpose of treatment the industrial wastes can be classified into three classes:

(a) **Wastes of animal origin:** These wastes are discharged from milk, dairies, fertilizers, glue, leather, soap, woollen textiles, etc.

(b) **Wastes of mineral origin:** These wastes generally come from chemical industry, dyeing, gas plants, mines, oil refineries, metal industry, water treatment plants, etc.

(c) **Wastes of vegetable origin:** These are wastes from beet-sugar industry, cotton textile mills, paper and pulp industry, rubber industry, etc.

The general methods have been adopted for the treatment of industrial wastes are as follows:

1. Aerobic biological oxidation
2. Chemical coagulation
3. Chlorination
4. Incineration
5. Screening
6. Spray irrigation
7. Anaerobic digestion
8. Chemical oxidation
9. Filtration
10. Logooning or ponding
11. Sedimentation
12. Vaccum filtration

6.8 Treatment of Waste or Effluents with Organic Impurities

6.8.1 What is Organic Waste?

- The organic waste stream is composed of waste of a biological origin such as paper and cardboard, food, green and garden waste, animal waste and biosolids and sludges. Organic waste is usually generated as a component of most waste streams. There are two common sources of confusion about the term organic waste. Firstly, the term is generally not intended to include plastics or rubber even though to an organic chemist, these polymers are certainly organic. Secondly, putrescible wastes are a subset of organic wastes with the distinction being that putrescible wastes, for instance food scraps, tend to biodegrade very rapidly whereas some other organic wastes, for instance paper, tend to require lengthy times or special conditions to biodegrade. For information on the treatments for managing Organic Wastes click on the links to the right.

6.8.2 Waste Volumes and Contribution

- Organic wastes are the single largest component of the waste stream. Approximately 1.2 million tonnes of organic waste was generated in Perth in 1996 (Waste 2020, 2001). 25% of this waste originated from green (or garden) waste with other main contributors to this waste stream being manures and sludges (20%), food wastes (18%) and paper and cardboard waste (15%). Land clearing, timber processing and wood combine to form another 18% of the organic waste. In addition to being a valuable resource for nutrient poor soils, this material generates the most significant levels of pollution when disposed of in landfills. Some forms of organic wastes can cause public health problems, such as disease, odours and pests.

6.8.3 Organic Wastes Degradation by Aerobic and Anaerobic Biology

- In landfills, organic wastes decompose an aerobically to produce biogas (predominantly methane, a significant greenhouse gas) and leachate that contains nutrients and soluble organics. The leachate has the potential to pollute groundwater and may release and mobilise heavy metals from landfills (Waste 2020, 2001). Some organic wastes such as sludges and biosolids can contain heavy metals or nutrient pollutants. Uncontrolled disposal of biosolids may lead to site contamination or water pollution. To protect our water resources we need to prevent pollution arising from uncontrolled treatment and disposal of organic waste.

- Open burning of organic wastes pollutes the air and contributes to the smoke haze problem in metropolitan Perth.

6.8.4 Recycling and Reuse

- Organic wastes are resources and can be processed into various useful products. Given the low organic content of soils in Western Australia, any soil improvement products could be utilised, provided that logistics can be made economical. Agricultural and degraded land in WA would also benefit from the application of recycled organics products. Potential products and markets include mulch, compost, vermicompost, soil conditioners, recycled timber, firewood and energy recovery.

- Successful recycling of organic waste depends on adequate separation at the source of generation, ensuring the production of a higher quality end product. Anaerobic digestion is an option for more noxious organic compounds such as biosolids and animal sludges, that would not normally be composted due to their offensive nature.

- The production of recycled organic products will also conserve landfill space that is becoming increasingly scarce and expensive.

6.9 Treatment of Waste with Inorganic Impurities

- The inorganic waste should be transported for scientific landfill site. The waste collector will deposit the recyclables at the identified spots from where the contractor will pick up the useful material. Only the refuse is transported to the landfill site.

Table 6.1: Various types of recyclables present in the waste

Sr. No.	Types of recyclable	Types of waste
1.	Unbroken bottles	Glass
2.	Ferrous and non-ferrous components	Metals
3.	Plastic sheet, piping, and plastic bags, cans and bottles	Plastics
4.	Old tyres and shoes	Rubber/Leathers
5.	Wooden logs, woody waste from garden.	Wood

6.9.1 Disposal of Waste

Wet Waste:

- As per the MSW-2000 rule, the wet waste, which is biodegradable is processed to obtain compost by mechanical composting or vermin composting. KCDC will provide the technical assistance and is desired to be operated by private sector participation on BOT basis.

Dry Waste:

- Dry waste which is inert is disposed by land filling at the landfill site as per MSW - 2000 specifications. Land fill site will be operated by private sector participation on BOT basis.

6.9.2 Recyclables

- Recyclables obtained from the segregation will be sold to the scrap merchants which in turn will be recycled using suitable process.

- **Waste from desilting** of drains, street sweeping, constructional waste will be used for filling low lying areas or as soil cover in land filling.

6.10 The Nature, Effect and Treatment of Some Important Chemical Wastes

6.10.1 Pulp and Paper Industries

- The paper-making process is one of the most water-intensive industrial production processes. The manufacture of paper generates significant quantities of wastewater; as high as 60 m^3/tonne of paper produced. The raw wastewaters from paper and board mills can be potentially very polluting. Indeed, a recent survey within the UK industry has found that their chemical oxygen demands can be as high as 11000 mg/l. In line with the majority of UK practice, it focuses mainly on aerobic biological treatment and, in particular, on the activated sludge process.

6.10.1.1 Chemical Processes

- The Kaft process is an alkaline process. The lignin is cracked by NaOH or Na_2S, which is very effective at different kind of woods especially the wood contains pollutions. Disadvantage is the odour problem, based on thiols and sulfides.

- The sulphite process is a procedure based on acids. The effect is not the same compared to the alkaline process. The procedure is more sensitive, against pollution. Branches and bark disturb the chemical process and will not solute as well as the wood. Also resin disturbs the process.

- Combinations of anaerobic and aerobic treatment processes are found to be efficient in the removal of soluble biodegradable organic pollutants. Color can be removed effectively by fungal treatment, coagulation, chemical oxidation, and ozonation. Chlorinated phenolic compounds and adsorbable organic halides (AO_x) can be efficiently reduced by adsorption, ozonation and membrane filtration techniques.

6.10.1.2 Advanced Treatment by Chemical Oxidation of Pulp and Paper Effluent from a Plant Manufacturing Hardboard from Waste Paper

- This chemical oxidation process is used to polish biologically treated effluent of a plant manufacturing hardboard from waste paper to comply with the discharge limit of 120 mg/l chemical oxygen demand (COD). In the first step, a chemically assisted settling was applied. The optimum results were obtained with alum plus lime with the alum dose of 200 mg/l. In the second step, chemically assisted settling effluent was fed into an activated sludge system and over 80% COD removal was achieved. In the last step series of ozone oxidation and Fenton oxidation methods were tested to remove residual COD. Ozone oxidation provided 80% COD removal. An ozone dose of 40 mg min^{-1} with a reaction time of two hours was found to be optimum.

Enzymes

- The use of enzymes for wastewater treatment in the pulp and paper industry is reviewed as a new possibility. There is currently a lot of research activity in the enzymology of lignin degradation. Ligninase, cellulase, peroxidase, etc. are the most important enzymes, especially peroxidase, which is used for colour removal in bleaching effluents. It is also possible to mix enzymes together with special microbes, which normally do not have high enzyme activity, and remove recalcitrant and harmless compounds from wastewater.

Paper Recycling

- Depending of the agents to bleach the pulp, waste water has to be treated. Bleaching with peroxides, oxygen and ozone is not as efficient as using chlorine or chlorine dioxide, but the water has generally a very low or no amount to treatment of chemicals. By using chloride or chloride dioxide, the water contains these agents which increase the AO_x. On the other hand, chloride bleaching is the most efficient.

- The waste water of paper recycling contains also particles which have to be filtrated. Rests of plastics, metal parts (paper clips, etc.) other waste have to be removed.

6.10.2 Soap and Detergent Industry

- The original soaps did not degrade in the environment and their residues remained in waterways and water treatment plants. By the 1950s, drains and rivers often carried persistent mounds of foam, and the water became toxic to small organisms living in the water. Manufacturers therefore sought to make washing powders 'biodegradable' - to decompose naturally as soon as possible after use. Water hardness is a significant factor in the effectiveness of modern detergents; to decrease the hardness of water the manufacturers added 'builders to soften' the water.

- Phosphates have been the builder most commonly used in detergents. However, because excess phosphates cause problems in our waterways, that is called Eutrophication. Some detergent manufacturers have developed 'phosphate-free' detergents. (Although these detergents are marketed as such, they are not always entirely phosphate free i.e. the biodegradable builders).

What does 'biodegradable' mean?

- The term 'biodegradable' refers to the ability of a material to be broken down, by a group of biological organisms called decomposers, into various other compounds. Decomposers are a necessary component of a balanced ecosystem present in natural waters and sediments, and are encouraged in sewage treatment works. Bacteria are the most common decomposers. Sometimes, biodegradation can change materials such as phosphate compounds from a biologically unavailable form into a form that can be taken up and used by organisms.

- When phosphate detergents are used, disposal of the wastewater is an issue. The breakdown of phosphorus complexes in detergent wastewater (and other household products, as well as human and industrial wastes that contain phosphates) creates freely available phosphates; these can contribute to an oversupply of phosphate in waterways and cause an imbalance of the aquatic ecosystem, with the following results:
    1. Excessive algal growth (sometimes in the form of algal blooms).
    2. Blooms of cyanobacteria (blue-green algae) may also be toxic.
    3. This toxicity may be acute (short-term severe) or chronic (longer-term low-level), and can be carcinogenic.

- (**Note:** Most algae are an important part of the ecosystem; only in excess are they a problem.) Decomposer organisms that require oxygen may increase, which can deplete the amount of oxygen dissolved in the water. Excessively large numbers of decomposers may reduce the oxygen levels to the extent that other aquatic organisms die from lack of oxygen. Decomposer populations grow in response to an increase in their food, such as detergent components and, in the drier summer months, the dying excess algae. This problem can be solved by biodegradable phosphate detergents only if detergent wastewater is directed to the sewage system and the treated effluent is re-used to grow plants. The reuse of treated effluent for irrigation on land. A well-managed reuse program can have an overall beneficial effect on the environment.

- Disposal of phosphate-free detergent wastewater is also an environmental issue. As an alternative to phosphates, manufacturers can use a builder, or combination of builders, including zeolites (aluminosilicates), sodium citrate and nitrilotriacetate (NTA). Detergent wastewaters containing alternative builders also have environmental impacts and must be treated by sewage treatment works. Some of them (alkyl phenols) are oestrogen mimics that can have serious detrimental effects on populations of aquatic animals, such as decreasing their ability to reproduce. Even after treatment, the environmental impacts of some alternative builders remain.

6.10.2.1 The Removal of Phosphate from Waste Water

- Phosphorus removal can be effected biologically in a process called enhanced biological phosphorus removal. In this process specific bacteria, called polyphosphate accumulating organisms are selectively enriched and accumulate large quantities of phosphorus within their cells. When the biomass enriched in these bacteria is separated from the treated water, the bacterial biosolids have a high fertilizer value. Phosphorus removal can also be achieved, usually by chemical precipitation with salts of iron (e.g. ferric chloride) or aluminium (e.g. alum). The resulting chemical sludge, however, is difficult to dispose of, and the use of chemicals in the treatment process is expensive and makes operation difficult and often messy.

- The soap and detergent waste minimization can be effected as follows.
- Biodegradable detergents cause problems if they enter our stormwater systems, streams, rivers and ultimately the ocean. No matter which detergent you use, always direct your wastewater to the sewer or use it to irrigate your garden (without allowing any runoff). Both phosphate and phosphate-free detergent wastewaters have negative impacts on our waterways, whether or not they are biodegradable. Directing the wastewater to the sewer allows wastewater treatment plants to remove upto 90% of phosphates. Help the environment by making sure contaminated water does not pollute our stormwater system. Some of the ways for the soap and detergent waste minimization are:
  - Wash your car on the lawn or take it to a commercial car wash that recycles its wastewater.
  - Dry-sweep footpaths and driveways and place sweepings in the bin. If you have an SA Water permit to wash down areas, make sure all of the water is contained and not allowed to run into the street gutters and stormwater drains.
  - Place an absorbent material, such as sand or kitty litter, on grease patches, then scrape it up and place it in a bin.
  - Do not hose down paths or driveways. Mop or scrub and direct the wastewater into the sewer as you would when cleaning inside your house.

6.10.3 Food Industry

- Wastewater generated from agricultural and food operations has distinctive characteristics that set it apart from common municipal wastewater managed by public or private wastewater treatment plants throughout the world: it is biodegradable and nontoxic, but that has high concentrations of biochemical oxygen demand (BOD) and suspended solids (SS). The constituents of food and agriculture wastewater are often complex to predict due to the differences in BOD and pH in effluents from vegetable, fruit, and meal products and due to the seasonal nature of food processing and post harvesting.
- Processing of food from raw materials requires large volumes of high grade water. Vegetable washing generates waters with high loads of particulate matter and some dissolved organics. It may also contain surfactants.
- Animal slaughter and processing produces very strong organic waste from body fluids, such as blood, and gut contents. This wastewater is frequently contaminated by significant levels of antibiotics and growth hormones from the animals and by a variety of pesticides used to control external parasites. Insecticide residues in fleeces are a particular problem in treating waters generated in wool processing. Processing food for sale produces wastes generated from cooking which are often rich in plant in organic material and may also contain salt, flavorings, coloring material and acids or alkali. Very significant quantities of oil or fats may also be present.
- All these waste of food industry can be treated with suitable method described earlier in general methods.

Exercises

(A) Answer the following:

1. What is meant by waste minimization?

2. Explain the different terms involved in waste minimization program.

3. What is the meaning of following terms:

   (a) Recycling and reuse, (b) Source control, (c) Incineration and (d) Landfill.

4. What is meant by assessment procedure? Discuss the different terms involved in assessment procedure.

5. Explain the different types of waste.

6. Discuss in detail the treatment and the disposal of industrial waste.

7. Explain in detail the treatment and the disposal of paper and pulp industry waste.

8. Explain in detail the treatment and the disposal of soap and detergent industry waste.

9. What is organic and inorganic waste? Discuss the treatment and disposal of these wastes.

10. What is meant by atom economy? Explain with suitable example.

(B) Multiple Choice Questions (MCQs):

(i) Modes of controlling pollution in large cities include ....

    (a) Less use of insecticides

    (b) Proper disposal of organic wastes, sewage and industrial effluents

    (c) Shifting of factories out of city areas

    (d) All the above

(ii) Domestic waste mostly constitute ....

    (a) Non-biodegradable pollutants   (b) Biodegradable pollutants

    (c) Effluents   (d) Air pollutants

(iii) Chief source of soil and water pollution is ....

    (a) Agroindustries   (b) Thermal power plants

    (c) Mining   (d) All the above

(iv) Eutrophication causes reduction in ....

    (a) Nutrients   (b) Dissolved salts

    (c) Dissolved oxygen   (d) All the above

(v) Phosphate pollution is caused by ....

    (a) Weathering of phosphate rocks only   (b) Agricultural fertilizers only.

    (c) Phosphate rocks and sewage   (d) Sewage and agricultural fertilizers

(vi) Proper management of disposal of household and industrial wastes can be done by ………

    (a) Recycling the waste material to give useful product again

    (b) Burning and incineration of combustible waste

    (c) Sewage treatment

    (d) All the above

(vii) By Green chemistry we mean ………

    (a) Producing chemicals of our daily use from green house gases

    (b) Performing chemical processes which use green plants

    (c) Performing only those reactions which are of biological origin

    (d) The use of non-toxic reagents and solvents to produce environmental friendly products

(viii) Which of the following is a biodegradable pollutant?

    (a) Plastics   (b) Sewage

    (c) Asbestos   (d) Mercury

(ix) Man-made sources of air pollution are ………

    (a) Increase in population   (b) Deforestation

    (c) War   (d) Pollen grains

(x) Which of the following is a secondary pollutant?

    (a) NO   (b) CO

    (c) SO_2 (d) Phenols

(xi) Atom efficiency is related only to ………

    (a) Reactants   (b) Products

    (c) Chemical process   (d) Reaction parameters

■■■